Praise for *Free Style*

"*Free Style* explores the compromises made on the road to adulthood. A fun debut novel from a fresh new voice."

— Marta Acosta, author of *Happy Hour at Casa Dracula*

"Linda Nieves-Powell really pulls you into these powerful characters' world and takes you on a roller-coaster journey of their frustrations, fears, and joys."

— Theresa Alan, author of *Getting Married* and *Girls Who Gossip*

"A completely engrossing journey of self-discovery. And the pop culture references were a blast!"

— Robyn Harding, author of *The Journal of Mortifying Moments* and *The Secret Desires of a Soccer Mom*

"*Free Style* is a delightful, insightful exploration of friendship, filled with honesty, humor, and Latina flair."

— Wendy French, author of *sMothering* and *Full of It*

"Idalis wants life to be like it used to be, before she had a husband, a kid, and a corporate job—when her biggest worry was what to wear to her old Bronx haunt, Club 90. But life doesn't stand still, and neither does Idalis. She gets over the past and gets real, then tells it like it is about love, marriage, motherhood, and all of the other parts of a working woman's life. Smart, sassy, and, above all, honest, Idalis is a character you will love."

— Heather Swain, author of *Luscious Lemon*

LINDA NIEVES-POWELL

Free Style

A NOVEL

ATRIA BOOKS

NEW YORK LONDON TORONTO SYDNEY

ATRIA BOOKS
A Division of Simon & Schuster, Inc.
1230 Avenue of the Americas
New York, NY 10020

Copyright © 2008 by Latino Flavored Productions, Inc.

First Atria Books trade paperback edition April 2008

ATRIA BOOKS and colophon are trademarks of Simon & Schuster, Inc.

For information about special discounts for bulk purchases,
please contact Simon & Schuster Special Sales at
1-800-456-6798 or business@simonandschuster.com.

Designed by Karolina Harris

Manufactured in the United States of America

10 9 8 7 6 5 4 3 2 1

Library of Congress Cataloging-in-Publication Data
Nieves-Powell, Linda.
Free style : a novel / Linda Nieves-Powell.
p. cm.
1. Hispanic American women—Fiction. 2. New York (N.Y.)—Fiction. I. Title.
PS3614.I374 F74 2008
813'.6—dc22   2007015020

ISBN-13: 978-1-4165-4281-0
ISBN-10:   1-4165-4281-7

To Valentina and Virginia and all the women who came
before me who dreamed of living free style

Free Style

1 When I removed my new digital Internet phone from the installation kit, I stared at it in awe. The same way I had when I bought my first CD by CeCe Peniston and placed it in my new portable Sony CD player.

I remember sitting on the lower level of the Staten Island Ferry, on my way to work, jamming to "Finally" early in the morning, across from my friends, who were jamming to the music playing in their Sony Walkmans. Even back then I thought about how much had changed since the late eighties when I was a teenager playing hooky from school, escaping Global Studies and taking a round-trip to Manhattan on the ferry with my other delinquent classmates. The lower level, before Sony Walkmans and portable CD players came out, used to be filled with the sounds of a hundred conversations. Strangers and friends talked loudly to be heard over a teenager's giant-sized boom box blasting Public Enemy cassettes.

I thought about how fast everything seemed to be moving these days. My life was beginning to look like that Madonna video with the cars and people moving at warp speed. The thought of having to quicken the pace of my own life, in order to catch up to everyone and everything else around me, gave me a mini anxiety attack. I placed the digital Internet phone back in the box and tossed it under the television console. I wasn't in a self-installation mood anyway. Besides, what's wrong with the phones we've been using for the past hundred or so years? I picked up my old trusty reliable landline phone and called Selenis. Thinking about the end of cassette players and old-school jams like Taylor Dayne's "Tell It to My Heart" and Soul II Soul's "Keep on Movin'" was making me feel nostalgic, and since I'd known Selenis practically all my life, who better to share this wistful moment?

She answered on the first ring.

"Hey, you up?" I asked, glancing at the clock over my kitchen table. It was 11:53 p.m.

"Apparently," she said, sounding half asleep.

"I need to talk."

"What's wrong?"

"You know what I've been thinking a lot about lately?"

"Blowing up Manny's car?"

"No. Club 90."

"Ah, Club 90."

"The memories just keep coming up, for some reason. Like the night you danced with that freckle-faced Colombian dude, I forget his name. You were so drunk you didn't realize that your left nipple was hanging over your dress," I said, laughing so loud that I almost forgot that my son, Junito, was asleep in the next room.

"Roland Sanchez," she answered, with a little more pep in her voice.

From the corner of my eye, I saw an instant message pop up on my laptop.

AN INSTANT MESSAGE FROM MACHOMAN1970. WILL YOU ACCEPT?

It was from Manny, my husband. No, correction, estranged husband. I hit the "No, I will not accept" button and continued talking to Selenis.

"He used to kiss you with his eyes open. Don't you ever wonder what he looks like now?" I said, staring at the laptop screen waiting for Manny's next move.

"Idalis, he's old like us."

"Oh, come on now, fifteen years didn't do much to us."

"Fifteen years ago we were wearing tiny stretchy pants and short bolero jackets. Let's try that shit now."

"So we went up a size or two because of the kids. Big deal. I would die to be able to go back to Club 90 and meet up with the old crew, like *la loca* Regina and Victor."

"You mean Panamanian Victor, who wore two different socks the night he met your parents?"

"Yeah, my mother had picked the most awkward moment, while we were all eating, to tell Victor that gray didn't go with brown. Victor had no clue what she was talking about until my mother told him to stand up and pull up his pant legs."

"Your mother is too funny sometimes. She cracks me up," Selenis said, laughing out loud.

"*Bendito*, I felt so sorry for him. He liked me so much, but he was no Trisco Mendez."

"Trisco and Kique."

When she said their names, I could hear the nostalgic longing in Selenis's voice. Kique was her first real crush and the "one" she wished she had gone all the way with. And that's how I felt about Trisco.

"I wonder where they are. Let me Google them," I said, typing the letters into the search bar.

"Idalis, leave that shit alone."

"What are you afraid of? That we'll find them? What happened to that happy-go-lucky, free-spirited *chica* I used to know? I'm Googling right now."

But before I could finish typing Trisco's last name into the Google search bar, Selenis fled.

"*Me voy*, Idalis. I have to go. Carlito is still up watching *Justice League* with his father and he has to go to bed."

"You're such a chickenshit! What's the big deal if I Google Trisco's name?"

"Later, girl. Go to sleep already," Selenis said, before hanging up the phone and leaving me with my memories.

I finished typing into the search bar and pressed enter. Wow, 123,358 matches; I guess that's what happens when you're looking for a Latino on the World Wide Web. Half the population comes up. So I tried narrowing the search.

TRISCO MENDEZ + BRONX, NEW YORK

I couldn't imagine what I would do if I actually found him. I wondered if he was married. I wondered if he looked the same. Some guys get better with time. I wondered what he'd think of me now. Then again, Trisco was one of those guys who, no matter how much time went by, was always happy to see me. He was the one I should've married. Trisco and I were always happy to be together. We never argued. I could always count on him for a good night of dancing and just plain fun. Not to mention that he had those nice full succulent lips that I wish I could've tasted.

Everyone knew us as the royal couple of Club 90. But it's funny how we never took our love outside of the club. Even though we used to dance with other people, Trisco always made me feel like I was the only one for him. One time I hurt my arm playing handball and couldn't go out for about a month, but as soon as I came back to Club 90, there he was waiting for me. Trisco and I had this unspoken agreement. If I was at the club, I was his and he was mine. Although our nightclub relationship never saw the light of day, it was ours forever. No questions. No doubts. We'd always be waiting for each other.

AN INSTANT MESSAGE FROM MACHOMAN1970. WILL YOU ACCEPT?

Of course, Manny, Mr. Macho Man to the tenth power, would ruin this good moment. That was what Manny did so well these days. What could he possibly want at midnight on a Friday night? I decided I wasn't answering. Let Manny find someone else to mess with.

So again I hit the "No, I will not accept" button.

If only Manny were more like Trisco. Trisco was so open with his feelings and was never afraid to show his sensitive side. After ten years I wasn't sure Manny had a sensitive side. Hell, I'd never

seen Manny cry. Not at our wedding, not when Junito was born;
I thought I saw a tear drop when the Giants lost the Super Bowl
championship in 2001, but he told me it was from the spicy buffalo wings he was eating.

AN INSTANT MESSAGE FROM MACHOMAN1970. WILL YOU
ACCEPT?

Why was he stalking me?

FreestyleChica:	What?
MACHOMAN1970:	Cálmate, I can feel your attitude. Where's my son?
FreestyleChica:	Out partying with a couple of whores. And don't tell me to calm down.
MACHOMAN1970:	Oh, is that what first-graders do nowadays?
FreestyleChica:	Oh, maybe if you hung around a first-grader you might not have to ask.
MACHOMAN1970:	Like you didn't know I had plans with my brother last week.
FreestyleChica:	Manny, I have to get up early to take Junito to soccer. Bye.
MACHOMAN1970:	I thought I was taking him.
FreestyleChica:	You didn't arrange that.
MACHOMAN1970:	I always take Junito to soccer.
FreestyleChica:	You didn't take him last week. Besides, he's getting very used to me taking him.
MACHOMAN1970:	Well, I guess we're both going then. See you there.
MACHOMAN1970:	Signed off. 12:06 a.m.

What didn't I resolve in my past life that I was being forced
to work out now? Manny was the only person I knew who could
challenge my spiritual peace. If I ever meet Oprah, I'd love to ask
her, "Ms. Winfrey, when Stedman gets on your last nerve, are you
as nice and patient with him as you are with the rest of the world?
Or do you just lose it and kick his ass from time to time?"

I didn't know what was going to happen to my marriage. I really didn't. I hated not knowing. Why couldn't I ever be the one

to make a decision about this relationship? I shouldn't be hanging around waiting for him to give me an answer, especially since he hadn't shown any signs of wanting to get back together. What if he'd fallen in love with someone else while I'd been waiting for him to decide what to do? That would just piss me off. I should be able to make a decision, stick with it, and not feel like I'm making the worst mistake of my life. Maybe I should send a declaration out into the universe.

Here goes: "There is no way that I'm going to get back together with Emmanuel Rivera. I'm going to be strong and learn how to live life alone. I don't need a man to define me. That's it! I will never go back to Manny. Never ever, *nunca!*"

"Ma?"

"Oh, Junito, did I wake you up?"

Me and my big mouth.

"Yes."

"Come here, *papito*. I'm sorry, *Mami* was just making a wish on a star."

Lord, please tell me he didn't hear what I just yelled out the window.

"It's okay, *Mami*."

"Let me wrap you up like one of *Abuela*'s delicious empanadas," I said. Junito jumped into my arms and sat with his back against my chest. I held him tight.

"Is it true?" Junito asked, looking at me with those beautiful long black lashes and hazel eyes, the only good things that came from his father's gene pool.

I cloaked the blanket around us as we gazed out at the full moon. A little six-year-old boy enveloped in his mother's arms; a wonderful fairy-tale moment, waiting to be narrated by someone with a sweet, light, airy voice.

"*Qué*, Junito?" I asked, in that voice, acting as if I had forgotten what I'd just offered the universe.

"You'll never go back with *Papi*?" Junito asked, continuing to stare at the moon, which seemed to be smirking at me and taunting: "Go ahead with your *pendeja*ness. Answer the kid. Try for once to tell him the truth. Would it kill you to finally be a grown, responsible individual and take control of your life? *¡Estúpida! ¡Pendeja!*" I guess the moon had an attitude tonight; reminded me of my mother.

"Junito, listen . . ." I paused for a second to avoid turning this beautiful children's story moment into a Chucky kills *Mami novela*. Why should I be the one to do all the dirty work? Let Manny be the villain for a change. It was his idea to separate. "It's late, *papi*. I think we should go to bed and not worry. Things have a way of working themselves out, *pa*; really, always for the best," I said, also trying to convince myself.

If only I could believe it.

2 The next morning I didn't feel like dealing with Manny's bullshit lines. The worst experience in the world is to be on the receiving end of a lousy pickup line coming from your soon-to-be-ex-husband. I decided to forgo the desperate but charming I've-been-separated-for-three-months-so-check-me-out look and put on that wonderful married, sweatpants look that screams out for a tube of Great Lash, luscious lip gloss, and a J.Lo apple-bottom implant. The look was complemented by a huge foot-long chili dog in the palm of my hand, and the onion breath was kicking up very nicely.

I watched Junito under the blazing sun, looking as adorable as hell in his long black soccer shorts and little black and white cleats. Boys are wonderful; it's when their pee-pees get longer that they become intolerable.

I looked into the sky and couldn't find one little obscure puff of God mist anywhere; a perfectly clear beautiful Saturday morning.

"Excuse me?" asked a male voice from the bleacher below.

I glanced down, and of all days, of all hours, there he was: the La-tino version of the Marlboro Man; less Tom Selleck, more a darker version of Jay Hernandez, wearing a tight pastel blue designer T-shirt with matching caramel-colored, softball-sized biceps.

There was something about a Latino-looking African-American that sent a shiver down my spine—like one of those chocolates with a cherry inside. It looks like solid dark chocolate but when you bite down, surprise! The sweet taste of cherry is oh, so famil-iar. But like they say, the darker the berry, baby, the more shit I have to hear from my mother.

"Yes?" I answered, pretending to be more concerned with the overflow of my chili dog than with his presence. As much as I loved men, I had this tiny little problem: I wasn't crazy about stroking their egos.

"I think our sons are buddies at school. My son is Lyle."

"Nice. Yes. Right," I said with clenched teeth and a big smile, hoping that the vapors wouldn't escape between the spaces of my teeth.

"I'm Edgar. Is anyone sitting here?"

No, Edgar, it's just me and Mr. Onion Breath. That's all. Please come join us.

"Sure. Come. Sit," I said, trying to think of some more one-syllable words that didn't start with the letter *h*, so that I could avoid releasing my deadly breath.

Of course, I now had to introduce myself, but once I told him my name, he'd surely catch a whiff. The name Idalis is worse than any *h* word—horrible, horrific, highly hysterical—like helium, flowing out of a humongous balloon.

I pretended to flick a wet crumb off my pink sweatpants as I introduced myself. "Hi . . . Idalis," I said, looking toward the bleacher below me.

"Excuse me? I'm sorry, I have a middle ear infection. I can't hear that well," he answered.

I'd swear he was pulling my leg.

"Idalis!" I yelled out in front of me, hoping that the morning breeze was blowing north to south and not east to west.

"I have a cousin named Idalis," he said with a smile so bright I thought I heard the clink of a sunbeam hit his teeth.

We sat awkwardly quiet for a few minutes, watching our kids, waiting to see if this moment meant something more than just a friendly exchange.

Junito blocked the opposing team's play and I screamed myself out of that bleacher and onto my feet. Edgar laughed as I made a fool out of myself. I noticed him checking out the caller ID on his cell phone, but he placed it back into his back jeans pocket without picking it up. He then reached into his front pocket and pulled something out.

"Would you like a piece?" he asked, extending his hand as if knowing that a piece of gum would probably speed things up between us.

Before I could say thank you with my new minty-fresh breath, I saw Manny walking toward us accompanied by a tall brunette. I saw all the soccer moms inhaling to make their waists smaller as she walked by. I felt a little arrhythmia coming on, but that must be normal when two people who have been married for ten years decide to cut the ties that once bound them to the same bedroom. I tried to ignore the feeling.

Manny and the brunette sat behind Edgar and me. I didn't acknowledge them. I couldn't understand how Manny could do this to me—at our son's soccer game. I knew that we were separated and I knew that I told the universe I would never go back to him, but I wasn't ready to deal with meeting my husband's girlfriends.

Manny pointed Junito out to his lady friend and then tapped me on the shoulder. For a second I thought about not turning around, but I didn't want Macho Man thinking I was jealous.

"What's up, Manny?" I asked, knowing it was inevitable that this moment would be uncomfortable.

"Damn, where's your makeup?" Manny asked, laughing to himself.

I so wanted to throw down and come up with a seriously clever ghetto-style comeback, but I didn't want Edgar to see that side of me and I honestly couldn't recover from the punch in my stomach quick enough to get up and punch back. Besides, I was tired of being creative with my fighting words. Instead, I took the high road, which could also be perceived as the *idiota* road.

"Edgar, this is Junito's father. Manny, this is Edgar, Lyle's father."

"Hey, bro, nice to meet you. This is Bonita," Manny said with a big stupid grin on his face, as if to say, "Isn't she so *bonita*?"

"*Hola*," Bonita said in her Conchita Alonzo accent.

I saw Edgar checking her out a little longer than he should have. I turned around to acknowledge Bonita and could smell her cheap floral drugstore-brand perfume mist. It reminded me of the gifts I used to get from *Abuela* when she came to visit from Puerto Rico.

Bonita tried to get friendly with me and asked me what the score was. I didn't want to give this chick the time of day, so I pointed toward the scoreboard and let her figure it out herself. What the hell, did I look like the umpire and shit? Okay, maybe that was rude. So then I answered, "Ten to five, we're winning."

Bonita reminded me of one of those *telenovela* actresses on Telemundo who were so damn perfect: tall, shapely, bronzed, and well poised. Not your average New York Latina. I'm neon-colored compared to her South American pastel-colored vibe.

"*Gracias*, I mean, thank you," she said, trying hard to make me feel comfortable in a non-Latina way.

"I understand Spanish," I answered, pissed that she'd made such a quick assumption. Did I look like I didn't speak Spanish, or did Manny mention to her how much he wished I could?

Manny always wanted me to speak to him in Spanish, especially when we were making love. I remembered how when we were dating I tried saying a few things to him like, "*Ay, Papi. Papi, qué bueno. Tú eres mi culito.*" But when he cracked up while I was going down on him, the foreign-language foreplay ended forever. I meant to say you are my *chulito*, a term of endearment, not you are my little ass.

So I lost my ability to speak Spanish growing up in a Staten Island suburb and now I sounded like Frank Perdue in a Spanish-language commercial. Big deal. I could still salsa my ass off and make a mean *arroz con gandules*. I'd also been seriously contemplating a Puerto Rican flag for the back window of my Jetta, but one smaller than the one Manny had that said, BORICUA YO SOY, POR EL MONTE YO VOY. Yeah, right, I'd really like to know when he was going to that mountain. Manny always had a problem with my Latina *gringa*ness; he made me feel as though I was never Latin enough for his Bronx-born ass.

Edgar and I listened to Manny and Bonita have a conversation about the importance of sports in a kid's life and how fathers should be there to help them with little things like throwing a ball. I already knew where he was going with this. It was what I heard often throughout our marriage. It was what I heard every time we drove past a baseball park. It was what I heard every freaking World Series. He'd always start the same way: "I probably mentioned this before or maybe not, but my father never wanted to play ball with me. My mother taught me how to throw a ball. How embarrassing is that?"

Before I could let out my sarcastic chuckle, Manny stood up, looked out into the field, and yelled, "Hey, Junito! Up here!" Junito looked over with a big grin and a new kick in his step. It was obvious that he was happy to see his dad, and it changed his performance for the rest of the game.

Edgar got another call and this time he did answer it. He waved good-bye to us and spent the rest of his time on the phone at the front gate. As I turned back around in my seat, I caught Manny staring at me. Our eyes met, but he quickly turned away and looked out into the field at Junito.

I couldn't believe that this was what happened after you had given someone ten years of your life. Ten years of sharing, trying, crying, fighting over what color furniture to buy, laughing in the middle of the night, getting over your first fart together, dreaming about winning the lottery and pretending you would still stay together, watching Junito play an orange in his first *Five a Day* play at school; only to suddenly be sitting alone on a cold bleacher while your husband was sitting behind you with a gorgeous female. If this weren't reality, it could possibly be a turn-on.

But this wasn't fun on the inside, because to the right and left of me sat no one. I looked up at the sky, took in the vast blueness, and tried not to feel sorry for myself. I was playing back some PBS show I had watched where this bald guy talked about how the bad moments in our lives are not really bad moments. They're just the moments necessary to help us reach our more enlightened, happier selves. No matter how much I wanted to believe that, I felt like the fat kid sitting alone on the other side of this park—the kid who's waiting for someone to care enough to give him a chance to play.

3

The following day Junito begged to stay with his dad. I told Manny that as long as Bonita wasn't around he could take Junito and bring him back the next day. He didn't act like it was much of a compromise for him, which left me wondering why Manny had her hanging around.

With a full day to myself, I decided to do something unselfish and go to Selenis's place and surprise her with her very own Happy Maid. I'd been holding on to a free coupon for months, and even though I could have used a free cleanup, Selenis needed it more. I'd heard that the male maids they sent out were delicious to look at.

"*Pero*, Idalis, that's so sweet of you," Selenis said, jumping up and down like a voluptuous teen whose robust tatas were spilling over her bright red Lane Bryant V-neck. Twenty years ago I'd have killed for my best friend's breasts. They were two perfect 36C mounds of gelatinous flesh pointing toward the heavens. But after she had three kids and gained a few pounds, hers lost their perkiness, and I had come to accept my little 34A's.

"The maid should be here soon," I said.

For the moment, Selenis's joy helped me escape my own problems. I was practicing what I'd heard a southern black minister say on an early-morning Christian show. He'd said, "When you're feeling down, do something for someone else." His advice was helpful even though the guilt of not having been to Catholic church since I was a teenager had plagued me for the entire day.

Selenis took my hand and led me to the spare bedroom in the back of the house. She was skipping down the hallway and I trailed clumsily behind her. She opened the door to her mother, Doña González, rocking back and forth in her rocking chair as she watched a Spanish television show. The adult actors were dressed in kids' clothes and acting like silly children.

"*Mami*, Idalis is getting us a maid for a day!"

"*Hola*, Doña González," I said, bending down closer so that she could see me better. Her eyeglasses were gigantic and the lenses were so thick, not even a BB gun could crack them. She didn't seem excited to see me. Instead she looked behind me and around, waiting to see someone else.

"*¿Cómo estás, idiota? ¿Dónde está el nene?*" she asked.

I tried really hard not to laugh or get offended. For some reason, the old woman always called me an idiot.

"I'm fine. *El nene* is with his papa," I answered.

I was hoping she wouldn't ask me anything else. She always got angry when I couldn't have full-fledged conversations with her in Spanish, as if my handicap was offending her.

I guess she didn't believe me, because she kept looking for Junito to pop up. She became so frustrated that she stood up and demanded to see someone named Jonathon, but Selenis sat her back down with a gentle hand.

"*No, Mami, es Junito,*" Selenis corrected her as she laid the pale pink knitted blanket over her mother's hairy thin legs.

As we left the room, I looked over my shoulder. Doña González was rocking in her chair again, looking at the comical Spanish-language characters on the small television set. She wasn't laughing; she seemed to be staring far away.

I watched Selenis as she closed the door behind her, acting as though this were normal. Unfortunately, it was. Doña González was forgetting a lot of things lately, and Selenis held on to the hope that her mother would return to her lively old self soon.

As I followed Selenis down the hallway and back into the living room, the doorbell rang. A young platinum-blond woman was standing at the door. She had on a perfectly fitted pink maid's uniform, cleaning supplies in hand.

"Hello, my name is Zaneta. I am from Happy Maids," she said in a rich, robotic Russian accent.

Selenis stepped back to let the pretty maid in and I could see her checking out Zaneta's curvaceous slim body as she made her way into the house. Selenis and I looked at each other, probably thinking the same thing. Why was this chick a maid when she could so obviously be a model? Damn, I'd been really looking forward to the male maid who I heard looked like that cute Latin guy on *CSI: Miami.* I guess next time I would have to put in a special request.

"Vat vould you like me to start doingkh?" Zaneta asked.

"Well, if you want, you can start in here, then the kitchen, and then you can leave," Selenis said, speaking louder than she should have.

"Tank you," Zaneta said, walking her perky derriere toward the large wood-colored IKEA wall unit.

"Why are you yelling? She's not deaf. And why don't you let her clean the whole house? I'm paying for it."

"I don't need the whole house cleaned," Selenis said, eyeing the dust on the coffee table in front of us.

"Yeah, you do," I said, picking up a recent fashion magazine from the bottom shelf and dusting it off. "I guess husband Ralphie is coming home soon, huh?"

"Please, Idalis. Don't be so ridiculous. And the next time you want to send somebody to clean my house, ask me first."

I laughed, knowing that if the maid had been a gorgeous hunk of man, she would have had every room in the house cleaned.

Selenis sat down with me and we tried to act like we were going about our regular business, but Zaneta was a serious distraction to our spiritual inner peace. I thought of having Selenis send her to clean the basement so that we could stop feeling like two busted old maids.

"Where is Ralphie?" I asked as I flipped through the pages of young supermodels in exotic locations.

"He took the kids to the park," Selenis said as she pulled her shirt down below her chubby midsection.

"*Ay, Dios,* would you look at this chick? Does she even eat?"

I said as I handed the magazine to Selenis. I glanced over at Zaneta, who was doing an incredible job of giving shine to furniture that I had never seen shine.

Selenis and I tried to get into a natural conversational flow, but the pretty little Slav was making us feel like we were in desperate need of emergency makeovers. I could tell that she was the kind of girl who did it with the lights on. Hell, she could do it in the middle of Central Park on a sunny afternoon during a volleyball game.

Zaneta finally disappeared into the kitchen, giving Selenis and me time to focus our attention on something other than her perfection.

"You know that she wouldn't get the time of day on Orchard Beach. Don't you think?" Selenis asked, looking at Zaneta's tiny butt walk out of the room. "Baby don't have back like us."

"Who you telling? Please, none of those guys on Orchard Beach would even give that a second look," I said, taking back the magazine, feeling better about my own imperfect body.

Whenever Selenis and I felt depressed about our bodies, we would pull out the culture card immediately. We knew that the Latin female bodies on Orchard Beach in the Bronx rivaled the bodies of some of the best porn stars. Latin women just had that thing that Latin dudes referred to as *sabor*, that thing that left construction workers drooling over their homemade sandwiches.

Honestly, though, I'd never felt like those girls. Selenis had been close to that back in the day. She had a curvy bottom, big boobs, beautiful dark eyes, and full lips that she painted Revlon red to draw even more attention. What made her less than perfect was her belly. Her big boobs always accented the thickness around her middle. But as for me, I always felt like the girl who the guys thought was nice. Instead, I wanted to be the girl who made them look up and yell out, "Goddamn!" I didn't have Beyoncé hips, a big high ass, or a set of knockers that jiggled every time I took a step forward. No matter how much makeup I wore and how tight my clothes clung to my five-foot physique, if you blinked, you might miss me walking by.

"Speaking of Orchard Beach, I heard that Gladys was having a barbecue there tomorrow," Selenis said, picking up a small bottle of fuchsia-colored nail polish from the coffee table.

"She's crazy. I wouldn't go there now. I heard it changed a lot," I said as I watched Selenis open the tiny bottle and start painting one of her big toes.

"Remember the time our parents brought all that food, and my father decided to start selling some of it? The *rellenos de papas* were a huge hit. He made his gas money back that day and then some."

I always had great memories of the times my parents took me to Orchard Beach. It became a family tradition to drive to the Bronx and spend Saturdays there during the summer months. It was the Puerto Rican version of the Hamptons—less the bling. For my parents, it was the closest way to connect to their vibrant Caribbean culture. They never really had enough money to take summer vacations to Puerto Rico.

I remember young and old people dancing in their bathing suits to boom boxes playing Tito Puente and Celia Cruz; coconut-flavored chipped-ice desserts, an unlimited supply of Bacardi rum for the adults; vendors selling Spanish limes (*quenepas*), weird little hairy jawbreaker-sized Caribbean fruits that you would suck all the pulp out of; *abuelitas* sitting under large umbrellas that weren't meant for the beach and their husbands playing dominoes and always flirting with the young women. But those festive excursions ended abruptly when we all moved out of the city and into the suburbs. Instead of seeing empty brown bottles of malta on the sand, we'd see bottles of lemonade and lots of blond and red-haired people who weren't sitting under umbrellas and weren't afraid of getting too dark. Instead of Tito Nieves playing on the FM dial, I'd hear Led Zeppelin's "Stairway to Heaven" over and over again.

The front door opened and Ralphie entered with Carlito, Symone, and Crystal. Little Crystal was holding her bloody knee and crying hysterically. When she saw her mother, she milked the moment and wailed even louder.

"What happened?" Selenis asked as she got up from the reclining La-Z-Boy chair. I could see Zaneta focusing intently on cleaning the microwave door, hiding that she was listening in.

"Carlito pushed me, *Mami*," Crystal said, trying hard to keep those crocodile tears coming.

"No, I didn't. You fell by yourself," Carlito answered as he took a seat on the sofa and continued to battle the little demons in his Game Boy.

"Yes, you did! He's lying, *Mami!*"

"Don't call your brother a liar. Symone, what really happened?"

"Ma, don't ask me."

Adorable little ten-year-old Symone was just like her dad, very hands-off, an uncommon trait for the oldest sibling, and also nothing like her mother.

"Hi, Idalis," Ralphie said in his unemotional monotone voice.

Ralphie didn't even wait for me to say hello back. He walked into the kitchen, leaving Selenis to organize the chaos. He easily could have taken Crystal to the bathroom himself and put a bandage on her, but Ralphie was always good at walking away from every messy situation, the way Manny used to do to me.

"Selenis, sit down, I'll take care of Crystal," I said, hoping that Selenis would give up a little control.

"No, she won't let you touch it. Believe me."

"Sure you will, right, Crystal?"

"No!" Crystal screeched with her piercing five-year-old poltergeist voice.

"It's okay, Idalis, I got it," Selenis said, picking up Crystal in her arms and not caring about getting blood on her new khaki-colored cropped pants.

"No, it's not okay, Selenis. Why do you even have a husband?"

Selenis looked at me as if it were the first time I had ever pointed out the brutal truth to her.

"Excuse me, Idalis. Let's not talk about husbands, okay?"

I hated moments like this for fear that they would turn into serious arguments between us. We were both so stubborn that there were times we stayed mad at each other for weeks.

Zaneta raised her hand, like a schoolkid trying to ask permission to go to the bathroom. "Excuse me, vould you like refrigerator inside cleaned?"

"Crystal is bleeding to death, Ma! Are you going to do something?" Carlito said, probably out of guilt.

I loved the way Selenis could always let stress roll off her chest; I wondered if she had a breaking point.

"Zaneta, you can clean the refrigerator," Selenis answered, leaving the room with Crystal in tow.

I looked over at Ralphie, trying to figure out what was going on with him lately. He was quiet and more distant than usual. Selenis was doing so much that she couldn't even see past her own to-do list to fix what was going on in her marriage.

I entered the small bathroom. Selenis had Crystal sitting on the edge of the sink.

"How's the boo-boo, Crystal?" I asked, trying to ease my way back onto Selenis's good side.

Instead of answering, Crystal just looked at me as if to say, "Duh, isn't it obvious?"

"Crystal, *Titi* Idalis is talking to you. You want *Mami* to take away your favorite toy?"

Crystal just rolled her eyes and folded her little arms across her white T-shirt, covering up the iridescent I'M A LATIN PRINCESS logo.

Selenis picked up Crystal and stood her on the floor. She patted her little flowered denim bubble butt and told her to go play in her room, away from Carlito.

After Crystal left, I watched Selenis in the mirrored shower doors as she put the first-aid kit back under the sink. I looked at her new khaki pants, now decorated with smudges of Crystal's blood. Her blouse a wrinkled mess, and her frosted brown highlights coming loose from the top of her ponytail. I was sure that

Selenis woke up this morning inspired to look nice, but she'd probably be back in her sweats tomorrow. It was times like this, these crazy-kid moments, that made us feel that spending quality time on our appearance was a futile attempt at resurrecting our inner divas. So why bother?

"Listen, I don't need you not talking to me right now, 'cause you hold grudges and, well, that shit is wack," I said, trying to find a way to make peace before the war broke out.

"That's an apology?" Selenis said as she flicked water into my face from her fingertips. "Idalis, I'm not blind, okay? I see a lot."

I followed Selenis out of the bathroom, using my sleeve to wipe the drops off my face. As I entered the living room, I noticed Ralphie chatting with Zaneta. They were both sharing a laugh while she was diligently cleaning the stove top. It was a hearty laugh, not a simple halfhearted laugh.

I purposely tried to block Selenis's view by walking in front of her, hoping that she wouldn't see what I was seeing. But when I turned to look at her, I could tell she overheard the two of them laughing.

"Ralphie, can you go change Carlito's clothes? They're dirty." Selenis yelled toward the kitchen.

"Yeah, babe," Ralphie answered, boldly taking one last glance at Zaneta before exiting the kitchen, a big smile on his face.

As Ralphie walked past us, Selenis couldn't help but ask what was so funny, and Ralphie answered, "You know what her name means in Russian?"

Selenis looked at him as if to say "What would I care?" but he told her anyway.

"It means 'gift from God,'" Ralphie said, laughing as he was leaving the room.

Husbands are such idiots.

4   I woke up the next morning, on my potholed sofa-bed mattress, to a heart-wrenching silence. I missed hearing my little man playing his video game in the next room. I missed him taking his morning pee and forgetting to flush the toilet. I especially missed hearing him play with his father, like two little boys at a slumber party. I imagined that the two of them were playing action figures. I always loved listening to both of them make up voices and dialogue for each character as they battled the forces of evil. It made me sad to know that the last time I heard Manny and Junito playing together possibly could have been the last time.

I hoped I could get out of this depressed mood by work tomorrow. I needed to be focused and energetic, since it was going to be a hellified day at the ad agency. With three new accounts, all the secretaries on the creative team were pulling twelve- to fourteen-hour days. In a way it was a good thing because I needed all the time-and-a-half money I could get. But it was still hard getting by with one salary since the separation. Even if Manny gave me a couple of hundred dollars a month, I still had to use my credit cards to buy things like groceries or even to pay doctor bills. Plus I had the extra expense of paying a babysitting service for Junito two times a week because Manny changed his hours at work and couldn't pick Junito up on time from the after-school Latchkey program.

Sometimes I wished I could leave my job and find something more flexible so that I could be closer to Junito and spend more time with him. Having Junito in school in Staten Island while I worked in Manhattan stressed me out for fear of what might happen if the Staten Island Ferry or the Verrazano Bridge were shut down like during the terrorist attacks. How would I get back home? Before the fall of 2001, I never worried about things like that.

For some reason, everything in my life was suddenly changing. It's like the other day I was cleaning out my closet and I found my old pair of size four Chic jeans, the ones that made my ass look round. I thought, What the hell, they should still fit, but I wound up breaking the zipper. I just stayed there, lying on the floor, looking up at the ceiling and thinking, Isn't it weird how everything in my life just doesn't seem to fit?

Like my job: any idiot could do what I did, because being a secretary on the creative team of Jones, White, and Maller felt more like being a clerk at an arts-and-crafts store than being an employee at a top-ten advertising agency.

When the art directors needed inspiration or visual aids for their ideas, I'd sometimes spend an entire day looking through stock photo catalogs for just the right white American family. I always thought it would be easier just to pull the pictures from a bunch of cheap eight-by-ten picture frames from the local drugstore.

I would stare at family after family wondering if perfect families like that did exist. Were there that many families that looked that good, owned houses like that, and looked that happy all the damn time? Working at the agency always made me feel as though I were born into some dirty, dysfunctional subuniverse. My world was a cheap polyester five-and-dime-store housecoat compared to their couture-designer world where everything was colored in rich shades of green and blue, the sun was always shining at the right angle, and the birds were always humming Bing Crosby songs.

There were times I might have—under my breath—voiced my views about the lily-white world of advertising to one or two art directors I trusted, like Levell Johnson and Marilyn McVee, two Caribbean black art directors responsible for the very clever Juice Me Up ads. They would just laugh and say, "Hey, when in Rome, Idalis."

When in Rome? Who the hell decided to give so much power to the Romans anyway? Why couldn't it be, "When in Rome, be like me"? But since I was the only secretary without a college degree from some fancy-schmancy college in Michigan, Connecticut, or Boston, I would always back down for fear that I'd lose the battle of the brainiest. I really didn't know or care to know what happened during the Roman Empire. All I knew was that I once saw this outrageously sexy movie called *Caligula*, and had no idea that Roman emperors were just as horny and hung as Ron Jeremy.

Dim-witted thoughts like that made me realize the mango doesn't fall far from the tree; those silly little bimboesque moments that I played off like I was just kidding. But with my mom, it wasn't a joke. She would say the stupidest things and be serious about it.

One Saturday she came with me as I dropped off some work at the office and she wouldn't stop rambling on about how lucky I was to work in a building that was so beautiful. She stood in front of my boss's office window looking down on Madison Avenue, watching the people and the traffic below.

"*Pero*, Idalis, you can never leave this job. This is beautiful here."

"*Mami*, a job isn't a location, it's a career. It's what's inside that counts," I said, realizing that my answer sounded as stupid as her comment.

My mother was always in awe of the people who worked in tall buildings. She assumed that people who worked at the Empire State Building or the Trump Tower had to be successful. She couldn't understand why my cousin Damaris, who was seven years younger, got a gig at the Citicorp Building and I couldn't.

"Ever since you read that stupid book *IMOK—YOU'RE OKAY*, you think you are too good."

"Ma, the title is *I'M OK—YOU'RE OK*," I answered, wanting to pee in my pants. However, the seriousness of her voice brought me right back to reality. I always wondered how my mother, with her limited capabilities, had been able to bring me so far in life.

What I wished I could share with my mother was that I aspired to do more than just work at a Madison Avenue business address. I wanted to move out of the creative department and find a position that allowed me to use my brain instead of my first-grade art skills. But the only positions like that required a college degree. I could never understand that, because from what I saw, those who had degrees were sometimes more ignorant than those who didn't.

What really pissed me off was when I had to work alongside these pretentious brats; like the account management trainees, who still had that college sorority vibe going on but tried hiding it behind a navy blue power suit.

"Samantha Leonard needs the Simon Brothers account file. Can you bring it up when you get a chance?" I daydreamed saying into the phone's intercom.

"Idilis, account management trainees don't deliver."

I'd press the ON button on the intercom so hard that I would chip the white off the index finger of my French manicure.

"First of all, it's *Idalis*! With an *a*, not an *i*. And second, Ms. Simone Dubois, you are under your boss, Ms. Leonard, not over, so would you like me to tell her you're too busy?" I'd say, trying to get the balance back in my brain after seeing nothing but black dots before me. My temper was so bad that sometimes I would actually lose my eyesight for a few seconds.

"Oh, so huffy, aren't we? It's business, Idilis, so let's keep professional about it."

"Then, if it's a professional place of business, why don't you try to act a little more professional? You're not at Wilson Community College anymore."

"Community college! Let me set the record straight—"

"Oh, sorry, gotta go. I'll see you in about ten minutes. Thank you so much, Simone, for your prompt attention to this matter."

I always had this crazy dream of making it big and coming back to the old job wearing the I'm-a-successful-bitch uniform—a sexy Armani suit, a kick-ass pair of Manolo Blahnik Mary Janes, a new sassy haircut from Frédéric Fekkai—holding my little Maltese in one hand and blowing air kisses to every asshole that had made me feel invisible and insignificant.

My phone rang and I snapped out of my daydream. Damn, always when I was in the middle of a good one too. It was my mother. She wanted me to drive her into the city so that she could go to the *botánica* on the Lower East Side of Manhattan. She felt a cold coming on and wanted to pick up some authentic eucalyptus crystals.

"Ma, it's Memorial Day weekend, there's gonna be a lot of traffic. It would be a lot easier if you just bought a bottle of Vicks," I said as I sat up on the edge of my bed staring out the window toward Bayonne, New Jersey, the ugliest view in New York City.

"Vicks?" she screamed into the phone.

Vicks had been everywhere in my house when I was growing up. It cured a cold, a stomachache, and it held the broken handle of a cup together—well, at least that was how I remembered it. But suddenly Vicks was old school for my mother, and in her quest toward becoming an enlightened and progressive Latino, like Uncle Herman, she began experimenting with alternative medicinal cures, like melatonin and Saint-John's-wort. But instead of just going to the corner pharmacy for that, she'd get the Latin version of it on Avenue B and Third Street, trusting that it would be a more exact match for her system.

"Forget it, Idalis. I'll take the bus, the ferry, and the subway so that you don't have to deal with me and your very sick *abuela*," she said after I gave her the well-deserved dramatic pause she probably expected.

"Ma, I didn't say that I wouldn't take you, but you never ask me if I'm busy. You just assume that I have nothing to do. And what's wrong with *Abuela* now?"

"Now? She's old, Idalis. That's what's wrong with her."

I always thought that my mother and her mother, my only living *abuela*, were frustrated actresses. The melodrama came so naturally to them.

"Besides, what are you doing that is so important?" she continued.

"Nothing right now, Ma, I just got up."

"You know, Idalis, sometimes instead of just fighting things you should be more compassionate and understanding and quietly do things for people you say you love. Life is *bien* short and then the flowers die."

What language did this woman speak?

I heard another call coming in and I told my mother to hold on. As I clicked over to the other line, I heard her sigh impatiently. It was Junito.

"Hey, *papito*, you ready to come home?" I asked, happy to hear his little voice.

"*Mami?*" By the tone of his voice, I could tell he was about to ask me for something that I probably would say no to.

"Yes?" I said, with a long-drawn-out hesitation.

"I want to stay here a little more."

"No, no, no, no, no, you have to come home, you have school tomorrow."

"Daddy said I can stay if I want."

"Put Daddy on the phone."

I heard Junito say, "Here, Daddy," as if I was about to be the crimp in their plans.

"Yeah, Idalis."

"I want him home today. Now. Not tomorrow. *Ahora!*"

"He wants to stay with me."

"Hello? Excuse me? You're not hearing me. That's it. He has school tomorrow."

"Like I can't take him to school."

"Manny, seriously, stop. I want him home now. Besides, he has no change of clothes."

"I'll buy him some. He needs new jeans anyway. The ones you have on him are high-waters."

"Manny, what are you not hearing? Listen, this isn't the way it works, okay? You can't have what you want every time you want it. He's coming home today. That's it," I said, now standing up on the edge of my bed, ready to win this round.

I felt like I was starting to become one of those crazy house-wives in a Lifetime movie of the week. I hated feeling like the incessantly bitchy wife, but Manny was making it impossible for me to hold down my own fort. I needed structure, stability, and some kind of organization in my life. He couldn't come and go as he pleased with my son.

Or was I wrong? Was I trying to be a control freak? Was I trying to get back at him for not caring enough to make it work while we were still living in the same house? Part of me wanted to let the stress roll off my shoulders, but the other part of me, the one that really cared about my son's future, wanted to put her foot down.

"Listen, if you need more time with Junito, then maybe it's time we talk to a lawyer and stop playing this game," I said, partly afraid and partly jumping for joy.

But I didn't hear anything back. No sarcastic comment. No laugh, nothing. He just hung up without saying a word and I took a deep breath and exhaled, before clicking over to my mother.

"Hey, Ma," I said in my pretend-happy voice, hoping she wouldn't detect my anger. No matter what happened between Manny and me, my mother always seemed to come to his defense, and I didn't feel like hearing her praise the same man that was breaking my heart.

"Well, it's a good thing I didn't have a stroke or a heart attack. How would anyone get in touch with me *por teléfono*?"

I could take the high road and keep it moving, ignore her comment and have a more peaceful afternoon, or I could jab her back with a sarcastic below-the-belt insult that would keep her pissed at me for the rest of the day.

"Ma, I'll pick you up in an hour," I said.

When I placed the receiver back down on the phone, I felt my stomach turn a bit. It was the first time since my separation that I'd actually made an attempt to take control of the situation. That moment of empowered inspiration was such a surprise to my system that it caused my heart to flutter with fear. Maybe because part of me, the part that I swear had ADD sometimes, didn't like to wait around for an answer. I didn't like gray areas and never had. I didn't even like the color gray. Gray has an identity crisis going on because it doesn't know what color it wants to be. It tries to be black and it tries to be white but it fails to be either. The colors black and white are so sure of themselves, that's it. Either we're married or we're not. I couldn't wait forever. I needed an answer now.

5 Rather than wait for Macho Man to bring Junito back to me on his time, I decided I would go pick him up myself. Manny was staying with his younger brother Johnny on the south shore of the island and it would take me fifteen minutes to get there and another ten minutes to get to my mother's house.

It was super-convenient to have everyone live in the same borough. The migration happened gradually starting in 1976 when *Mami*'s brother, Uncle Herman, decided he had had enough of running numbers for the neighborhood folks down on the Lower East Side and was ready to become a serious entrepreneur.

He used to say, "*Ese hombre* Ronald McDonald deedn't go to *escuela*. He was a born entrepr—enterprenu—entre—*contra*! He was like me, a person with a lot of balls. That's what you need to be a big-time businessperson, a big set of *huevos* and a dream."

"*Tío*, you mean Ray Kroc, not the clown you see on television," I would say, time and time again. For some reason my uncle never wanted to listen to me, or anyone else, for that matter. He made up his own rules. He was a risk-taker, and as annoying as his rebellious tendencies were sometimes, I had to admit that I found them admirable.

Uncle Herman was a short hairy man with a big ego. He had long black hair that grew out of his back and up around his neck. His potbelly hung down below his belt, but you could never tell him he was putting on weight because he'd suck up his belly and say, "*¿Dónde?* I don't see any fat." He had an olive complexion and a beauty mark on the left side of his upper lip.

He was easily mistaken for Greek wherever he went and once in a while we'd kid that he was a male Cindy Crawford. He'd laugh and answer, "Oh, *sí*, then I could suck my own *tetas!*" He was a nasty horny little man too, but one thing I always gave him credit for was being ballsy enough not to care about what anyone else thought of him.

When he first moved to Staten Island to open his business, he immediately realized a Spanish bodega wouldn't be the smartest thing to open in a predominantly Italian borough. Instead he opened up a luncheonette and called it Constantine's Webos. His logo was a face with two large eyes, above a little fuzzy mustache and a long nose somewhat in the shape of a penis. The slogan read, "Two *webos* are better than one." I remember his brother, Uncle Sammy, the only one of my mother's brothers who attended college for a minute, and so acted like he had earned a Ph.D., would tell Herman that his logo was too phallic for an eatery. Uncle Herman, always paranoid that Sammy was trying to crush his dream, would answer, "Ay, phallic *ni* phallic."

"Do you know what *phallic* means, *Tío?*" I would ask Uncle Herman, trying to help him out before Uncle Sammy got to him.

"*¿Qué tu crees?* What do you think?" he always answered. It was better to answer with a question than admit to not knowing something.

Uncle Herman, however nutty he appeared, was a brilliant man. His phallic little logo made him a popular local businessman, and that caused Uncle Sammy much distress. Uncle Herman made such great egg sandwiches that his business became the favorite truck stop en route to the New Jersey Turnpike. Uncle Sammy couldn't understand how someone so ignorant and uneducated could actually become so successful.

As the business grew, so did Uncle Herman's pocket, and he was able to buy his family a house on Staten Island. My parents followed soon after. Selenis's mother moved a few years later and before you knew it, most of my close friends and immediate family lived twenty minutes away from each other.

When I got to Johnny's place, I noticed a new dent in the back of Manny's white Dodge Durango in the garage. My stomach dropped; I hoped that Manny hadn't gotten into an accident with Junito in the car. I ran up the stairs immediately and rang the doorbell. Once, twice, and then I just banged the hell out of the door.

The door opened.

"Junito! How many times do I have to tell you that you shouldn't answer the door like that? Don't do that again, okay? You want some crazy person taking you away forever?"

I immediately saw his gap-toothed smile turn into a frown. This was my greeting? This was the first thing I said to my little miracle after missing him?

"But Daddy was in the shower," he answered, with his face to the floor.

I walked into the apartment, closed the door behind me, and picked Junito up in my arms, giving him a tight hug and drowning him in a million kisses.

"I want you to stay with me forever. I don't want somebody taking you away, *papito*. Okay?"

His smile returned and I could smell orange juice on his stinky little morning breath.

I carried Junito to the sofa and as soon as we sat down, Manny sprinted out of the bathroom with a towel wrapped around his waist. I could see a thin mist of water on his broad tan shoulders. It looked to me as if he had been working out. It's funny how those muscles had lain dormant for the last five years of our relationship. His ass looked nice and tight too, and I could see a few muscles bulging at his stomach. I quickly remembered why I let him dance with me to Janet Jackson's "Alright" the night we finally danced at the Pegasus Dance Club.

He was unusually tall for a guy whose father and brother stood at five-foot-six with shoes on. He was almost six feet tall and when his thick light brown hair was blow-dried out, it added another half an inch or so to his height.

"He opened the door?" Manny said, without looking for an answer, and gave a look of disappointment to Junito before walking back into the bathroom.

"We're just gonna leave, okay?" I yelled out while picking up about half a dozen of Junito's X-Men action figures from the floor.

Either Manny couldn't hear me or he didn't want to answer. I told Junito to pick up the rest of his toys so we could head out to my mother's on time.

Manny came out of the bathroom. He had dressed so quickly it seemed like a David Blaine magic act.

"Can I talk to you?" he asked.

"I've got plans today, Manny," I said, hoping to evoke a look of curiosity.

"A minute, Idalis, that's all."

The desperation in his voice almost made me feel sorry for him, but I thought about how happy he seemed the other day at the soccer game and decided not to give in that easily.

"People are waiting for me," I said, wondering if he was curious to know who was waiting for me.

"Hey, Junito, *Little Bill* is on. Why don't you go in *Papi*'s room for a second?" he said.

I watched our little boy race to watch one of his favorite shows.

I plopped my ass on the sofa, placed the Spider-Man backpack down with a slight hint of impatience, and stared up at him. My heart was fluttering through the anger and I knew there still had to be something there for him. How can you suddenly fall out of love after so many years together? The more confident Manny appeared, the more I hid my feelings by reverting to some childish animated being, like Dora the Explorer.

"Idalis, I don't like what you said. I don't understand why you have to bring lawyers into all of this."

Can you say because you are a *cabrón*, motherfucker? *Excelente!*

"What's so funny?" he asked.

Sometimes I had a habit of laughing at my own internal dialogue.

"Manny, I'm not trying to be a bitch just to be a bitch, but for real, we need some order here. Well, I need it. I don't know what you need," I answered, accidentally ripping Wolverine's head off.

He stood there staring down at me as I tried to click the bearded guy's head back on.

He took the Wolverine action figure from me and I felt his fingers rub against my hand. They felt warm and familiar. It reminded me of the times we lay in bed together and held hands before falling asleep.

"This isn't working," he said as he tried over and over again to snap the plastic head back onto the neck of the body.

"Well, then let's just get this shit done already. Why are we here playing games? You're obviously moving on."

"I was talking about the doll, Idalis."

"Daddy, it's not a doll, it's an action figure!" Junito chimed in from the back room.

For the first time in a long time we shared an intimate laugh. Thank God for kids; as crazy as they can make your life, they know exactly what to say at the right moment.

"Listen, I'm not trying to be difficult either. I agree we need to get our shit together for Junito's sake, but I can't afford a lawyer right now," he said as he bent down on one knee, meeting me at eye level.

I sat there looking into his face, wondering if he was feeling all the same anxiety that I was feeling. Was he afraid? Men—you can never really tell. They've been trained so well to swallow their emotions. In that moment, I realized that maybe I was being too hard on Manny. Maybe I needed to step back and look in the mirror. I knew it took two to tango and, I mean, maybe I contributed to our separation in some way, just maybe.

I felt a door open within my heart. I wanted to talk and share with him the way I had before we split. I wanted to tell him that I was tired of living in the land of uncertainty, of floating in a highly emotional state of limbo and not seriously dating anyone in case we still had a chance to fix this marriage. I thought about all those couples I'd seen on *Dr. Phil* who actually did get back together after long separations. Yes, I knew it would be tough and I'd probably ask him a million times, "How far down did Bonita go?" Or maybe I didn't want to know. Because if we loved each other and got through this, what did it matter if Bonita kissed him down there? What did it really matter? Who cared? I was bigger than that. Hell, we were bigger than that. I didn't need to know stupid things like that. Because we would have braved the storm and I would have come out the champion and we'd live happily ever after. Like that character that Jim Carrey played in *The Truman Show*: I would have escaped the surreal hell that I was put through because it was a test, a little quiz given to me by the creator of my own TV show to see if I had what it took to keep this marriage together.

As soon as the birds in my little universe sang their last melody, I heard the basement door creak open and out walked the last person I ever expected to see at that moment. Bonita.

There were more than a million black dots floating in front of my eyes at this point. I actually thought I was going blind. But more so, I felt that reality had given me the biggest kick in my little naïve ass.

Bonita swung her flowered straw bag around her shoulder. She seemed upset; the nerve of her. I couldn't move. It was as if I were watching the climax of one of my *abuela's novelas*.

"Bonita, what are you doing?" Manny asked as she whizzed past me in her tight blue jeans and yellow high-heeled sandals.

"Manny, I wunt to live." To the average non-Spanish-speaking American it would have sounded like Bonita just talked herself out of suicide, but I knew what she meant as she raced to the door without even acknowledging my presence.

As the door almost closed behind her, Johnny came running up the stairs and followed her out of the house dressed only in boxers and holding a loafer in each hand.

"Bonita, wait!" Johnny screamed as he skipped to the front door trying to put one loafer on at a time. But Bonita was so quick she beat him outside. The door closed behind her with such force, Johnny had to move his hand quickly out of the way to avoid getting his fingers caught. Then Johnny opened the door and followed her out and screamed, "But I do love you!"

I sat there wishing I could change the channel. I could not believe that Manny hadn't told me the truth about his brother's girlfriend.

"Are you serious, Manny?"

"I know it was stupid of me. I don't know why I did that."

"Fuck you. Really, fuck you right now and forever. Because I can't believe you were trying to make her out to be a friend of yours. No, excuse me, your girlfriend."

"She is a friend."

"No, Manny, she's really Johnny's friend, stupid."

I ran into the spare bedroom where Manny was staying, grabbed Junito's forearm, and dragged him and the Spider-Man backpack out of the house.

"Wait, Idalis, listen to me," Manny said.

As I ran right past him without saying a word, I could feel his heavy breathing behind me. I ran out of the house and down the stairs to my car, passing Bonita, who was crying along with Johnny, who was holding her in his arms.

"Idalis, would you wait a minute?" Manny screamed from the top of the staircase.

Before I got into my car, I looked at us in that moment and my internal dialogue recognized the humor of it all: four Latin people screaming and crying loudly in the middle of the street. I could hear the old rich white couple driving by in their Mercedes E500 saying, "Those Latinos are such lively people."

But the thing that wasn't so funny to me was that Manny wanted to give me the impression that he was moving on when he wasn't. Why would someone I spent an entire decade with lie and try to hurt me?

It made me wonder what else he wasn't telling me.

6 I dropped my mother off at the *botánica* on Avenue B and Seventh Street on the Lower East Side of Manhattan and decided I would take Junito to Tompkins Square Park across the street. I wasn't in the mood to listen to my mother and Señora Topacio talk about homemade remedies that could possibly cure arthritis, migraines, and menopause while at the same time warding off evil spirits. Señora Topacio, the owner of the *botánica*, was the ultimate salesperson. She had a way of talking you into buying her DIY concoctions, as if you were missing out on the world's best-kept secret.

I sat on a park bench, watching Junito run up the long steps to the top of the slide.

"Look, *Mami!*" he yelled as he made his way down.

His little happy voice pressed pause on the pity party playing inside my head so that I could share his fun moment with him.

"Good, *pa*, but be careful," I said, trying to smile.

Junito seemed so happy and oblivious to the realities of our family's present emotional state. I wondered if kids went through the motions the way adults did when they were trying to get through the bullshit of life. I wondered if underneath it all he was stressing out just as bad as I was.

My thoughts were interrupted by the hint of a urine smell coming from the homeless woman a few benches away. I watched her sitting with her legs wide open, reading a newspaper that she had rested between them, the same way construction workers riding to work on the subway often do. She was absorbed in the pages of the science section of the *Times*, and one would wonder why someone so seemingly sane would be living on a park bench. But that thought ended when she broke out into hysterics at every turn of the page.

I couldn't help but wonder if this woman had had a normal life at one time. How did she get here? Where was her family? Her husband? Her kids? Weren't they worried about her? This was a woman who was once a little girl. Watching her sent a feeling of uncertainty through me. How did a person get so lost that she didn't realize she was wearing a wool coat and a scarf in ninety-degree weather?

My heart raced as I thought about the three credit card bills sitting on my kitchen table waiting to be paid. Not to mention the payment reminder from Con Edison that I'd taped to the refrigerator this morning. I was trying to fight the urge to go over and ask the ragged woman if credit card debt had brought her to this park bench. I hoped she might give me information that would help me avoid the same ill fate.

"Excuse me," I said, trying hard not to allow my face to twitch from the killer ammonia-like odor. "Here you go." I offered her a dollar bill.

I held a very tiny corner of the dollar bill so that she wouldn't touch my hand. To my surprise, she looked at the dollar bill, went into hysterics, and went back to reading her paper—without taking the money. I thought, Wow, she's really off her rocker. In an instant, she closed the newspaper shut, slid her smelly ass over to the next bench, and opened the paper back up and kept reading. She made sure to give me one last look as if to say, "Bitch, you're trespassing on my property."

As I walked back to my bench, I waited for Junito to come back down the slide. I never saw his brown hair reach the top of the metal staircase, so I walked closer to the slide. He wasn't there.

"Junito!" I immediately scoped the swings, the monkey bars, the seesaw, and saw no sign of Junito anywhere. My heart was beating out of my chest. I'd had this happen in a dream and I could never get myself to scream his name loud enough, as if someone had removed my voice box.

"Junito!" I yelled louder, and with such panic I scared the homeless woman out of her seat. I ran to the park entrance but didn't see his little orange Sean John T-shirt or his blue Nike nylon pants. God, please show him to me. Don't do this. This was my biggest fear. I wouldn't be able to handle this one. That was why I hated coming into the city now; it wasn't what it used to be when I was a kid. Every person on the street was now a suspect in my eyes. I ran from the front entrance of the park to the back entrance and screamed his name louder each time, hoping that I would see his little head peek out from under a bench or from behind the small brick house in the center of the park.

I walked toward the men's room, and I noticed a pair of boy's black leather Jordans standing behind a tree. They were Junito's black Jordans. I saw another pair of larger Jordans standing next to him.

"Surprise!"

Both Manny and Junito jumped toward me.

Manny must've found out that I was coming here. I snatched Junito by the sleeve so hard I took half his shirt off him.

"Don't ever do that to me again," I said, pulling him out of the park and trying to get his arm back into the sleeve.

"Daddy told me not to say anything."

"I don't care. You don't scare *Mami* like that."

"Are we gonna wait for Daddy?"

"I have to pick up *Abuela*, come on."

"Daddy, come on, we have to pick up Grandma," Junito yelled over his shoulder.

"Daddy isn't allowed to come with us."

"Why not?"

Because he's a pathetic confused asshole.

"Junito, please stop asking me so many questions."

"Why are you always running away?"

"I guess you want to get punished for two weeks," I screamed, knowing that in a few seconds I would feel like crap for doing that.

I walked back up toward the *botánica*, passing the homeless woman on the other side of the fence. She was laughing.

"Idalis, please stop!" Manny yelled, a few steps behind me.

I didn't want to hear him. I didn't even want to look at Manny. I was so tired of trying to figure out where he was coming from. Just when I thought he was being sincere and truthful, he pulled something stupid and I was left feeling like a *pendeja* once more. Well, that wasn't happening again.

"Ma, you're walking too fast."

"I have to get *Abuela* right away."

"Idalis, wait, stop making me chase you. Idalis!"

I felt Manny getting closer and before I could step off the curb, he grabbed my arm and turned me toward him.

"Manny, don't you dare. I don't want to hear anything come out of your mouth. Nothing!" I said, pulling my arm away.

"Don't be like that in front of you-know-who."

"Like he doesn't know who you-know-who is."

"*Por favor*, Idalis, *cálmate*, calm down."

"What's the problem, Manny? You wanted to separate, and now what? Did you have a change of heart? This isn't a game show."

"I wanted the separation? Oh, yeah, that's a joke. Who told who to pack up and leave because she wasn't sure if she was in love with you-know-who?"

"What the hell is with the you-know-who shit? Manny, you tell so many stories that I think you're beginning to believe your own lies."

My mother was sitting on a small wooden bench in front of the *botánica* waiting for me to pick her up. She was pretending not to hear us as she browsed through the large shopping bag sitting on the ground next to her feet. But I knew that Manny and I were loud enough for her to hear.

"I am calling a lawyer first thing tomorrow," I said, wondering how one went about finding a divorce lawyer. Should I use the yellow pages or AskSimon.com? "And stop following me!"

"Here, these are for you. Can you just hear me out?" he said as he handed me the most beautiful roses he had ever given me.

I looked at the roses for a second, taking in the long stems and the firmness of the petals. They were perfect. He'd spent good money for these. These weren't the roses you pick up at the Korean market, the twelve-for-ten-dollars bunch. These were the eighty-dollar roses you get at a florist either at the South Street Seaport or uptown on Lexington Avenue.

"First of all, I'm calm. Second, I don't feel like talking to you right now. I seriously can't figure out why my husband is suddenly acting like Mr. Big," I said, taking the roses and throwing them in a nearby garbage can. "You always did say that flowers were a waste of money."

"Who in the hell is Mr. Big? *Quién en carajo* is Mr. Big?" was the last thing I heard Manny say before I walked away from him feeling like a winner and a loser: a winner for standing my ground, but a loser for standing my ground while our son was watching.

I finally made it across the street and my mother waved hello to Manny as if all were normal. I could feel Junito yearning for his father to be a part of us again, because he looked over his shoulder to say good-bye more than once. I couldn't imagine what I was putting my son through right now. I wondered if his six-year-old heart knew what was really going on.

I just wanted Junito to know that it wasn't my idea to break up the family unit. I never told Manny that I wasn't sure if I loved him. He was manic. Okay, maybe once in a stupid fight about him spending endless hours playing video games instead of helping me clean the house I might have said I wasn't sure if this marriage was working. But that was just something I said because he told me I was becoming a nag. I agreed that maybe we'd fallen into a rut and things had gotten a bit stale for us. I did get tired of wearing Victoria's Secret lingerie to bed. It made no sense in the winter because you just froze your ass off and it cost a fortune. So I wore cotton jammies for a minute, what's wrong with that? At what point did I get to stop having to impress my husband? For God's sake, the man had seen placenta fly out of my vagina. But no, nothing was enough for Manny. How many different ways could a couple have sex? Because once you've played the you-numba-one-fucky game a hundred times, what's next? Maybe we were a match gone wrong. I'd thought I really knew him. I mean, his idea of kinky sex was totally different than mine. Kinky sex to me was watching *The Bridges of Madison County*, making out for an hour, and then having our souls dance to a slow jam by Donny Hathaway. Dance with me, *pendejo*! Be more like Trisco. Trisco never would have let me dance alone. Trisco never would have broken up our little family—that is, had we had one. Thanks to Manny, our once-happy little family was now broken and in desperate need of love.

I could feel my eyes tearing up, but I didn't want Junito or my mother to see me cry. I put the key in the ignition and kept my eyes wide open to let the breeze from the open window dry up my tears before they fell down my face. It worked as long as I could concentrate on the road ahead, but after ten minutes of forcing my mind not to think of Manny, my mind won. I could feel the tears fall onto the steering wheel. I wiped away the wetness as I tried hard to keep the rest of my emotions from flooding out.

"*¿Qué pasa*, Idalis? Why do you and Manny need to be fighting so much? It's bad for Junito and it is very stupid. Stop wasting time and get back together, because marriage is a contract," my mother said as she browsed through her purse looking for something.

I looked into the rearview mirror and noticed that Junito had fallen asleep, giving me the opportunity to speak without having to use big-people codes.

"Ma, today people are different. They don't stay together for the sake of the kids anymore. When it's over, it's over. You move on."

"You are going to get divorced after all that money you spent on the wedding and *esa comida?* Now you have to stay married because that would be too much money to throw away."

She handed me one of her tissues.

"Ma, money? You're worried about money that I spent on vows that mean nothing?" I handed her back the unused tissue.

"*Ay, mi madre,* I didn't know that I was sitting next to Elizabeth Taylor. Go ahead. Spend all your *dinero.* Go ahead. Use some more credit cards *para un divorcio y después,* get married again. The problem with kids like you is that they want to throw something away as soon as it doesn't work."

As stupid as my mother could sound, there were those times she made sense.

I couldn't deny that I was guilty of throwing away a lot lately. But it was different today than it was back in the day. I remember Selenis and I would wear a pair of no-name smiley-faced sneakers until the toes ripped a little in the front or the soles became uneven. And we never would have thought of spending more than ten to fifteen dollars on a pair of hangout shoes. Back then, fifteen dollars would buy us at least two or three pairs of different-colored jellies. We didn't have it to waste, so we'd make sure that we really used the stuff we had until we couldn't use it anymore. It was rare that we would send five bags of clothes and shoes a year to the Salvation Army.

But *Mami* was right. The other day I threw out a bunch of Junito's VCR tapes: Elmo, *Blue's Clues, Sesame Street,* and *Baby Einstein.* I had to. No one I knew owned a VCR anymore except my mother, and as she used to say after babysitting Junito for an entire day, she'd seen enough of that shit. But hell, it wasn't my fault that DVDs came out. It wasn't my fault that they kept adding new features to cell phones and computers. How was I supposed to share my pictures with my family and friends with a Pentium III and dial-up? And there was a really good reason why I couldn't wear last year's Coach bag this year, because, well, then everyone would know that I was wearing the little *c*'s that were out last year instead of the big *C*'s that were in this year. I wouldn't be caught dead in old school if old school wasn't really in. So in the meantime, I thought I might start wishing for a new pink iPod to come my way, since my iRiver MP3 doesn't do iTunes.

"Ma, that's why they invented eBay, so you don't feel guilty about getting rid of your stuff," I said, breathing a sigh of relief knowing that I figured out the solution to the problem.

"Oh, so why don't you find a husband on eBay?" she said, laughing to herself while searching the depths of her purse.

If only I could bid on a husband. That would be hilarious. But I was sure I'd be outbid by a PowerSeller whose life wasn't as screwed up as mine and who had great credit on PayPal.

The tears wouldn't stop. I grabbed a tissue from the top of my mother's purse and I squeezed the tears back into the corners of my eyes. I didn't want to cry anymore. I was tired of crying. Tired of figuring out why my life suddenly seemed to be out of whack.

"Idalis! *Virgen Santa, Idalis!*" my mother screamed.

"What, Ma?" I asked, watching my mother frantically go through her shopping bag and purse.

"*Dios mío,* please, son of *em bon bitche.*"

"What?"

"*Mi dinero. Yo creo que está en la botánica.*"

Oh, my damn. Was she serious? She'd left her wallet in the *botánica*?

"*Mami,* are you sure? Look through everything again. I can't go back to the city now, I just paid the toll."

"Idalis, *mi tarjeta de* Medicare *y* Social Security and everything is lost. I will give you two dollars."

I wanted to tell her that her offer was off by another seven dollars, but the real headache wasn't about the money, it was having to go all the way back into the city.

This had been one long-ass weekend, and all I wanted to do was lie down in my bed alone and listen to Josh Groban's "Un Amore Per Sempre" and cry myself to sleep. But instead I dropped my mother and Junito off at her house and drove another thirty-five minutes back into Manhattan.

I couldn't help but remember that bald motivational speaker I'd seen on PBS. It was as if he were sitting next to me in the car on my ride back to the city. "Sometimes you may not understand why you are being dealt the hand that you are being dealt, but you created your own universe from the very beginning of your birth. The things that happen to you happen because you planned it that way. The people in your life are there because you ordered them there. Remember what it is your heart really wanted when you first got here."

Could someone shut him the hell up?

7 As I walked into the *botánica*, I was overwhelmed by the heavy smell of musk incense. I immediately experienced a feeling of déjà vu. The song "Un Amore Per Sempre" was playing, but it wasn't Josh Groban's version. I suddenly stopped to listen. It was one of those crazy coincidences I'd been noticing a lot lately. Like last week I was driving behind a guy whose license plate read 917 and when I looked to see what time it was, the clock read 9:17. This made me feel like I should look around the store a bit more. Maybe there was a message here for me. Who was trying to talk to me? Hello? What are you trying to tell me? Please speak to me. I can't decode any more signs and I can't figure out this Rubik's Cube I live in.

I walked over to a makeshift altar. I recognized Saint Martin, a black saint that my grandmother used to have on her own make-shift altar back at her home in Puerto Rico. I looked at the dark little man in the brown robe and I asked him to please tell me if Manny and I were meant to be together. He didn't answer or give me a sign. He just stood there, holding his cross to his chest, staring at the two little dogs sitting at his feet. I picked up the statue and stared at him, hoping he could hear my thoughts. Saint Martin, here's the deal: Just because Manny brought me flowers, actually expensive flowers, doesn't mean he wants to be with me. He could just be as scared as I am about being alone for the rest of his life. Maybe I'm just a backup plan for him. It'll be a cold day in hell—oops, my bad—it'll be a cold day in July if he thinks I'm waiting around for him to decide what's going to happen to us. We know each other too well to play games. We've invested too much of our time together to pretend that there is no pain living in this eternal state of limbo. I feel a huge lump in my throat, Saint Martin. Aren't you the saint that heals people? I can't swallow. There's something really big stuck in my throat that won't let me swallow.

I placed Saint Martin back down on the altar, and the lyrics of the song, the thoughts running through my head, and the lump in my throat finally got the best of me. It all came out—in one big sloppy sob.

"Idalis," Señora Topacio said, stepping out from behind the burgundy-colored velvet curtain that separated the front room of the store from the Room of Dreams. "*¿Qué pasa, nena?*"

"Señora Topacio, I'm just having a really bad day," I said, in between heavy sobs that could be heard even louder now that my song was over.

"*Siéntate, mija*, sit down." Señora Topacio took my hand and led me to one of two wicker chairs that smelled like cat.

I looked up at Señora Topacio. Her foundation was so thick I could make out all the lines and pores on her face as if I were looking at her through a magnifying glass. She wore dark eyeliner on both the top and bottom lids of her eyes and sparkly blue eye shadow. She hid her gray hair behind an old Versace kerchief.

Sitting at my side, she sandwiched one of my hands in between hers and tried to comfort me. As my sobs were mellowing out, she looked into my eyes with such passion that it made me pull away. I browsed the inside of my bag, pretending to look for something.

"I'm better, thank you," I said, with my head practically in the bag.

"Talk to me, *nena*, I'm here to help," she said, looking so deeply inside my pupils that I thought I had an eye booger. I slid my index finger into the corner of my eye to make sure. No booger. She continued to stare deeper and deeper. She was so close that I could smell her sweet breath. To my surprise, it was the only thing in the whole place that smelled pleasant.

"*Nena*, I see something," she said, inching closer to my face. She continued to stare as if she were playing the no-blinking game that I sometimes played with Junito. First one to blink loses. I blinked. She kept staring. Our lips were almost touching and I wondered how much closer she needed to get before she could see into my future. Didn't she have a crystal ball? She pulled back and looked toward the cash register. I knew it. I knew that I was going to be suckered into one of her fixes. She knew I'd believe anything she told me because I was just so tired that I couldn't possibly have the energy to put up a good enough fight. I couldn't defend myself. I couldn't think straight.

"What do you see?" I asked, hoping it would be good news.

"You are flying," she said, looking into my eyes as if they were a crystal ball.

"Where am I flying to? Los Angeles? Hawaii? San Juan?"

What the hell did she mean by flying? Was I going on a trip? Shit, I felt like I'd been tripping all weekend. Oh, right, this was the part when she asked me for twenty dollars so she could figure out where I was flying to.

"No, *nena*, wait." She thought for a moment, trying to find the right words, or trying to make out the visual in her head, or in my eyes.

"You are dancing."

Was I flying or dancing? Make up your mind, I thought.

"*Sí, sí, sí*, you are dancing and you are happy," she said.

She was bugging me out. Should I be taking this literally, or was this some metaphor or just plain old bullshit? I was dancing? Freestyling or salsa dancing? If I was salsa dancing, then I wasn't really alone because I would need a partner to do that, but if I was freestyling, then that probably meant I was doomed to be a lonely old woman. She took her hand away and walked to the cash register. She opened it and asked me what I wanted as she counted the dollar bills.

See, I knew it. This was the part when she handed me the bill and told me that as soon as I paid her she'd tell me what it was I really wanted.

"What do I want?" I asked, trying to find the answer in me.

I noticed a little girl a few years older than Junito pressing her dirty face up against the store window. Señora Topacio picked up an old Café Bustelo can, walked toward the little girl, and opened the front door. She held the can out and the little girl reached in and pulled out a lollipop. The little girl peered inside the can again, looking for something more, reached in and pulled out a second lollipop, then she skipped away. Señora Topacio walked back into the store, turned the OPEN sign to the CLOSED side, and walked back to the register, where she continued counting her money.

"Yes, *nena, ¿qué tú quieres?*"

"Well, I guess I want to be happy."

"But what will make you happy?"

What would make me happy? What would make me happy? What would make me happy? Why was that such a difficult question to answer? World peace would make me happy. The end of racism would make me happy, but that actually fell under world peace. Who was I fooling? A size four would make me happy. A whole closetful of designer shoes would make me gloriously happy. Actually, winning the Mega Millions would make me ridiculously happy. But for some reason, I didn't think that was the answer Señora Topacio was looking for.

"When you are ready to experience the dance, then you will be free."

Holy shit! This was worse than a Rubik's Cube. This was like playing Pictionary with your eyes closed.

I handed Señora Topacio a ten spot before leaving. To my surprise, she pushed it back, along with my mother's wallet. I left the *botánica* thinking hard about the dance I was supposed to experience and replayed her last few words:

"When you are ready to experience the dance, then you will be free."

The next day at work, I was so anxious to hear what Selenis thought about Señora Topacio's prediction that I skipped the usual routine of grabbing my second cup of morning coffee and borrowing the newspaper's daily horoscopes from T-Zone (the wannabe rapper/mailroom clerk) and called Selenis as soon as I got to the office.

"Are you nuts, Idalis? Stay away from that lady, *ella es una loca.* My mother told me she made some lady disappear from the face of the earth."

"You know, Selenis, your mother's been saying a lot lately; things that don't make sense," I said, tiptoeing around the obvious.

"Don't diss my mother."

"Not for nothing but she calls me an idiot every time she sees me."

"That doesn't make her crazy, that just makes her smart."

"Nice. Listen, Señora Topacio can't be all that crazy; she wouldn't be in business this long if she were. Besides, my mother trusts her."

"I have to take my mother to her doctor's appointment. Are you done?"

Selenis rushed me off the phone and said she'd talk to me later. She was too preoccupied with her own life to help me out with mine. Nice, considering that I'd spent money I didn't really have to buy her her maid service.

I placed the receiver down on my desk and stared at the screen-saver of Junito standing next to the number 20 NASCAR car at the Home Depot. Thinking about my weekend, I didn't realize that my boss, Samantha Leonard, was standing at the foot of her office door staring at me.

"Idalis, can you step into my office, please?"

She sounded pissed. But then again, I could never tell when that bitch was happy. She'd been the same way for the past nine months. She was the complete opposite of Angie Reynolds, her predecessor.

As I entered Samantha's office, Levell Johnson and Marilyn McVee were sitting on leather chairs in front of Samantha's desk. I said good morning, but I didn't get much back. I looked over Samantha's shoulder and saw the storyboard from last week. Someone had painted all the faces brown and had drawn Afros on top of their heads.

"Oh, my God, who did that?" I asked, slightly pissed that someone would ruin my work. Not that I illustrated the faces, but I had to print out the pictures and glue them down evenly.

"You have no idea who did this?" Samantha asked.

"No, not at all," I said, looking over at Levell and Marilyn. Their faces suggested that they had some information on the perpetrator.

"Take a seat, Idalis," Samantha said.

I sat in the only chair available, between Marilyn and Levell.

"I want all of us to be very open here. Okay?" Samantha said, getting up and pacing from one side of her desk to the other.

"Okay, but I hope you know that I would never do anything like that, Samantha. You know that," I said, feeling as though they were thinking otherwise.

"We never said you did, Idalis. Why would you assume that?" Levell said in his high-pitched voice. He sounded like Dave Chappelle mimicking a white guy.

"Idalis, did you tell Levell and Marilyn on several occasions that you felt the executive creative team was racist?"

My stomach dropped like I was getting ready to free-fall. I could feel the blood rush to my face, but I knew that my olive complexion would never give away my embarrassment or surprise.

I couldn't believe that Levell and Marilyn, the only two black people in my department, would betray me. I tried to think fast about what I'd said to Levell and Marilyn. Oh, yes. I'd said I just wished that the creative team would consider using ethnic actors in the ads instead of the typical blond-haired, blue-eyed characters all the time. Okay, so would I get fired if I told the truth or should I just lie my ass off right now?

"Well, do you remember saying that?" Samantha asked, quickly glancing at a memo on her desk.

I looked over at Levell and Marilyn, wondering how two people could be so disillusioned. Or maybe I was the one who was disillusioned. I should have known by now that I shouldn't ever speak the truth inside corporate walls. I'd seen too many get fired for that.

"I don't remember saying anything like that," I said, using my best poker face.

"You didn't say to me that you were tired of the devil white man and that what this place needs is some real color?" Marilyn said as she placed both hands on the arms of her chair, looking like she was getting ready to give me a beat-down.

"First of all, I would never use the term 'devil white man.' What I remember saying was that it would be nice to see someone in a commercial that looked like me. That's all I said."

"So what you're saying is that you feel the company executives should consider using more urban types, people from the streets, perhaps?"

Levell chuckled and tugged at the sleeves of his dark blue Ralph Lauren button-down shirt, one at a time. Marilyn crossed her legs just at the right moment to show off her new Gucci flats. Perhaps they were trying to suggest that they had no affiliation with urban or street types, since they could afford designer duds.

"I don't understand what's going on here. Is this about what Levell and Marilyn think I said, or are you trying to find the person that messed up the boards?" I said, trying to take control of the situation.

"Both," Samantha answered, sitting down in her leather chair, taking back the control.

"Samantha, I've been with this company for ten years. You can ask anyone that's been here for that long about my behavior and they'd tell you that I earned my place here. Why would I risk my job to make a statement like that?" I said, pointing to the storyboard.

Samantha stared me down, analyzing me to find the truth, but I didn't know if she believed me or not. She got up from her chair, walked to the window, looked out, and turned to all of us. She was smiling, and it scared me. It reminded me of the time when my next-door neighbor, the hermit that everyone thought killed his wife, walked out of his apartment with two big suitcases and smiled at me, making me feel that if I reciprocated the gesture, he'd think I was accepting an invitation to be his friend.

"Let's be real here, off the record, okay? You have to understand something about me," Samantha said, looking only at Levell and Marilyn. "I have a couple of African-American friends. I do, and they are very close friends."

Levell and Marilyn smiled awkwardly, and for the first time I saw them fidgeting in their seats.

Then Samantha looked at me and continued.

"Quite honestly, I don't have many Latino friends. Well, my best friend's nanny is Ecuadorian, and I love her to death. I can't wait to have kids so I can hire her. The woman works like an ox."

Levell and Marilyn laughed harder than they should have; it wasn't that funny. It wasn't even a little funny.

"So, I understand what you all must go through. Believe me."

Samantha turned her back, walked to the edge of her desk, and leaned her zero-size derriere against it. She continued speaking.

"You know, I have an old college friend; she's an investment banker at Financial America. She happens to be part African-American, German, and Swedish."

"Magnificent," Marilyn said.

Samantha could've said "I spent the weekend in a cottage in

Vermont playing with myself" or "I have a big snot stuck in my left nostril," and Marilyn would have a list of exclamatory adjectives under her tongue, waiting for the right brown-nose moment to use them.

"After we leave the gym, we walk into the supermarket and everyone stares at us. It's sad, yes. But the reality is that as much as we want to change things, the advertising world cannot be held responsible for that. We are in the business of helping our clients sell their products. That's how we all get paid. Make millions of people fall in love with our clients' products, and we can be assured a paycheck. We fail at reaching those millions, and we end up in the unemployment line. Besides, Idalis, isn't Cameron Diaz Latina? She definitely doesn't look like you, but she is one of you, isn't she?"

Oh, my Lord. It was the sermon from Valley-girl hell. I didn't want to get into the whole Cameron Diaz thing (why confuse matters?) and decided that this wasn't the time to get all Malcolm on her ass. I needed to pay my bills and figure out the rest of my life. I needed my job.

I couldn't get a read from Levell and Marilyn. I guess they were too far up Samantha's ass. All I knew was, this was the last time I'd open my mouth about the lack of people of color in the advertising industry. You know what? From this point on, I wasn't going to care. Why did I worry so much about crap like that anyway? It wasn't like anyone else cared enough to do anything about it. Why was I always trying to teach diversity to the people I worked with? How could I, some non-degree-having Latin chick, with no real job skills, on her way to becoming a single mom and living in a park next to a homeless hyena, possibly change the world? Why risk my job, my paycheck, change my lifestyle, for a problem that honestly had been around since the first pilgrim landed on Plymouth Rock? Or maybe it started way before then. Whatever the case, this ain't no Jerry Maguire movie. I couldn't walk out of here with fish in my hand and the newly arrived assistant who thinks I'm cute. There were no fish here and there wasn't a gorgeous male assistant that I felt would complete me. I had no backup plan. This was reality. I would sit my quiet, little, nonactivist ass back into my cramped gray cubicle and learn to accept my place in society, no matter how small it was.

"Yes, Samantha, you're right. Cameron Diaz doesn't look like me, and she is Latina," I said, giving in.

"Well, that's what I thought. So one could say that the blond-haired, blue-eyed characters featured in our own commercials could conceivably be Latino. Isn't that correct?"

Even though I knew that really wasn't the case, I just wanted to end the conversation.

"Yes, I guess you could say that."

I hated that I was letting Samantha have the last word and I also hated that I didn't own a pair of Erin Brockovich–sized balls to cleverly fight my way out of this argument.

Samantha walked over to the two-foot storyboard, picked it up, and placed it outside her door. She walked back to her desk, dialed an extension, and asked that someone in the mailroom promptly remove the garbage that was sitting in front of her office. When she hung up the phone, she asked Levell and Marilyn to kindly leave, as the meeting was over. I could tell by the uncertain look on their faces that they weren't too happy that I was staying behind. Once Levell and Marilyn walked out of her office, Samantha closed her office door, walked behind her desk, and sat down.

"You miss my predecessor, Angie Reynolds, don't you?" she asked.

Here we go again. Do I lie or tell her the truth?

"We had a chemistry that worked, I guess."

"Yes, I know. She called the other day and I got a chance to speak to her."

I could feel a slight pang of jealousy in me.

"Idalis, it's no secret that you don't like me."

"Did Levell and Marilyn tell you that?"

"They don't need to tell me. I could figure that one out on my own. Here's the situation: I don't know who marked up the boards, and regardless of what office gossip got back to me, I don't think you would have done something that chancy. You don't seem the type that takes risks."

I could if I wanted to.

"Now, I do think we need to fix our professional relationship. I also think you need to accept that Ms. Reynolds is no longer your boss and that you work for me now. If you cannot accept this, then I think it's best that you consider being transferred to another department, such as bookkeeping or human resources."

I knew Samantha had no choice but to give me an ultimatum. It was her way of keeping me in check. For the first time, I felt my job was no longer a sure thing and I'd have to learn how to keep my comments to myself.

"Samantha, I'm a team player and I always have been. You can count on me to do the right thing. I'll do whatever it takes to make this work," I said, fighting the urge to gag.

9 On the ferry ride back home to Staten Island, I felt good about my new life strategy; my new Americanized perspective; the old, don't-give-a-shit-about-anyone-but-me American way. Anyway, I'd always felt that the biggest setback for me was that my family came from a small island in the Caribbean that honestly hasn't had a chance to show what it could be without the help of its American big papa. It didn't know how to stand up on its own and be the independent beautiful little island of enchantment that it longed to be. It had always, in some way, belonged to someone else, while at the same time trying hard to find and maintain its original voice. And maybe that was me too. Maybe that same codependency was in my blood and I'd never get a chance to find my original voice because there would always be someone or something holding me back—trying to keep me from being free.

As I glimpsed the majestic lady in New York Harbor holding her torch to the sky, I realized the irony of my thoughts. Was this another one of those signs?

"Excuse me, is anyone sitting here?" a deep male voice asked.

I moved my purse off the seat and onto my lap without looking at who the voice belonged to. Commuting with hundreds of other commuters a day, I disconnect from people sometimes. Maybe it's just the native New Yorker in me. It's too many people to have to look in the eye.

I continued looking out the window into the harbor and attempted to revisit my last thought. But I couldn't. Whatever cologne this guy sitting next to me had on was calling me toward him. I pretended to look around the boat to get a sneak peek at the face attached to the voice and the seductive aroma. He was

brown-skinned, clean-shaven, with a strong chin, handsome profile, flawless. We sat so close our arms touched and for some crazy
reason I felt a surge of electrical energy. He must have felt it too,
because he turned to look at me and smiled before going back to
reading his *Fortune* magazine.

From what I could see, he was well put together. I could tell
by the look of the fabric and the tightness of the weave that the
suit was not your average Banana Republic suit. It was custom- or
designer-made. I could see the cuff of his crisp white shirt under
his black suit jacket. His hands were perfect: pretty but masculine, with clean fingers. No metrosexual look, just clean, no-shine
fingernails. As if he knew I was scoping him, he crossed his legs.
I could see his shoes. They definitely were not like the ones that
Manny wore with the rubber soles. These were Italian all-leather
designer shoes. Bruno Magli, maybe? This guy was the guy that
pops up in Terry McMillan novels. The one brother that you
know all the women want to marry or at least want to see naked.

It was a quiet ride and the ferry was fast approaching the pier
on Staten Island. I knew better than to get up before the boat
had finished docking. This was the part where you hung on to
something or someone to keep from losing your balance as the
boat made its way into the narrow wooden pier. I guessed he was
thinking the same thing, because he stayed seated, which meant
he took the ferry often. Either he lived or worked in Staten Island
or he knew someone who did.

I didn't want to get up from my seat, even after the boat docked.
As I watched the commuters make their way toward the front deck
of the boat, my curiosity about the handsome stranger beside me
took me by surprise. I wondered if I really knew right from wrong
these days. Knowing that I still had unfinished business with
Manny, I was wishing that this guy would talk to me.

My heart started racing and I felt nervous. Was I crossing into
a new place in my life? What exactly did this mean? Had Manny
and his machismo finally pushed me over the line? I sat there,
drawn to this stranger, feeling wonderful just sitting next to him.

Could I just stay here? It felt too good to leave—even though I felt like I was cheating on Manny.

He looked over at me, smiled, took his leather laptop case from the floor, stood, and before walking away he said, "Have a nice night."

"Thank you, same to you," I said, feeling my heart skip a joyous beat.

I felt excited and pretty again. The feeling was familiar. It reminded me of the time I'd first laid eyes on Manny.

As I exited the boat, I could see the nicely dressed dark stranger in the distance as he disappeared into the crowd of commuters running for their buses. But while everyone else was racing toward their appropriate ramps, the guy with the deep voice appeared to be in no rush. He had that Denzel Washington strut going on; that nice, smooth, it-ain't-nothing-but-a-thing walk.

I couldn't stop following him with my eyes. Why didn't I just talk to him when he was sitting right next to me? Hell, why didn't he talk to me? I was feeling anxious again. It was that feeling I got when there were too many people in my cubicle or when I got on an elevator during lunchtime and felt like I was losing air. What if I could never attract another man in my life that loved me the way Manny used to love me? I didn't want to be alone. I turned to take one last look and noticed Denzel walking toward me, against the mob of oncoming commuters. For a moment, I wondered if I was making this all up in my head.

Someone accidentally stepped on the back of my shoe and I tripped a little. Denzel smiled. At least I knew that I wasn't dreaming.

"I never do this, really I don't, but can I call you sometime?" he said, with a hint of shyness.

I laughed and I said, "I never do this either, and yes, you can."

He was tall, about six-foot-three with broad shoulders, like Manny. He looked a lot like the actor Blair Underwood, but there was something else that reminded me of Manny and I wasn't sure what that was.

He took a fancy gold pen out from his laptop case and handed me the *Fortune* magazine so that I could write my number on it. Hmmmm, that seemed weird, surprised he didn't have a business card.

"I just got a promotion and I'm getting new cards printed," he said, reading my mind.

As I placed the ball of the pen onto the magazine, I realized that the last time I gave out my number was when Dwayne Wayne was trying to get with Whitley. The only number I gave out back then was my beeper number. Beeper? Did anyone even use a beeper anymore?

"Idalis," he said as he watched me dot the letter *i* at the end of my name.

"Yes, Idalis," I confirmed, giving him the sexiest smile I had.

"*Dominicana?*" he asked.

"No, Puerto Rican," I answered, surprised that he knew the right way to refer to a Dominican female in Spanish. He'd probably had a Dominican girlfriend or two, but I also knew from the way he articulated his words that he probably wasn't Spanish himself; but then again, who was I to judge his language skills?

I decided to write down my cell number. Too much was going on at work and there was no way I could have this guy calling me at home.

"My name is Cameron. I will be calling you," he said, emphasizing the *will*, and placed the pen and my number back into the leather bag.

"Sure," I answered.

Before turning to walk away, he left me with a smile that felt sincere and true. I didn't sense a hidden agenda, but he did forget to give me his number. Maybe he was nervous. Whatever the case, this was the most natural and organic moment I'd ever experienced with a stranger. It seemed that this moment was meant to happen.

10 I got to Joanne's Babysitting about ten minutes late, but I wasn't stressing because I was still happy dizzy from the Cameron moment. I walked through the back door and I could tell that Joanne the owner was pissed. She was sitting in a kid-sized chair in the blue section of the room with her arms folded across her chest—reminded me of Crystal. Junito was sitting alone in the red section watching *Yu-Gi-Oh!* and I waved hello to him before approaching Joanne.

"Hi, Joanne, the traffic on Staten Island is getting so bad, isn't it?" I said, hoping she wouldn't make me pay the dollar-a-minute late fee again.

Before answering, Joanne took a deep breath and rolled her eyes on the exhale. I immediately wanted to ask her what the hell her problem was, but I didn't need to catch an attitude with the woman who took care of my son. I needed her more than she needed me.

"Ms. Riviera, can I tawk to ya for a second, please?" she said in her Carmela Soprano voice. She walked away from the blue section of the room and into the yellow section—farther away from Junito. I assumed she wanted me to follow her, so I did.

"Let me put this out there right now, this ain't a personal thing, ya know. But I have ta tell ya, this *is* a place of business. And I find myself waitin' around fa ya till the very end of the day. Your son has been here fa two months now and ya been late ten times. I have my own personal schedule too, ya know."

"I understand and I'm really sorry. I promise I'll try harder to get here earlier. It's just that I'm coming from the ferry at rush hour. You know how that is," I said, walking away from her and toward Junito.

"I'm not finished, Ms. Riviera," she said with a slightly angry tone. I inhaled but caught myself before letting out the sigh. I tried to keep my body stiff for fear that my neck would involuntarily do the ghetto neck roll. I turned back toward her and gave her my best fake smile.

"We've been havin' some problems wit your son."

"Excuse me?" I said, trying to recall all Four Agreements, especially the one about not taking things personally.

"He's been actin' very detached and he doesn't want ta play wit any of the otha kids. The otha mothas are a little concerned. He sits in the corna and doesn't want ta talk ta anybody. He actually pushes us away."

"Physically?"

"No. But he's actin' a little 'different' and that makes some of the other kids and some of us, to be quite honest with ya, uncomfortable. Honestly, they think there's something wrong wit him."

Acting different? Something wrong with him? What the hell was this chick talking about? This didn't sound like the Junito I knew.

There must have been a missing piece that she wasn't telling me. I could feel it. None of this felt right to me. Yes, I knew that there was a lot going on in Junito's life, but he'd never been antisocial. He'd never pushed any of us away. I glanced over at him, and he didn't seem anxious or uncomfortable—in fact, he seemed fine. But as much as I wanted to tell Ms. Joanne what I really felt, I had no choice. My hands were tied. I knew there was no other babysitter on the island that I could take Junito to. I knew that if I messed up our relationship, it would eventually affect my job; I couldn't afford that. I needed Ms. Joanne.

I stood there just staring away at my baby, who was laughing along with a Billy & Mandy commercial. Above his head, I noticed the Joanne's Hall of Fame poster: little Polaroid shots of all the kids who came to Joanne's after-school program were posted on red poster board. Each picture was set in a different-colored balloon. Junito's picture was in the center, surrounded by kids who didn't share his ethnicity or anything close to it—reminded me of my own eighth-grade class picture.

"Joanne, I'm sure we can fix this. Junito, come here, baby. I need to talk to you," I said, confident that I was going to walk out of here just as chipper as I walked in.

Joanne kept her arms folded across her chest as she stepped aside to let Junito pass her.

"Junito, why don't you want to play with anyone here? Ms. Joanne says you push people away."

Junito didn't answer. He glanced over at Joanne for a quick second, as if he needed to know why she'd said that.

"Ms. Riviera, please. This is not somethin' ya should be discussin' in front of me. Why don't ya take him home and tawk to him tonight?" she said.

I was beginning to think that there was something ugly underneath all of this crap.

"If my son is a problem, I'm going to fix it."

"Frankly, I don't think there is anything to fix. This is not the right place for ya son," she said, walking away from Junito and me. She started picking up some loose crayons and throwing them in one of the clear plastic bins at the center of the table. She threw one so hard that it popped back out of the box.

Whenever someone had something to say about my kid, it was as if they were saying something about me. I could feel my blood pressure rising, but I had to make this situation work.

"Why isn't it the right place?" I asked, trying to squeeze the truth out of her.

"I just think that it may be best ta find anotha babysitta."

I felt like she wasn't telling me everything she needed to tell me.

"Why is that?" I asked, still trying to stay calm.

"Because I just said, it's not working out," she said, picking up the Elmer's glue stick that she'd dropped on the floor.

"You know, I'm trying really hard to understand something

here. My son doesn't hit anyone. He's just quiet and you think that because he's quiet we need to find another place? Listen, I'm separated. I don't want to beg you, but I really don't have any other options here. I happen to think that Junito really likes it here."

"What kind of name is that?" she asked out of left field.

"Excuse me?"

"Junito. Doesn't Junito have a real name?"

"Yes, he shares his father's name, Emmanuel. We call him Junito instead of calling him Junior." I didn't like the way she emphasized his name, as if it were a ridiculous nickname to give my kid.

The front door opened and a tall red-haired woman in tight blue jeans and holding a Louis Vuitton Denim bag walked into the house, and suddenly Ms. Joanne got really happy.

"Hey, Joanne, how was Tyler today? Betta?"

I watched the red-haired woman walk into the house, confident that she wasn't too late.

"Yes, much betta. And ya have ta see what he made today. Ya gonna die when you see it," Joanne said.

The redhead glanced at Junito and looked over at me. No smile, just a look. It reminded me of the look my mother and I got from a couple of older ladies when we first visited Jones Beach.

"Ms. Riviera, have a nice night, and I hope it all works out for ya," Joanne said.

Where was she going? What the hell just happened here? Did I have a babysitter or not? I didn't know whether to leave that house or force her into giving me a concrete reason that I could live with. This was wrong, but I couldn't prove anything. I should have known better, though. I'd lived on Staten Island long enough to know that there was still a dirty little secret that nobody wanted to talk about; the same sort of secret that eventually got out in Howard Beach and in Bensonhurst. But was I being paranoid? Was I making this up, or did this lady just tell me she didn't want us here? It wasn't like she came out and actually said we don't want you here anymore, but she did tell me that she hoped it all worked out for Junito and me. But why did she take my money in the first place? Maybe Joanne now felt that the "otha mothas," as she called them, had a right to feel comfortable. And, of course, it was easier to remove one picture from the Hall of Fame instead of five or six.

I held Junito's hand and walked out of that house for good. My most precious possession had been in the care of someone who didn't really care about him. Even though I thought I had been doing the right thing, I hadn't. What was wrong with me? I'd sworn that when I had Junito, I would never make mistakes like this. I would never place him somewhere he wasn't safe.

How dare she make me feel this way?

Before driving off for good, I beeped my car horn a few times to get Joanne to come back out. A few of her neighbors stepped out instead before she finally stuck her head out of the top floor window.

"Yes, Ms. Riviera?" she said. I could see the red-haired Louis Vuitton chick standing right next to her.

"First of all, you need to add more color to your stupid wall of fame, and number two, my name is pronounced RRRRRivera. Not Riviera, right, Junito?" Junito high-fived me and I got energized. "RRRRR! Can you roll your *R*'s like that? No, I don't think so!"

She didn't answer. She just closed the window and I drove off. So I looked like an idiot; at least I felt like I got the last word. Now all I had to do was go home and beg Macho Man to change his schedule and help me out. This was a fun day.

11 After I put Junito to sleep, I tried to call Manny, but he didn't answer. So I lay in bed staring at the flickering shadow on the ceiling from the lit candle on my dresser, thinking about how unpredictable life could be sometimes. One minute I was happily married, the next I was planning a divorce. One minute I had a babysitter, the next I found out she was really the Imperial Wizard's wife. My mind was racing, but I could feel my body giving out from all the stress. I was hoping that the lavender scent from the candle would do its thing and put me to sleep. But as soon as I tried to relax, another thought or worry would make me tense up again. I wished that Manny would return my call so I could at least figure out what I was going to do with Junito.

Where could he be at eleven at night? I picked up the receiver next to the sofa bed and rolled my fingers over the numbered buttons. Should I call again? If he really wanted me back and gave me those flowers as a sign of wanting me back, then why wasn't he up my ass trying to get me back? This was what I hated about separation. I hated that I had no idea what he was really doing while we weren't together. If we ever got back together, I was going to wonder where he'd been tonight. But would he really tell me the truth? Hell, no. So for the rest of our lives, I would always wonder what he really did while we were separated, and that thought alone made me not want to get back together, so I placed the phone back down.

It was so hot in the room that I thought about ripping off the silk teddy that Manny had given me one Valentine's Day and sleeping naked. But that was never my style. Sleeping naked is like not wearing underwear under your clothes. Anyway, I had too many nosy dead relatives and I was sure that when they got bored they started snooping around in my life. I needed to be fully dressed at all times, just in case they showed up.

I wanted to turn the air conditioner on, but I knew that a moment of cool convenience would give me a month-long worry about the electric bill. Instead, I waited for the next breeze to come through my window, hoping that it would cool down my sticky body. Even with the saunalike heat, I could feel that my mind was starting to drift further away. I leaned over the sofa bed, blew out the candle, and tried to find a cool spot on the pillow to rest my head. I could hear Junito's faint snoring coming from his bedroom next door and I closed my eyes.

In the back of my mind, I could swear that I heard fingers tapping on the front door. I must have been dreaming. That happened a lot in my sleep. When I thought I heard something like a loud noise or a scream and woke up only to realize that it wasn't real. But the tapping got louder and it sounded like someone was talking outside my front door. I opened my eyes. Now I was awake. I started trembling from the sudden noise. I could feel my knees shaking. I stumbled onto the floor, made my way to the door, and looked through the peephole. It was Manny and it was now midnight.

"Manny, I'm sleeping," I whispered as I stood behind the door.

"No, you're not, you're talking to me," he mumbled.

"It's late, I'll call you tomorrow."

"Let your husband in, Idalis," he said, laughing to himself.

Was he drunk? He sounded it. What a jerk.

"Idalis, come on, open the door. I want to give Junito a kiss. I miss my son."

I didn't want to open the door because I was afraid of what could happen. I had to be stronger. I was thirty-five years old and I still hadn't figured out what I was going to do with the rest of my life, and I knew that if I let him in, I might never find out. I couldn't be playing these games forever, I had a kid. I needed to find a real career and the meaning of true happiness. I needed to let go of the past and move on. But, of course, the *idiota* in me always backed down for fear of really finding an answer to my problems. Whoever said that looking for the meaning of life was fun must be the one person who dances to the sound of fingernails on a chalkboard. I grabbed my terry-cloth robe off the kitchen chair, put it on, and tied the belt real tight.

I opened the door. I was too tired to talk him out of it, plus I needed to know if he could help me out with Junito.

Manny strolled into the apartment with a suave tilt to his step, dressed in his UPS uniform and looking more tan and muscular than he did the other day. He turned to look at me. I could see a glaze in his eyes.

Something in my stomach, or maybe it was my sixth sense, was telling me that this was all wrong. I tried hard (okay, maybe not hard, but I tried) to place our future in the ready-to-throw-out compartment of my head. But the universe, for some stupid reason, wasn't giving me the chance to do that just yet.

Manny placed his knapsack down on the floor and walked into Junito's room without saying a word to me. I sat in the center of the bed, yoga-style. I turned on the television and waited for him to come back in.

"You look beautiful," he said.

I didn't realize he had been staring at me from Junito's doorway. He came back into the living room, moved the kitchen chair out, and sat in it. He stared at me with a big grin on his face.

"Right, listen, I have work tomorrow, so we have to get this shit with Junito figured out," I said as I tied the belt to my terry-cloth robe even tighter. I held the remote in front of me like a gun, shooting the television every two seconds. "The babysitting service won't be able to pick up Junito from school on Tuesdays and Thursdays anymore, and I can't get to him in time," I said, pretending that his presence didn't faze me.

"What happened to the babysitter?"

"It didn't work out. You have to do something," I said, giving him no choice to back out of his responsibilities.

"That's rough, Idalis. You can't ask her to watch him for a few more weeks?"

"No. I need you to do it and you know I wouldn't ask if I didn't really need the help."

"I have to talk to my boss 'cause they just changed my hours again."

"Well, I can't change my hours, so . . ."

"Listen, I don't want to fight. I'll talk to him tomorrow, okay?"

"Well, do that, because I need to know by Thursday or else I have to leave early from work, and things at work aren't that great."

He didn't bother to ask what was going on at my job, so I guess he didn't care to know.

I sat on the bed watching television. The extra layer of terry cloth was making me feel hotter than I was before. I was suffocating and also trying to figure out why Crockett was so pissed at Tubbs. I could feel Manny staring at me.

"I was thinking a lot about you and Junito today," he said.

I felt my heart flutter for a second, but I kept staring at the television. I couldn't let him see my heart flip-flop because I didn't trust his intention for coming over. He could have just called me back on the phone, so I knew that he was here for something else.

"You heard me?" he said in a desperate tone of voice.

"I heard you, Manny," I said, pretending to be absorbed in the scene.

"You don't have anything to say?"

"Nope," I answered.

I was trying to hurt him for hurting me.

"That was messed up that you threw those flowers out the other day. I paid a lot of money for them."

I didn't say anything.

"Are you seeing somebody else?" he asked.

"After the shit you pulled the other day, I wouldn't ask that question right now," I said, getting off the bed and walking toward the fridge.

"*Yo te amo*, Idalis. I love you."

Damn, I felt that big-time. I could feel the same throbbing sensation that always happened between my legs whenever Manny spoke Spanish to me. I stood in front of the open refrigerator pretending to look for a snack, but I wasn't really hungry and closed the door. If this kept up, I'd eventually be a size four again. I stood in front of the closed refrigerator, browsing through all the late payment reminders that were hanging on the fake food magnets. I was also trying hard to avoid acknowledging his feelings. Damn you. Don't speak Spanish to me. Don't tell me you love me. I haven't had sex in three months. Don't do it.

"Can I hold you?" he asked.

I hesitated and realized that I shouldn't have done that.

"I have to go to sleep," I said, now back on the bed.

"But can I hold you?"

"For what reason, Manny?"

"Because I miss my wife, that's why," he said, putting his head down as if the pain in his heart was too much to bear.

"I got one word for you: Bonita."

"I never introduced that girl as my girlfriend."

"No, you just acted like she was."

"No, I didn't."

"I guess you forgot that you admitted to me how stupid that was to do."

He knew that he was wrong, but he kept the smile on his face the way Junito did when he knew he'd done wrong but hoped I wouldn't get angry.

I kept watching the television the way Doña González did, not really paying attention.

"I just want to hold you, Idalis. Why do you always have to control things? Man, nothing changes with you," he said, removing what looked like a Gatorade from his knapsack. "You could tell me the truth, you know, I can handle it."

I could tell he was nervous by the way he was chipping away at the label of the bottle with his nail—or maybe he was just pretending to be nervous.

"Listen, I need to go to sleep, okay? Just let me know when you talk to your boss," I said, getting up from the bed and walking toward the front door.

Before I could reach the door, Manny sprinted up from his chair, grabbed my robe by the belt, and pulled me into him. He wrapped his arms around me and I could feel his hands tightening up on the small of my back. When I looked up at him I could smell his real motivation for being here.

"You're drunk?" I asked, knowing now that everything that took place from this point on was probably meaningless.

"No, well, yes, but no. Listen, I made a big mistake letting you go. *Perdóname*, Idalis. I miss you and Junito a lot. I don't want to lose my family."

I looked into his eyes. I didn't know if what I saw was pure horniness or real love. I couldn't get a sincere read. It's a terrible thing to look into your husband's eyes and not know what he's really feeling, to not trust him. I pulled away and walked to the opposite side of the sofa bed, farther away from him.

"You only feel like this because you think there's somebody else in the picture," I said.

"Is there?" he asked.

I immediately thought of Cameron, but it wasn't like we really had anything; just a little spark among strangers.

"No," I answered, feeling a little guilty that I was keeping this new information to myself.

"Well, you know that you can't compare ten years to a little fling. It's real easy to feel good about somebody you don't know, but you don't really know them until you live with them."

I wondered why he was sharing this bit of wisdom with me. For a second I thought he knew about Cameron, but then I thought that maybe things in the single world weren't really working out for him.

I moved away from Manny and sat at the edge of the bed, closer to the television. Crockett and Tubbs were friends again, so I skipped through the channels over and over, looking for something to keep me away from Manny. What, exactly? I didn't know. Maybe the longer I sat here pretending to be disinterested in him, the quicker he'd get up and leave.

By chance, I found a channel that was playing one of my favorite movies: *My Cousin Vinny*. It was the best part too. The scene when the stuttering attorney addresses the witness and asks him if he had his reading glasses on when he saw the perpetrator speed off.

"Oh, man, I haven't seen this in the longest time and shit," Manny said, moving his body forward in the chair to get a better view. It was his favorite scene too.

I raised the volume a bit more, hoping that a good joke could turn the tension between us into something less nerve-racking. Manny and I watched the attorney stutter his way through the examination process and we laughed softly. We waited for the climactic moment to play out on the screen and I wondered if he could sense the subtext in our own reality. I waited, knowing that sooner or later the punch line was going to make us laugh our asses off. I could feel us working in sync, being in the moment. I could also feel the fear and insecurity starting to release from my back, neck, and shoulders. I thought about how bizarre it seemed that after living so much of our lives together, we were now acting like strangers. As soon as the stuttering attorney sat down next to his client and said, "Boy, he was a tough one," we lost it. I fell back on the bed and Manny was bent over in his chair. I could feel that the tension between us was almost gone. We laughed so hard. It was exactly what this moment needed.

"I don't care how many times I see that movie, that shit is still funny," he said, moving off his chair and closer to me on the bed.

"Yeah," I said, pretending not to notice that he was making a move.

I stayed on my back, staring at the ceiling, chuckling to myself as I repeated the punch line and pretended not to notice his sweet-smelling sweat; never pungent, always mild and seductive. I didn't want to lose control, so I tried to think of something funny. But I couldn't find Dora the Explorer to help me out with this one, and I was trying my best to keep from falling apart in front of him. For the first time I realized that Manny and I were starting over. This was it. My husband and I were in a different place. It didn't matter what history we'd had together. It was different now. It was as if someone had dropped our Etch A Sketch and now we'd have to shake the remaining lines and begin again.

I didn't know whether to relax and let things be or to keep holding on to that thick brick wall between us. Sometimes that wall just got too heavy for me to carry. It would be nice if I could let it fall and not worry about what was going to happen next. I just wanted to enjoy the fun moments, like I did back in the day.

But back in the day, it was much easier to bounce back from a broken heart. I guess the older I got, the harder it was to trick my heart into thinking it had another chance at love. Besides, I didn't know if my heart could handle another breakup.

The day I watched Manny remove all of his clothes from our closet, unplug his PlayStation, take down his favorite family pictures, and place them all into moving boxes was worse than the day when we had our first big fight at the Great Adventure amusement park in New Jersey. That was before we were even engaged—the warning fight.

A woman I knew who was obsessed with studying relationships once told me that every couple had a warning fight in the beginning of their relationship. The one fight that gave them a little taste of what their life would be like with each other. She said that couples were so in love in the beginning that they ignored the warning signs and stayed together anyway. That was funny to her because that same argument would continue to resurface over and over again in different ways. She also said that that fight would eventually become the reason that the couple would split up.

I thought a lot about that after Manny and I separated because we did have that warning fight. I could swear he was checking out this girl. He said he wasn't. But then for some reason this woman would appear at all the same rides we were on.

It was ninety-five degrees that day in the park and I was thirsty. I told Manny that I was getting off the line to get some water and that I'd be right back, even though I knew that the park rule was that once you leave the line you couldn't go back on. But there was no park security around, so I took a chance. As soon as I left, I turned around and found that same woman talking to Manny. Little did she or he know that I was watching all of this from where I was standing. Any idiot could see she was flirting, and I couldn't understand why Manny didn't shoo her away or do whatever men do when they want a lady to know they're not interested. I swear I wanted to go up to him and ask him what he was doing, but I didn't want to look like a crazy jealous girlfriend. So when the woman saw me coming back onto the line she walked away, sneakily. When I got back to Manny I asked him if everything was okay.

"Yeah, let me have some of that water," he said.

"No, you should've gotten your own water."

"Come on. I'm thirsty."

"Nope."

As I gulped down half the bottle of water, I noticed a few beads of sweat falling from his forehead onto his Roberto Clemente T-shirt.

"Why can't you give me some water?" he asked.

He grabbed the bottle of water out of my hand, but I yanked it back. He looked at me while I kept drinking and I could see that chick he'd been talking to staring at us. She was with a group of girlfriends who were now laughing at us. Manny quickly stepped over the ropes and walked off the line. I followed him, still drinking the water, and still trying to play it cool.

"What the hell is wrong with you, Idalis?"

"Nothing, I'm thirsty and I want to drink my own water. If you wanted water, then you should've gotten your own, right?"

"That's some stupid shit right there."

"Oh, no, I could show you what stupid shit is."

I drank the rest of the water.

"You know what, you can stay here by yourself and drink all the fucking water you want," he said, quickly walking away.

"Good, because I don't like needy guys anyway," I yelled back.

I watched him walk back toward me.

"You know what? You're crazy. I have no idea what you're talking about, Ms. Life-Is-Always-About-Me."

"Are you saying I'm selfish?"

"Yeah, a little. We've been going out for six months now and I don't know if you even like being around me."

"Oh, like spending all day and all night with you isn't enough proof."

"Why do I feel like I'm always coming after you? You never come to me. I feel I'm the one always apologizing first. I'm the one always kissing you first, I'm the one that always makes the first move."

"Please, Manny, don't exaggerate. I come to you all the time."

"Then come to me now and apologize for what you just did to me."

I knew he wanted me to go to him. I could see it in his face. He loved me more at this moment than I loved him. Which was why I didn't stress when I gave him my cute smile and said, "If you don't like the way I am, then leave."

He didn't leave. I guess my cuteness won him over, because an hour later, he apologized.

Yet the day that Manny packed up his stuff and didn't come back was the first time I felt like maybe we had tested our love one too many times.

All I knew was that it started as a fight about how Manny forgot to help Junito with his homework. I had to go to a co-worker's birthday party one night and told Manny to help Junito while I was gone. When I woke up the next day I asked Junito if he had done his homework, but of course he said no. The one thing that always made me lose it was when I'd tell Manny to do something important and he would forget to do it.

I hated the feeling that I was the only person in our house who kept track of every detail in our lives. I had to remember doctor appointments, replacing the old toothbrushes, the expiration date on the eggs and the yogurt, bringing Junito's violin on Fridays, karate on Tuesdays, laundry on Saturdays, every password for AOL, for Kids' AOL, the bank, the credit cards, the three stupid security questions they ask so that you can log on to your bank account— even the little bowling game I liked to play online had a password. I had to remember every stupid little thing and I was tired of it. I walked into our bedroom and screamed, "Manny! Didn't I tell you that you needed to help Junito with his homework last night?" He jumped up out of his sleep, but he wasn't sure what I had said. I repeated it without the same intensity, feeling stupid for wasting my breath.

"Oh, shit, I'm sorry. I forgot," he said, trying to keep his eyes open.

"He's going to get a zero today. Did you know that that's what happens when Junito doesn't do his homework?"

"*Mami*, I don't want a zero. I'm not going to school," Junito said, standing outside our bedroom door.

"Junito, it's your responsibility too, you know. You knew that you had homework, why didn't you tell Daddy to help you?"

"I did and he said we would do it after the next level of Spider-Man."

"Go in your room, Junito!" I screamed, before slamming my bedroom door closed.

"I'm tired of this shit, Manny. You take nothing seriously. I told you before I went out last night that you had to help Junito with his homework. Every day is the same shit here with you. You sit around and don't clean the house. You don't give Junito baths when I tell you he needs one. And you do that because you know that if you wait long enough, I'll wind up doing it anyway. What the hell is your purpose here? What do you do?"

"Idalis, stop. I'm not a kid. So stop the fucking yelling!"

"I'm not yelling! I do everything around here. This is your house too—clean it, damn it. He's your kid—clean him too. If I left it up to you, Junito would never get a bath and he'd be toothless because you never help him brush his teeth. I'm telling you I can't take this shit anymore. Something has to change. I can't do everything!"

"Okay, then let's get a divorce," he said, placing his head comfortably back on his pillow.

"You know, you always bring that shit up. If that's how you feel, stop talking shit and do it already."

I stood at the foot of the bed with my arms crossed, the car keys in my hand, and stared at Manny. He was acting as if nothing I said mattered and he just wanted to get back to sleep.

"Stop pushing me, Idalis."

"How else am I going to get you off your ass? You tell me. I have a list of shit I have to do; what do you do?"

He lifted his head off the pillow. His eyes were wide open now.

"I go to work, Idalis. And sometimes I work fucking double shifts, like the other night. How the fuck do you expect me to work all night, do dishes, and remember to do homework and give Junito a bath? Shouldn't he be taking his own *maldito* baths already?"

"He's six, Manny. At six did you know how to clean behind your balls? No, I don't think so. And hello, you didn't work a double last night. And besides, I work and still have to remember all that shit. I don't understand why you're so fucking lazy."

He hated when I told him he was lazy. His reaction was so over the top you would've thought I told him he had a two-inch penis.

"Fuck this shit!" Manny said, throwing the covers over the bed and onto the floor. He opened the door and walked out of the room.

"Fuck you," I said, staying put.

He walked back in.

"Fuck me? Fuck you too. All you fucking know how to do is nag anyway," he said, stepping out again to check on Junito in the next room. I heard Manny turn on Junito's TV and close the door to his room before returning to our bedroom. "What the fuck is your problem so early in the morning?"

"You, Manny. All you do is lay your ass around this house after work and do nothing. You take me for granted. You think I'm gonna bust my ass like this forever? I'll be damned. You don't want anything more in life? You want to dress up in a brown uniform every day and deliver boxes for the rest of your life? You just sit and play video games all fucking day and night. You're a grown man—when are you gonna stop playing kid games?"

"Never," he said, with his face an inch away from mine.

"Fine. We need to figure some shit out here, then," I said, getting ready to leave the house.

"Fine," he said, mimicking me.

"You suck."

That was the comment that led to the most damage that day. It was also the day that I realized cuteness wasn't going to win him over any longer.

"What would you know about sucking?"

"What?" I asked, knowing exactly what he'd said.

"Nothing."

"Really? Well, if you knew how to go down on me the right way, then maybe I'd know how to *suck* better. Ten years and you're still nibbling on the fucking outside. What the fuck? You don't know by now that that shit is annoying. Maybe I'd have a freakin' orgasm if you knew how to do it right," I said, knowing that I was crossing dangerous territory.

Manny just stood there staring at me, and then in a surprisingly calm tone he said, "You know, Idalis, I had a lot of chances to do shit. You know what? I was stupid. I should've gone for it."

"Knowing you, you probably did," I said, unsure if he was just lying or confessing to having an affair.

"Yeah, maybe," he answered, leaving me and going back into the bathroom.

"Yeah, maybe I did too," I said, knowing that it wasn't true at all. He turned to look at me before entering the bathroom and closing the door.

When I came home from work that night, I figured that Manny and I would do the usual after we had had a fight. I'd go to Junito's room and read him a book or two before going to sleep and Manny would be thumbing his way through the new James Bond game. Then he'd ask me a stupid question, like, Do you want me to turn the air conditioner on? And I'd say, Yeah, why not, we always keep it on. And he'd laugh to himself. Then I'd laugh to myself because I knew in my heart this was the way we always made up. But when I walked into the half-empty living room that night, I knew that this one was serious. The PlayStation was gone.

I looked at the bare wall near the TV stand and it left me thinking about how fragile relationships really are. One minute they're boring and quiet, the next they're dramatic and unsettling. One minute we're willing to work it out, and the next something clicks and we risk losing everything just to make a point. It was as if someone had cast an evil spell on my life and no matter what I did, things were completely out of my hands. Now the universe was controlling everything. For the first time in a very long ten years, I wished that I had shut my big mouth and had given Manny more hugs and compliments. Just overnight my life became Madden-less, the NBA was no longer live, and Spider-Man had spun his last web.

Now Manny moved in closer to me, but I continued to watch the television, pretending that I had no idea what was going to happen next.

Manny grabbed my chin and pulled my face closer to his. He drew a line from the bridge of my nose to my lips, tracing my lips slowly as if preparing them for something. I watched him as he placed his lips on mine. I wanted to stop watching us from the outside and instead I wanted to be lost within us. I wanted to let go. My body shivered. I couldn't fight it. I didn't. I wanted him as much as I think he wanted me.

He reached down and massaged my inner thigh. He slithered down toward my feet, gently slid my panties off, and tossed them on the floor. He didn't nibble; he did exactly what I always wanted him to do. It was as if I had a new and improved husband—if only he would have cared enough to do that when we were together.

I wanted to cry but didn't know exactly why I felt like crying. I didn't know if it was because it felt good being touched again or because I didn't know where this moment would eventually lead us. He climbed on top of me and looked into my eyes. I could have sworn that his eyes were saying he loved me. I believed it for the moment. I had to. I let the tears go and I told him I loved him too, hoping maybe that would make me feel safe again. But he didn't answer me with his voice. He just spoke to me with his eyes. And then it was over.

We didn't hold hands like we always did after sex. We didn't talk about what just happened. I waited for him to say something or do something. I waited for a period at the end of the sentence or an exclamation point, but all I was left with was a question mark. We were lying there, staring at the ceiling, waiting. Maybe I was the one waiting. I wanted him to tell me something, because I didn't know myself where we were going. Perhaps I was afraid that what had happened would be the last time we'd ever experience that.

The alarm clock rang at six in the morning as it always did during the week. I snapped out of a deep sleep, so deep that my mind was clear of any thoughts from the night before. But as the sunlight fought its way through the blinds, everything that had happened the night before started to play back in my head. Like a good book, all the details slowly unfolded until the climax revealed itself.

I rolled over on my back and noticed that Manny wasn't lying next to me. Was I so desperate for love that I had dreamed all of what had happened?

I felt the stress again; the tightness in my stomach, that horrible lonely feeling that doesn't go away; that forever nervous feeling in the pit of my stomach, also known as the best fucking appetite suppressant in the world.

I heard Junito moving around in his bed and onto the floor, his little feet stepping out of his room, into the living room, and onto the sofa bed with me. He got under the covers and made himself comfortable.

"Good morning, little man, how'd you sleep?"

He didn't answer.

"*Mami* said good morning."

"I'm tired. Can I stay home today?" Junito said, pulling the covers over his head.

"You have to go to school, Junito."

"But I didn't sleep good."

"You didn't sleep well. Why is that?"

"Daddy's big butt is in my bed."

It wasn't a dream. I got out of bed quietly and tiptoed into Junito's bedroom. Manny was snoring loudly with his face pressed against Junito's SpongeBob SquarePants poster.

"*Mami!*" Junito called from the living room. "Look on my TV. Daddy brought me a surprise."

There it was, sitting on top of Junito's TV. That black box of evil was back in my life: the PlayStation.

12 After I dropped Junito off at school, I was surprised to see Manny's car still parked in front of my apartment. As I put the key in the door, it opened on its own. Then Manny stepped out from behind it.

"Oh, hey, you're back?" he said, surprised to see me.

"Yeah, I decided not to go into the office today. Too tired." I hoped that he needed a mental health day as well.

It shouldn't have been an awkward moment, but it was.

"Listen, I have to get to work, I'll call you. Okay?" Manny said, looking preoccupied.

I wanted to ask when he was going to call me, but instead I held that brick wall up again.

"I'm busy today actually, I have things to do. So we can talk whenever," I said, trying to walk past him and into the apartment, again fighting the urge to ask when I'd hear from him.

"Hey, I brought my game over for Junito," he said.

"I noticed that. I guess you plan on playing it here? 'Cause we both know you can't live without that thing," I said with a smile on my face.

I figured that this was the part when he'd say, "Yes, I thought I'd bring it over so I can spend more time with you guys." But no, that's not what he said. Instead he said, "Yeah, some crazy shit happened to me the other day at work, they had a raffle and I won a free Xbox. Life is funny."

Yes, it is. It's hysterical.

Then he left, again.

I could smell Manny's powder-fresh scented deodorant when I walked back into my apartment. The memory of smelling that every day for the last few years of our marriage hurt my heart. I didn't feel like going to work. I couldn't focus on anything but this stupid marriage. Were we together or were we not?

There was no way I could deal with Samantha standing over my shoulder and watching me pick the right photos for the new Nature's Oatmeal Cereal storyboard, so I decided to take a mental health day. I drank some milk to give me that temporary phlegm thingy in the back of my throat and I called in sick. To enhance the effect, I cleared my throat after every sentence in my voice-mail message.

I also wanted a day to myself to practice what I'd read in a women's magazine the other day about how important it was to make a date with yourself. I thought about Uncle Herman and how I hadn't seen him in a while, so I decided to get in my morning exercise and walk to his luncheonette. I'd have the chance to say hello and get some free breakfast. It was another sticky, humid day but at least there was a little breeze.

My little red iRiver was jamming and after a few minutes with the help of Lisa Lisa and her Cult Jam, I picked up the pace and exhaled all my stress away, beat by beat, step by step. I thought about Manny and wondered if he was thinking about us this morning. I wanted to know if his feelings were still there. Maybe he was just afraid of showing them to me so soon. I suddenly felt guilty about talking to Cameron and thought that I never should've given my number to someone who I'd just met on the ferry.

I walked up toward the business district on Richmond Terrace in the direction of the ferry and watched the morning commuters rush to catch the next boat into Manhattan. Older conservative men in business suits made their way past me and up the steps to the courthouse. A few feet away a group of women stood on the public library lawn and gathered around a large-sized African-American sister with bright burgundy braids in her hair waving a book in the air. I was curious about what she was talking about. I watched as she held the book close to her heart and then up to the sky as if it were the Holy Scripture.

When I first stepped up to the group of women, they were in

the middle of exclaiming "Amen!" like some born-again Oprah witnesses in need of inspiration. I stood at the back of the crowd just in case I wanted to sneak away, but as I listened to the large sister speak, I knew I had come to the right place at just the right time.

"All y'all women need to get real with yourselves. Stop believing the fairy tale. There is no Prince Charming that's gonna ride up to your doorstep and carry your ass away. No, honey! You have to stop believing the myth or you are gonna be some unhappy triply divorced women. Can I get a witness?"

The women answered, "Amen!"

The preacher lady continued, "When a man breaks up with you, what's the first thing he thinks about?"

A woman from the crowd answered, "My home cookin'."

"Well, are you talking about the cookin' in the bedroom or in the kitchen, honey? 'Cause I could tell you right now, he ain't missing no stove-top cooking. Nah, honey! The answer is he missing the cookin' in the bedroom. He misses the S-E-X. He don't want nobody, and I mean nobody, touching your coochie, just in case he wants it back."

I couldn't believe what I was hearing. It was as if the universe had arranged this walk today. I could feel goose bumps up and down my arms as I listened to the sermon that seemed written for me.

"See, he remembers what that coochie could do on a good day. He doesn't want nobody messing with that. So you know what he does? He holds on to you. Like a dog on a leash, girl. He holds on to you. He'll even say he misses you and that he made a mistake, but believe me when I tell you he will not, and let me repeat this, he will not get back with you if he's tasted the ocean again. You know why?"

We all looked at each other trying to figure out the answer before the preacher lady could tell us.

"Because the ocean tastes *mmm, mmm, mmm* good," she said, stomping her wide gold flats into the grass after every *mmm*. "He knows there's a fish out there looking to get with him for free, with no strings attached, no nagging, and no demands. Come on, you know what we do in the beginning. You know how that is when we first meet a man. We want to impress him. We take care of ourselves and look pretty all the time."

The preacher lady got up close to us and whispered, "We will ride that man like he's never been ridden before. Won't we?"

We all giggled like fifth-graders in a sex-ed class.

"He knows this. That's why it's hard to let you go. He remembers the good ole times. That's why he has to make sure that the next fish he reels in is a keeper. And when he realizes that he found somebody else to buy his sorry-ass ways, then he's ready to let you go. In the meantime, he's careful not to mess with you or make you angry. 'Cause you are loyal, woman. Aren't you? You a good woman with a big heart. That's 'cause your mama's taught you right."

A tissue was passed in the crowd to a woman who was sobbing near me.

"He doesn't say or do anything to mess up his chances if there's no other fish that would take him."

I could feel the anger rising above the confusion inside me. Manny didn't say a word to me last night or this morning. He hadn't let me know what last night meant to him. Why hadn't he called me? I double-checked my cell phone. There was no tiny envelope waiting to be opened.

"'Cause he knows that no matter what, you gonna be there waiting. He knows this. Because you're always there waiting. Isn't that true?"

I looked around the crowd, wondering who else was going through the exact thing I was going through. Could she be talking to me?

"Even though he don't want to let go of the leash, he knows you a dying fish to him now, because you know his secrets. The man has baggage, he knows you know that. Now, that can't be no fun for a man. Because a man wants two things stroked, ladies, two things, do you know what they are?"

I raised my hand and yelled out, "His dick and his ego."

The women laughed.

"Now, that's what I'm talking about: a sister who tells the truth."

I felt proud that I got the answer right, but then I thought about all the people I knew who separated or broke up and got back together and actually stayed together happily. I mean, good things do happen sometimes. Why else would someone have said, "Absence makes the heart grow fonder"? So I raised my hand.

"Yes, my lovely goddess?" she said, wiping the sweat off her thick hairy brow. I could feel the crowd parting like the Red Sea until I was visible to everyone.

"Would you say that separation is a waste of time, then?"

"Let me tell you what separation really is. It's a time-out. 'Cause I know, child. I've been down that road. Separation, my ladies, is time off to play. That's it. It's two people saying, 'Let's take a little vacation to mess with other people and see where it takes us. Let's test the will of the almighty spirit that brought us together. Let's not rush into an expensive divorce just yet and get our freak on for a minute or two until we decide whether we want to be together.' That is what separation is to me."

I raised my hand again.

"Yes, my inquisitive little brown sister?"

"Then how do you know when something isn't really working?"

"Ah, the million-dollar question. You know how you can tell when something just ain't right? When things ain't working, but y'all still hanging on? It's called using your intwaition. Intwaition, ladies! That little feeling right in your little pouch area."

For a second I thought about correcting her, but then I saw the cover to her book, *Using Your Intwaition!*

"Y'all always ignore that feeling because you're too scared to wake up alone. Or even worse, you pay no attention to your intwaition because you're afraid of your own greatness. You are one big success story waiting to happen. But y'all don't think you deserve that, do you? Instead you try to find a man to fill your emptiness. Get married 'cause you need that 401(k) plan. But I'm here to tell you that every one of you is destined for greatness and your own individual 401(k) in your own name! Yes, you are. But first you have to find the love. It's there. Believe me, the love that you look for in the fancy bars and in nightclubs is already in your life."

"Where is it?" someone from the crowd yelled out.

"Now, sister, if you need to ask that question, then you have no idea where the love is, do you?"

I felt like I needed to help defend that lady. She asked the question, but I didn't know where the love of my life really was either.

"Lovely ladies, I leave you with this: listen to the silence."

The preacher lady took her book, her purse, and stepped into a taxi that was waiting for her across the street. She disappeared, and she left me hanging. I wanted to know where the love of my life was.

So there I was, standing on the corner of Bay Street and Richmond Terrace, looking at the three-mile trek ahead of me, trying to listen to the silence. It was me, myself, and I. There was no group of bitter housewives and ex-girlfriends standing around me, no born-again Oprah witnesses. The preacher wasn't preaching anymore. It was me alone, and for the first time in a long time, I realized that I had been alone before. Why, then, did I suddenly feel paralyzed without my ball and chain?

When I passed Salvatore's Italian Ice Stand, I knew I was just a few blocks away from Uncle Herman's place. I had picked up the pace with the help of one of the few rock songs that pumped me up like no other rocker song could, Nirvana's "Smells Like Teen Spirit."

No matter how fast I walked, I couldn't get Manny out of my mind. Maybe I was the one holding on to Manny. Maybe he wanted to let go and I wasn't letting him go? I didn't know anymore. I just wanted to find that place again that made me feel at peace. Where was the love that the preacher lady said was already here in my life? Was she talking about Cameron? Was Cameron the one I should be with? I waited for an answer. Why was it that the universe couldn't give me a sign when I asked for it?

The walk was a good idea; I felt victorious and less defeated. I felt like I was breathing in pink air and blowing out blue. A good walk always made me feel renewed. With a touch of my iRiver, I was able to make it to the homestretch in record time with the help of C+C Music Factory's "Gonna Make You Sweat (Everybody Dance Now)."

I loved the way that little bell rang as I walked through the front door of the luncheonette. I sat on the cracked white plastic stool at the counter.

"Well, look who's coming to visit finally. *¿Cómo está la vida, nena?* How's life?" Uncle Herman asked, anxiously looking over piles of little receipts at the end of the lunch counter.

"Life is okay, Uncle Herman. It's okay," I said, browsing the same old menu.

"Don't lie to your *tío*, you know better than that," he said, still looking at the receipts.

"It's fine. Really. I'm hungry, *Tío*, can I get the Webo Special Number 2?"

Uncle Herman called the order in to the new cook. I looked around the run-down luncheonette and noticed one patron sitting at the farthest booth way back, an old man with salt-and-pepper hair, who looked up from his newspaper and smiled—I think he was flirting with me.

"It's quiet here today, *Tío*. Where's everybody?"

Uncle Herman walked toward me. And for the first time I noticed how old he was getting. He wasn't as fast on his feet as he used to be and I thought I noticed a new frown line on his forehead.

"*Nena*, didn't you hear? They built an Amos's Big Breakfast House two blocks up," he said, followed by a soft sigh.

"No way," I said, reaching out to hold his hand.

No wonder he wasn't acting like his old happy-go-lucky self. My poor *tío* invested so many years in making his dream come true and now a greedy corporate chain was going to take that all away from him.

"What are you going to do, *Tío*?" I asked, concerned that this would destroy his other dream of retiring rich in Florida.

"*No sé*. I don't know. Hey, make sure you don't tell your Uncle Sammy."

"Don't even worry about that, *Tío*," I said, letting go of his hand and browsing the menu again. I glanced through the breakfast items, looking for a way to help fix his problem or lend some advice.

"*Mija*, I came here to start something big. I wanted to be a successful businessman. Like *ese pendejo* Amos but better. He doesn't make better eggs than me. He makes lousy eggs."

I knew on the outside Uncle Herman was trying to stay strong, but I had never seen him like this before. For the first time, he seemed unsure about his future. Like me.

"You're right, his eggs are terrible," I said, never having tasted Amos's own *webos*.

"The family is always busy and nobody wants to help an old man and his dream. Your cousins, they don't like working here. They want to be big shots in New York making big money. So much for family business, eh? That's why our people have nothing; they don't stick together and build *como los mexicanos y los cubanos. Verdad*, Guillermo?"

In the middle of flipping one of my eggs, Guillermo turned around toward us and smiled politely, holding on to his personal views. Smart move.

I felt bad for Uncle Herman, knowing that he was the reason our family got a better chance at life. Being the first to take the risk of moving out of the ghetto was a courageous thing. He inspired all of us to have a better life, and now, when he needed help, no one was there to help him.

From where I was sitting I could see the young Guillermo

alone in the back, waiting for my eggs to finish cooking, and I wondered if he aspired to anything more than what he was doing at the moment. I wanted to go up to him and ask him what made him happy. It would just piss me off, though, if he had a very detailed plan laid out.

"Now, if I had someone working for me that was *bien inteligente* like you, ah, that would be the answer to all my *problemas*. Why don't you come work for me?" Uncle Herman asked me.

"*Tío*, you know I can't do that."

"Yes, you can. I'll let you run the place."

I smiled the way Guillermo had, hoping I wouldn't have to answer.

For a split second, I toyed with the idea of managing a luncheonette, but then thought, my mother would be so disappointed if I did that. Not that my mother had that power over me. It's just that if I compared working in a gray cubicle to working in a gray luncheonette, the cubicle won hands down. Besides, what could he possibly pay me? Definitely not what I was making at the agency.

I looked around and thought about how the place needed a new look. The black wooden tables were rickety and tilted—he'd have to buy new ones. The posters hanging on the walls were bleached yellow from the sun. The place unintentionally had that Johnny Rockets old-school look to it. Didn't Uncle Herman know that you had to invest time and energy in something you loved in order to get anything back? You just couldn't expect great things when you took it for granted. Times changed and you had to change with them. He had to know that.

Guillermo brought me my juice and eggs and I thanked him. He answered with a shy "*De nada*." I took advantage of the moment and decided to practice my Spanish on someone who I felt wouldn't be as judgmental and critical as my parents or husband could be.

"*¿De dónde es usted, Guillermo?*" I said, feeling proud of my language skills.

"*Guatemala.*"

"*¿En México?*"

"No, *Guatemala.*"

For a second I was a little confused. Uncle Herman had told me Guillermo was Mexican. I thought Guatemala was a place in Mexico.

I then asked him how he liked his job. "*¿Como tu gusta la trabajo?*"

He laughed a little, served me my food, and told me that the job was great, but it was *el trabajo*, not *la trabajo*.

"Okay, Guillermo, masculine and feminine forms are not my strongest skill set," I answered in perfect English, feeling a little embarrassed about my mistake but also realizing that I had the advantage of not having had to learn the language of the land. I took a bite of my food and I guess Guillermo took that as a sign that our very funny Spanish lesson was over.

It was so quiet in the luncheonette except for the faint sounds of *bachata* coming from a radio in the kitchen. I looked around the space, thinking of ways to make it more presentable and modern. The one thing about working at the agency was that I got a chance to learn about colors and about putting ideas together nicely before presenting them to our clients and eventually to the television audience.

The salt-and-pepper-haired old man got up from his seat and threw a few dollars on the table. As he made his way to the front door, he stopped to talk to me.

"Do you know Herman well?" the old man asked.

"Yes, he's my uncle."

"Well, maybe you need to tell Herman to get on the ball. The coffee in this joint sucks. That's why all my buddies eat at Amos's."

"Then why are you still coming here?"

"His omelets are still the best I've ever eaten, but it would be nice to get a good cup of coffee to go with it. Nowadays coffee can make or break a business, you know what I mean? Just thought I'd mention it."

The old man gave me one last look, which confused me. I didn't know if he was still flirting or whether he actually cared about Uncle Herman's little place.

I noticed the old coffeepot sitting on the opposite side of the lunch counter, and I could smell the bitterness from where I was sitting. Why didn't Uncle Herman buy one of those fancy espresso machines? He served instant coffee, for God's sake. Did people actually drink instant coffee anymore?

I took another bite of my breakfast and the eggs were scrumptious, cooked to perfection with a hint of garlic and onion, not overpowering, just right.

"*¿Tío?*"

"*¿Qué?*"

"How come you don't serve *café con leche* in here?"

"Do you think the *italianos* around here want to drink that?"

"They would pay two dollars a cup for it, guaranteed. And *Tío*, everyone in the family knows you make a mean *café con leche*. Besides, your shop is closer to the express bus stop. People wouldn't have to walk all the way to Amos's to get their breakfast. Try it and see what happens."

"Only if you help me," he said, with his head tilted to the side and with a sly grin on his face. "You know, it was always my dream that you would come work for me."

"Why me?"

"Because, *nena*, you are my special niece. You remind me of me. I can see you want more the way I want more."

How could I avoid breaking this man's heart? He thought I was the luncheonette's saving grace? I couldn't tell him that working in a luncheonette was not a stable enough career for someone like me.

"I'll think about it, *Tío*."

"Ah, thinking is very good. Very good."

Why couldn't I ever say what I really felt?

13

After my walk, I skipped the shower and drove to Selenis's place. I rang the doorbell twice, but she wasn't answering. I was starting to get worried because she'd asked me to come by right away.

"Selenis, you okay in there?"

I smelled something burning inside her house. Doña González must've been cooking and probably burnt a pot again. That old woman just didn't listen.

Selenis finally opened the door with rubber gloves on both hands and a dishrag in one. She gave me a pissed-off hello and walked back into the kitchen. The smell was worse inside the house, like burnt metal.

Doña González was sitting at the kitchen table holding a tissue to her left nostril. Her eyes were red. She looked like she was crying.

"*Hola*, Doña González," I said.

Doña González didn't answer me.

"What happened?" I asked Selenis.

"She forgot to take the fork out of the oatmeal when she was heating it up," Selenis said, cleaning out the inside of the microwave.

I didn't want to make Doña Gonzalez feel any more embarrassed than she already was, so I kept quiet. I felt bad for Selenis too because I honestly didn't know how she could deal with having to watch her mother's every move. It was as if she were taking care of four children instead of three.

"*Mami*, it's time for a nap," Selenis said.

Doña González obeyed her daughter's orders and headed straight to her bedroom. I could hear her *chancletas* hitting the

back of her heel with each little step. It was as if she were deliber-
ately walking at turtle speed to get us to feel sorry for her.

"You okay?" I asked Selenis.

Selenis gave me one of her are-you-for-real looks.

"I feel like doing a Thelma and Louise, that's how okay I am,"
she said as she pulled the rubber gloves off her hands, dumped
them into the sink, and pulled a piece of paper from the middle
of a bunch of bills and recipes that were sitting on the countertop.
She handed it to me.

"As if this shit with my mother isn't enough," Selenis said, "look
what I found on the computer."

I unfolded the page and it was a picture of a naked woman. She
was blond, brown-eyed, hefty in the thighs, with a small waist and
little breasts. If she was supposed to be a porno chick, she wasn't
the best-looking one I'd ever seen.

"Carlito or Ralphie?" I asked.

"The big-ass *sángano* that I'm married to, that's who. And that's
not the only one. There's tons of that shit up there."

"Why is he doing this?"

"I don't know, Idalis, but I swear that you and I are gonna be
roommates real soon if he keeps this up."

"Well, at least he's not *cheating* cheating."

"That is cheating, to me," she said, sounding as though she
wanted to cry.

Why was life kicking Selenis and me in the ass so badly? What
the hell did we do to deserve all this drama? Or was this what
happened to everyone in their thirties? I had to remember to pick
up that book *Passages* again. I only got up to the Trying Twenties
part.

"Girl, you're right, we do need to do a Thelma and Louise. Let
everybody figure out how to take care of themselves for a change,"
I said. "Or we can get away on a mini vacation?"

"I can't go on any vacation right now. Who's gonna watch
Mami?"

"Let her stay with my mother."

"Oh, yeah, right," Selenis said.

After thinking about it, I realized that maybe that was a stupid idea. My mother hated babysitting Selenis's mother because Doña González would call my mother a whore the same way she would call me an idiot. But my mother wasn't as forgiving and understanding as I was. My mother thought Doña González was doing it on purpose, not accepting for a minute that old age was making her say those things.

"What did the doctor say about your mother?" I asked.

"That she had a mini stroke and lost some of her memory."

I could tell by the way Selenis slumped into the kitchen chair that she'd had all she could handle. I knew there was nothing I could say that would make her feel better; just like there was nothing that anyone could tell me to make me feel better about my own life. It was as if someone had performed some serious witchcraft on the both of us and taken away all our happiness in one huge wave of a rooster's foot.

We sat in her kitchen quietly, in our own heads. My mind was doing a hundred and ninety in a thirty-mile-an-hour zone. I was tired too, but I wasn't going to let a spell of bad luck drag down our spirits. I was going to figure out a way to get rid of the evil that was creeping into our lives. Selenis and I were going to be happy and have fun again even if it meant abandoning our to-do lists temporarily.

"Too bad we don't smoke weed anymore," I said.

"Yeah, and it's a good thing we don't; the munchies alone would send me over the two-hundred-pound mark. But I got to admit a good stiff joint would do me good right about now."

"Men have all kinds of shit to escape to. Manny has video games, and now Ralphie has cybersex." I laughed a little.

"Laugh, *pendeja*, laugh, at least my husband's women are fake," she said, trying to keep from laughing or crying.

At first I didn't want to laugh. In fact, that little comment stung more than I expected it to. But the quirk of fate that we were both faced with forced me to laugh.

"You're such a bitch, but I gotta high-five you on that one."

The laughter trailed into silence again.

"What would happen if we disappeared for a day or a few hours at night?" I asked.

"Let's see. The kids would be malnourished. My mother would have piles of shit in her panties because nobody would be able to help her to the bathroom. Everybody would be on their own because Ralphie would be too busy Internet-fucking every porn star with his mouse . . . let's see, what else?"

"You know what, Selenis? We don't know that that would happen. For all you know, everybody's leaning on us because we let them lean on us, but if we disappeared, how much you wanna bet things would change around here?"

"So where we gonna go?"

"I don't know."

"Let's take a ride to the Bronx. Visit the old stomping grounds."

"For what?"

"I don't know. We'll just ride. Wherever the road takes us is where we end up. Besides, we're always planning our life. How about we don't think about it and just do what we feel like doing? Let's be spontaneous the way we used to be."

Selenis got up from her chair and opened the freezer door. She pulled out a tub of ice cream, picked up a spoon from the dish rack, scooped a spoonful of Vanilla Bean, and shoved it into her mouth.

"I don't know, I think we're turning into two old *viejitas*. Maybe this is our destiny now," she said, with a mouth full of ice cream.

"Speak for yourself. Don't include me in that shit. You know, Selenis, if there's one thing I've learned from reading all those self-help books, it's that we create what is or isn't in our lives. It's us, girl! It's gotta be something we're not doing. Like the other day I couldn't figure out what would make me really happy. That's really messed up when you think about that."

"A million dollars right now would make me happy."

"I thought the same thing. But chances are you won't get a million dollars, right? So if you knew you couldn't get a million dollars, what else would you want?"

We stared at each other with blank looks.

"See, maybe that's our problem. Maybe we need to figure out what makes us happy. It's like we're going through life without a mission and everybody else is trying to fit us into theirs."

"I'll tell you what would make me happy: if I could be the old me from back in the day. Thirty pounds lighter and more fun, that's what I want. I want to be fun again, Idalis. And skinny," Selenis said, shoving a huge spoonful of ice cream in her mouth.

"You're fun, *chica*."

"I don't mean that kind of fun. I'm talking about freaky fun. I was a freak back in the day. Shit, I can't even have sex with the night-light on," she said, stuffing a double spoonful of ice cream in her mouth this time.

"Why not?"

She let the ice cream melt in her mouth before answering.

"Because he'll see my fat."

"You don't think he can feel your fat in the dark?"

"Yeah, *estúpida*, but feeling fat is very different from looking at it."

"Well, if I had a chance I would've asked Trisco to marry me."

"I would've kissed Kique."

We stayed sitting there for a while, imagining life differently. I knew that it was just a matter of time before the next dramatic event would have us doing a Thelma and Louise over the Grand Canyon.

14

I left work early the next day and decided that my little man deserved some playtime. So after eating at Mickey D's we hit Funtown, his favorite and Staten Island's only indoor amusement park. I promised Junito that tonight was our night alone and no one and nothing was going to interrupt our time together.

"How do I use this thing?" I asked the plump Goth teenage girl with the nose ring behind the Laser Tag booth. She took the laser gun from my hand, pointed it in front of us, pulled the trigger, and handed it back to me as if that question were a waste of her precious five seconds.

After Junito and I got all laser-geared up, we walked into the dark fluorescent maze and fired invisible shots at any moving vest. I had to admit, it relieved a little stress, but for a very short moment. After twenty minutes of obnoxious little boys aiming their stupid guns at me, telling me they got me and that I suck at this game, I realized why fathers were so important to a boy's life. If mothers had to play these games all the time, somebody would get whacked for real.

Why do boys play so differently than girls do? Girl games are simpler and a lot more fun. I think Cyndi Lauper said it best when she said girls don't like GI Joes, they don't want to shoot someone 975 times in the chest in order to build their self-esteem, they don't aspire to become villains or compete 24/7, they just want to have fun. Well, that's the long, unabbreviated version. There was only one girl I knew that loved playing with Hot Wheels when we were nine; her name was Kiki Vasquez. I always thought Kiki was into girls, but then I got an e-mail from a friend of a friend who said that she had a Boston marriage. Now I tried not to assume things like that anymore.

After the game was over, Junito got super-energized. He was jumping up and down and sweating and asking for more, more, more. I hoped this kid never tried crack; his addictive little personality scared me sometimes.

I told Junito that we should sit out the next game so that I could catch my breath and get reenergized. I felt a little guilty that I was lying.

I sat on the bench in front of the Rubber Jungle Gym and watched Junito play with two blond-haired twins. He was having a ton of fun racing to the top of the gym where there was a little window that he could look out of.

My cell phone rang. I stared at the phone, wanting to pick up, but held back because of my promise to Junito that I'd give him a hundred percent tonight. But what if it was important? What if this call could change my life? What if it were Cameron? It was amazing how I lived most of my life without a cell phone attached to my ear. A busy signal today would cause me to have a panic attack.

"Hello," I said into the phone while looking up at Junito, who was waving down at me. I waved back, feeling a little guilty again.

"Is this the beautiful *boricua* I met on the boat the other day?"

"I don't know, it depends," I said, acting as though I weren't expecting his call.

"We sat next to each other on the six o'clock ferry the other day," he said, trying to get me to remember, as if I gave my number to guys on the boat all the time.

I laughed and said, "Well, let me see, are you the guy who waits for the last minute to talk to a girl?"

He laughed.

The laughter trailed into a bit of awkward silence and I could feel my face get red-hot with embarrassment. Maybe that wasn't funny to him. So he said, "Idalis, I'm not a big phone person. Would you like to go out to dinner with me? Tonight?"

I hesitated for a second. Maybe it was my "intwaition" telling me something. For a second I thought, Yeah, he's fine, but I hardly know him. It would be nice to talk to him for a second to see what he's like. But unless dating rituals have changed in the new millennium, I was still sticking to the old-school method.

"Hello, you still there?" he said.

"Yes, I was just thinking."

"About?" he asked, laughing a little.

"How I don't even know your last name," I said.

"I have the same surname as Michael and Jesse," he said playfully. "Now will you go out with me?"

"*Mami! Mami!* Look at me!" Junito called out from the top of the jungle gym. I gave him a thumbs-up.

"Am I interrupting something?"

"No, not at all," I said, purposely withholding any personal information that might turn him off.

"Okay, so is it a yes or a no to dinner tonight?"

Was it me or was he really determined to have me go out with him tonight? His pushiness put me off a little but excited me at the same time.

I looked up at Junito again; he was at the highest point of the jungle gym.

"Actually, tonight is not a good night," I said.

"You're not going to tell me you're married, are you?"

Wow—now, how do I get out of this without lying? But he saved the moment by asking me another question: "Or has it been a while since you've been out on a date?"

"Well, maybe."

"Okay, I'll make it easier on you. Here it goes, then. I'm a Leo."

Which meant he liked a lot of attention and the sex would be out of this world.

"I work out five times a week."

Which meant he would tell me I needed to tone up the minute we had sex.

"I have no kids and I've never been married."

He was either self-absorbed or a perfectionist.

"I love Latin women."

Okay, I got that.

"I own my own home."

I had never dated a man who even rented his own apartment, never mind owned his own real estate.

"And I'm thirty-six, looking to meet a woman that will complement my life. Is that good enough?"

Hmmmm, he was getting more and more interesting.

"Yes, that's good."

"Now that I put myself out there a little, I'd like to know a few things about you."

"Okay," I said, feeling a little nervous about the quiz.

"I won't ask you how old you are, but tell me what your favorite year is."

"Definitely 1991," I answered, without a doubt in my mind.

"Okay, and what's your favorite color?"

"Favorite color?" I repeated, hoping that one would pop up in my head, but it didn't, so I picked Junito's favorite color. "Green."

"Ah, *verde*, that's my *color favorito* also. So we have one thing in common."

I wasn't crazy about him speaking Spanish and I was tired of the questions. Please let the quiz be over.

"Last question," he said, pausing before asking. "What makes you the most happy?"

The dreaded fucking happy question. I still don't know the answer to that one. So I laughed first, hoping to buy some time when at that very moment, from the corner of my eye, I saw something or someone fall from the top of the Rubber Jungle Gym.

"*Mami!*" Junito screamed on the way down. I dropped the phone on the bench and immediately ran to Junito. He was just lying there, not moving, his eyes closed.

"Junito, are you okay?"

He didn't answer.

"Junito!"

I slapped him.

"Ow," he said. He opened his eyes and started laughing.

"I was just kidding, *Mami*. I got you good," Junito said, laughing hysterically. The two blond-haired twins started laughing and even some of the other mothers standing outside watching did too. I wanted to choke them all. Especially Junito.

"If you do that again, Junito, I will punish you for one week."

I went back to the seat and stared at the cell phone on the bench.

"Hello, Cameron?"

"Yeah, yes, hey," he said. I figured he'd heard my conversation with Junito.

"Sorry about that," I said.

"Kids are funny, huh?"

"Yes, especially the one that I have."

Again there was silence. I didn't know what he was thinking.

"How old is your son?"

"Six."

"He must be cute."

"He is."

He didn't say anything. Maybe he was disappointed that I had a kid, but I wasn't sure.

"So you never answered my question."

Was he talking about the happy question or going out to dinner?

"Listen, we don't have to go to dinner right away if you don't want. We can take a walk in the park instead. How does Silver

Lake Park sound?" he said, sounding a little less excited than when we started our conversation.

Maybe Cameron was in my life for another reason. Maybe it wasn't so much a love connection as a way for me to receive the information I needed to reach the next level of my life. My intuition told me I should say yes.

15

"*Mami*, it's only for a couple of hours. I'll be home no later than ten o'clock. What's the big deal if Junito stays here with you tonight?" I asked, hoping my father wouldn't come upstairs from the basement and put in his two cents. It was bad enough that I had to deal with my mother and my *abuela*.

"This has nothing to do with my grandson. This is about how you are acting lately. Is this what you are going to do now? Run the streets?"

"Ma, it's not even a real date. Please, okay? Besides, I'm sure *Abuela* would like to spend time with her great-grandson before she goes back to P.R."

Abuela was glued to the television watching her stories. She heard me say something about her and just mumbled, "*Sí, sí, sí.*"

"*¿Él es latino?*" my mother asked, wanting to know my date's ethnicity.

"Um, no, but he's nice," I said, trying to avoid the obvious question that was coming.

"*¿Americano?*" she asked, going down the list.

Not what you think is *americano.*

"Does it really matter, Ma?"

"*¿Él es negro?*"

"Maybe."

"*¡Ay mi madre!*"

My *abuela* gave me a disappointed look and went back to her *novela*. Incredible, since the woman was darker than all of us. It was the twenty-first century, for God's sake, and my family was still in denial about their roots.

"Next time I see your friend Sylvia, I'm gonna tell her how you really feel about her," I said, trying to invoke some guilt.

"*Yo no soy racista.* I am not racist. *Y Sylvia es diferente.*"

"No, Ma, she's not different, she's black."

"Why are you defending this man? Did you have sex with him already?"

Abuela looked up at me, waiting for an answer.

"This is ridiculous," I said.

"You are having sex without Manny?"

For a second it sounded like she was encouraging me to have a ménage à trois.

My *abuela* let out a heavy sigh.

"Do you know that I'm separated? Separation means that we are temporarily not together."

"Manny is trying to be with you, but you are so busy trying to be *una* wonder woman or something. Go back to your husband."

"You don't even know what happened to us, so how can you tell me to go back to him?"

"Whatever he did, it wasn't so bad, I'm sure."

"To you it might not be, but to me it is."

"What did he do?"

Three months after the fact, my mother finally asked what the reason was for our separation. What did she think? That we were just taking a vacation? None of this was serious for her, so why bother telling her anything?

"Are you going to take care of Junito or what? It's only a few hours, Ma."

"Why didn't you have Manny take care of him?"

"Manny has his own life, Ma, and I really don't know what he's doing tonight or the next, because you know what, Ma, he hasn't called me."

"Does he know about this person you're seeing?"

"No, and he doesn't need to know because it's none of his business."

"He's your husband, Idalis."

"Well, right now he's not acting like one."

"And neither are you."

"That's because I'm the wife, Ma!"

Did she ever listen to herself?

"You know what I mean," she said, finally realizing her slipup.

I heard my father coming upstairs from the basement. He walked into the living room with a toolbox in his hand, dropped it on the floor, and Junito ran to give him a hug.

"Hey, men don't hug. Give me a handshake."

Junito stepped away and shook his grandpa's hand.

"And why are you dressed so nice?" my father asked me.

"I'm going out, and by the way, it's okay for men to hug."

"Not in my house."

"She has a date," my mother said, like a little sister trying to get her big sister in trouble.

"A date? Isn't that against the law when you're still married?"

"No, *Papi*, it isn't. I'm just going to meet a friend."

"Male or female?"

"Male."

"Well, then that's a date."

"And Manny doesn't know anything. *Ella está loca*, Freddy. She's crazy."

"I'm not crazy, Ma, and in case you didn't know, Manny gave up on me first."

"That's not what he told me."

"You've been talking to him?"

"He calls me to say hello. He's a good son-in-law."

"He's a liar, Ma."

"No, Idalis! He loves you. *El problema* is that you want to control everything. *Él es un hombre*, he is the man, and you think that you can tell him what to do all the time. You have to let men be men. Do I tell your father what to do?"

I looked over at my father and he pretended to act like he wasn't listening.

"Ma, all the time."

"Oh, no. Your father and I are married for forty years because I let him be."

"*Mentirosa*," my *abuela* said.

"*¿Qué?*" my mother said.

"I think *Abuela* just called you a liar," I said.

"*Vete*, Idalis. Go. And let me tell you something. If Manny asks me anything, I'm going to tell him the truth because no matter what, he is still part of the family. That's it. And if you come back *un minuto* past ten, I'm locking the door and going to sleep. You can pick up Junito in the morning."

I kissed Junito on his head, but he was too busy playing with the ratchet set on the floor to kiss me back. I walked out of the house and into the car feeling like an irresponsible teen mom who had left her son to go out partying. My mother was so good at giving me guilt trips.

For a second, I thought about not going. Maybe she was right. Maybe Manny and I still had to work this out before we let other people into our lives. Maybe he did want me back and Bonita was just a test to see how much I wanted him. Maybe he was trying to make me jealous? But that couldn't be. I slept with him the other night and he still hadn't called me back. Why hadn't he called me back? If the love was still there, wouldn't we have gotten back together already?

My mother had a lot of nerve. What did she know about separation? She was a spoiled brat and she was trying to tell me how to deal with my problems? It was easy for her to talk when my father never pulled the security blanket away from her. And he would never do that because they were two needy codependent people. That had to be the key to a long marriage. If you could take care of yourself, why would you need anyone else?

The thought of Manny talking to my mother behind my back pissed me off so much, I stepped hard on the gas and decided I would go ahead and meet Cameron at Silver Lake Park.

Who cared what my family thought? This was my life anyway. So what if I broke a little rule from time to time, was a little irresponsible for a change? Everyone else could have their fun, why couldn't I? And you know what else? I wasn't going to say the Act of Contrition before I went to sleep anymore. By tomorrow I'd know if Sister Donna had lied to me. Sister Donna told my whole third-grade class that if we didn't say the Act of Contrition prayer every night before we went to bed, we would die. Something never sounded right about that.

I finally reached the park and I was ready to meet Cameron. I was feeling like I was going to have a really good time tonight. When I got out of the car, I saw him sitting on a park bench, waiting, with something in his hand. I walked toward him. Okay, the butterflies were back, but I wished them away. I vowed to have a good time and pretend that I didn't have any obligations to anyone.

"Wow, you look beautiful," he said with a big smile. He handed me a lavender rose and kissed me on my cheek. His lips were warm and that made me feel tingly inside.

"Thank you," I said, realizing that maybe he thought I said thank you for the kiss. "For the rose, it's beautiful."

He took my hand in his. His hands were soft, like Manny's. I felt a little panic attack coming on. For some strange reason I felt like I was cheating on Manny.

"Can we walk a little? I've got a lot of energy, for some reason," I said, hoping a little walk would calm my nerves.

As we walked down toward the lake, the sun was setting, filling in the spaces between the clouds and the horizon with a beautiful burst of purple and orange. I could feel myself loosening up.

"So?" Cameron said, smiling at me. He had his hands in his baggy jeans pockets, and his white button-down short-sleeve shirt was hanging loose. He looked very Caribbean, very stylish and very GQish.

"So," I answered, not knowing what else to say.

He reached out and touched my arm with his hand. I felt the electricity again.

I looked at my arm to see why he'd touched it.

"I was just testing something."

"Okay," I said, wondering if he was checking to see if he felt the same thing I did.

"So, Ms. Idalis—I love saying your name, Idalis—tell me about yourself."

"I'm not good at starting; why don't you start?"

"Okay, hit me."

"Let's see, what do you do for a living?"

"I'm a banker at Morris and Chestnut Financial."

I laughed.

"What's so funny?"

"It's just that . . . oh, forget it."

"The Morris Chestnut thing."

"Yeah, exactly."

"Yes, I've heard that before."

"Sorry."

"No, don't be. What sister doesn't know or appreciate a brother like Morris?"

We walked a few seconds without saying anything.

"So, you look like a Lambda Theta Alpha girl. Am I right?"

"Not sure what that is."

"It's the oldest Latin sorority. Started at Kean University. I'm sorry, I assumed you might have been in a sorority in school."

This wasn't fun anymore. It felt like I was being interviewed.

"No, didn't go to college."

"Oh."

"Yeah, couldn't afford it."

"So what do you do for a living?"

"I work in advertising."

"Advertising, nice."

I was getting the feeling that Cameron was one of those bougie dudes who was looking for a brand-name bougie wife.

We walked a little longer. This time, we let a good three minutes go by without saying a word. We were probably taking in the information to see how it worked for us. We reached the lake and leaned our arms on the fence that overlooked the water. I concentrated on the rippled bright line in the center of the lake, cast by the reflection of the sun.

"It's a beautiful sunset, isn't it?" he said, admiring the same thing I was.

"It is. Isn't it weird that the sun is always up there? Every day. It always comes up."

He laughed.

I looked at him, wondering if he was laughing at me or with me.

"It's true. I don't think people think about that enough. To think we are rotating around the sun right now. One big planet, moving around the sun, lucky enough to have gravity."

"Makes you wonder, doesn't it?"

"About?"

"Life."

"Yeah, it's funny how busy we get that we don't really think about the randomness of it all."

"I think about it all the time, actually."

I looked up at the sky, surprised at how easily I shared my thoughts—thoughts that I usually kept for my journal.

"I think about how everybody is so busy doing stuff. Worrying about buying a house, saving money for retirement, climbing up the corporate ladder, and everything else. When you think about it, nothing is really in our control."

He looked into my eyes.

"You're right. Nothing is in our control."

He kept staring, long and hard, the way Señora Topacio gazed into them the day she told me I'd be dancing freestyle. It made me nervous and I wanted to look away, but the thought of dancing alone made me even more nervous, so I stared back.

"I don't know, Ms. Idalis. I like you."

"You don't even know me."

"I feel you, though. I can feel you." He stopped looking at me and glanced into the water. I could feel his sincerity. "How come someone like you isn't taken?" he said.

I guessed there was no way around this one. Sooner or later, I was going to have to tell this guy the truth. Let it be later.

"I don't know, how come someone like you isn't taken either?" I answered.

"Well, I was in a relationship for five years. Actually, I was engaged. She was a lawyer and lived in D.C. We had one of those long-distance relationships. It didn't work out. She didn't want to move up here and I didn't want to move down there."

"But you obviously loved each other if you were going to get married."

"Yes, we did."

"See, that's what I'm talking about. Then what is love? Because I thought that, come hell or high water, nothing gets in the way of love."

"It should be that way, but I don't know. It gets complicated."

We kept staring into the water, quietly taking in everything. Someone roller-skated past us. I heard the skates suddenly stop and U-turn.

"Idalis?"

I turned to look at the skater, and it was an old friend from high school that I hadn't seen in at least five years.

"Desiree?"

We gave each other a sister hug and a kiss on each cheek.

"How the hell are you?" she said.

"Good, girl, real good. Where have you been?"

"I moved to Atlanta and hated it so much I came back here. Where's the little guy?"

"He's with my mother."

"I see."

I felt I was being rude to Cameron and Desiree, especially because she kept checking him out, so I introduced them.

"Desiree, this is Cameron; Cameron, Desiree."

They shook hands.

"And Manny, how's he doing?"

Oh, lord, must this happen now?

"He's okay."

I wondered if Cameron was wondering who she was talking about.

"My sister said she saw him the other day at some club in the city."

"Really?" I said, trying to act like I really didn't care to know, but I did.

That was probably the night he came to my house late. Asshole.

"Yes, but she didn't bother going up to him. He was with a bunch of guys."

"Okay," I said, hoping that she'd pick up on the fact that I didn't really care to hear anything more.

"I was surprised because you and Manny are like two peas in a pod, girl. From what I remember, you two were inseparable."

I wanted to cry. I really wanted to cry, because the universe had to be doing all of this for a reason. I looked at Cameron and he was looking out into the lake. I was wondering what he was thinking. This was why I had a love/hate relationship with Staten Island. It looked like a major borough in New York City, but it acted like a small town in the Midwest.

"I know, well, you know, things change sometimes and people move on."

"No! You guys aren't together?"

This is one clueless chick. Why couldn't she pick up the vibes?

"No, we're not."

"What happened?"

"Listen, do you have a number? You know, we could catch up later, 'cause I know you probably want to do another lap around the park or something."

"Oh, no, I was on my way home, girl. I did a bunch of laps

already. I can't believe that. Damn. I could swear you two were meant to be together." Now she turned to Cameron. "Their wedding was beautiful. Smaller than what I would've had, but beautiful. It was perfect, actually. It was so perfect, I was jealous."

Well, too bad I didn't have any popcorn to go with this comedy.

"You know, I have to go back and pick up Junito. Can we catch up later?"

"We better, girl. I'm at my mother's and her number is still listed. Good seeing you, Idalis. And Cameron, nice meeting you."

Desiree skated herself out of the park.

Cameron looked at me, looked over at the water in the lake, and looked at me again.

"You're married?"

I wanted to say no, but I couldn't.

"Yes."

"Oh." He looked into the water again.

"I'm separated, actually."

"Oh."

"It's been three months."

"Only three months?" he said, as if it wasn't enough time for us to be talking.

"Yes."

"I guess you guys are trying to work it out, then."

I looked at the water, looked at Cameron, and then the water.

"I don't know if we are."

"Oh."

He looked at his watch. "Maybe we should get going?" he said. He started walking toward the entrance to the park.

"I'm sorry," I said, trying to catch up to him.

"It's okay," he said.

I couldn't tell what he was feeling, since he wasn't looking me in the eyes as much.

"I mean, I didn't think I should tell you anything, since we just met and all."

"I told you I was engaged," he said with a forced grin.

"I know, but we just met, Cameron, and I didn't really have a chance."

"Okay, no problem," he said with a fake smile.

"You're making me feel bad, and I really wasn't planning on feeling bad tonight."

"It's okay."

We quietly walked to our cars. He walked me to mine, waited for me to get in, and then before starting toward his, he said, "I'll call you," and continued on.

"You're just saying that," I said, trying to get him to turn back.

He turned around, tilted his head a bit, and looked at me as if I were pushing the issue. I didn't want to push, so I opened my car door and got in. He walked back to close the door for me, and then I watched him walk across the street to his BMW, get in, and drive away.

I went home that night, put Junito to bed, stared at the ceiling, and thought about my luck lately. I decided that right now wasn't the best time to play with my fate and so I made my peace with Sister Donna.

> *Now I lay me down to sleep,*
> *I pray the Lord my soul to keep.*
> *If I should die before I wake,*
> *I pray the Lord my soul to take.*

16 It had been two days. Cameron hadn't called and I honestly didn't think he would. Manny called to talk to Junito at my mother's house the other day, but hadn't called to talk to me. So no one was talking to me. That Thelma and Louise drive was starting to look more and more appealing right about now.

I could understand Cameron not calling, but Manny not calling? I couldn't shake the feeling that maybe I had been taken advantage of, that I had had a one-night stand with my husband. Was it even possible to have a one-night stand with your husband? The more I sat there on my stoop, staring out at the Bayonne Bridge and trying to find a reason why the industrial drums in the water might be pretty, the more I couldn't shake the feeling I had when Bonita popped up out of the basement the other day. I was a sucker, a naïve little girl caught in a grown woman's body who for some reason didn't learn from her mistakes.

I wondered if other people had gone through what I was going through right now. Maybe I was just not lucky in love. Or maybe I had toxic people in my life, as Les Brown calls them. Or maybe, like my parents and Selenis, I couldn't let a lot of shit fly off my chest.

Mami and *Papi* had had some serious fights in their day. They would yell at the top of their lungs, and during the really bad ones they threw chairs and pots and pans around the house. One day I heard my father tell my mother that he'd never wanted to marry her. I thought that this would end their marriage for sure. *Mami* left for a two-month so-called vacation to *Abuela*'s house in Puerto Rico, but when she got back, she went into the kitchen the next morning, made my father his regular *café con leche*, placed it in front of him, and talked about her trip. How could couples say such crappy things to each other and still find a way to stay together? Did being married make it okay for them to say whatever they wanted to say? Was I supposed to just shrug it all off and pretend that I was happily married, the way all my *tíos* and *tías* did in their own marriages? Even Selenis had been through a lot with Ralphie, and they'd managed to stay together longer than Manny and me. Why was it that some couples could stay together for forty years and others couldn't make it past their tenth anniversary?

I didn't know what was wrong with me. Why couldn't I be like the rest of my family, complacent? I had to go and ruin it by wanting more. But maybe marriage wasn't meant for some people, or maybe I hadn't found the right person. Maybe it was like that poem that the secretaries in the office e-mailed around every time they broke up with someone. The one that said that some people are around for a season, some longer or shorter than that, depending on the reason you need them. Maybe Manny came to me for a season and maybe he had filled my reason. But I didn't know what that reason was. When would I find someone who would love me for my entire life the way I needed him to love me?

Mami might have been right. Like she said, "Marriage is work, *nena*, and sometimes a woman must do the things that she doesn't want to do to keep the *familia* together." But wasn't that old school?

If Manny and I had to hold down jobs, then which one of us was responsible for what had to be done at home? My mother thought it was a woman's job, and so did Manny. Did anyone know whose job it really was? All I wanted was a fair partnership. That was it. Was I asking for the moon? What did it take for the rules to change a little? How many couples were going to get divorced before someone came up with a solution?

It wasn't like I was twenty-five anymore. I didn't have time to make another mistake. In fact, I had to find someone soon, because the other day I found my first gray pubic hair. Who the hell was going to want me with a mound of gray hair down there? It was the ugliest and scariest discovery since the nipple hair I found a year ago.

In five years I'd be forty, and in fifteen years I'd be fifty. So there was no doubt during that time I would have inherited a new set of unwelcome and repulsive bodily issues. I would be so grotesque that I'd have to settle for some fat, short man like Danny DeVito, a bald old man with hair on his ass, permanent cheese between his teeth, and balls that smelled like a Blimpie sandwich, and who during sex would want me to suck his dirty stubby fingers. Or I could just remain a lonely old maid highly skilled in the art of masturbation.

When I thought about my journey, I couldn't help but think about the day Manny and I got married. How perfect that wedding was. It *was* beautiful. Desiree was right. It was small but perfect, because you could feel the love. We didn't have money for a huge fancy event, so we rented an American Legion hall. It was $250 for six hours and we got the food catered from El Borinquen and Nunzio's restaurants. Manny's cousin Joey deejayed for us because we couldn't find a DJ who had a nice mix of salsa, R&B, and pop music. It was simple, the way we used to be.

I didn't know how things suddenly became so complicated. When did life become so grown-up?

I thought about how every decision I made was for someone else: for Junito, for Manny, and for my parents. I never made decisions for myself. I'd never been to the West Coast or Europe, because how could I leave my mother or Selenis behind? I felt guilty for wanting more out of life. Why did I feel that way? Should I be happy with what I had and just shut the hell up? Should I stay in a marriage that didn't work because my parents expected me to? I didn't know who I was anymore. Something happened along the way and I just wanted it to stop.

I wanted to go back to simpler days, when all I worried about was what outfit to wear to a club, and whose number I was going to get, and how I was going to watch *Soul Train* so that I could learn the latest dance and try it out the next weekend. Life was so simple back then. If only I could turn back the hands of time.

17

It had now been four days since I'd heard from any male of the species. I hated men. I despised them. I'd come to terms with the fact that I could live without them, easily. I was through.

I so missed Manny.

"Ma, can I go outside and play?" Junito asked as we both stepped into my apartment. "I'll stay right in front. Please?"

"*Mami's* tired," I said, trying to find a way not to feel so guilty. "Maybe we could play Uno later."

"But I'll stay right in front. You can watch me from the window. Come on, Ma."

"I'm tired, Junito, I don't want to stand near the window. *Mami* needs a nap."

"You're always tired," Junito said.

"Excuse you?"

Junito stomped into his room and slammed his bedroom door so hard that the little I LOVE MY PARENTS THIS MUCH plaque on the door fell off. I placed my purse on the table and wished he hadn't done that, because now I had to find the energy to play mother and father. I didn't have an ounce of energy even to play mother. For a second, I thought about letting it go; letting him vent his own frustrations couldn't be so bad. But suddenly I had a vision of Junito in handcuffs on the front page of the New York *Daily News* looking like Babyface Finster.

I opened Junito's bedroom door and entered the room, feeling as though I were on my last energy cell. He was standing near his bookshelf; he had Storm and Wolverine in his hands. Wolverine was punching Storm in the stomach. Not a nice thing to do to a woman, even if she was plastic.

"Sit down," I told him.

"No," he answered boldly.

"Sit!"

Junito finally sat on his bed.

"Why did you slam the door?"

He didn't answer.

"I asked you a question, Junito."

"I didn't slam the door, it closed by itself," he said without looking at me.

"I'm going to ask you one more time, and if you don't tell me the truth, I will throw away Storm and Wolverine right now. Why did you slam the door?"

"Because I'm mad," Junito said, looking at his feet.

"Why are you mad?"

"Because you never let me do what I want to do. You always say no."

"No, I don't."

I sat on the floor and put my hands on his knees. I looked into his eyes and noticed my little man's face was changing. It seemed like just the other day I was carrying him around the house on my hip. He was getting bigger and filling out more and I could see more of me in his face. His upturned nose and his smile reminded me of me. But even though he was getting too heavy to carry, he was still a little boy and I wondered if I was expecting too much from him.

"I know you can't understand why *Mami* and *Papi* are going through what we're going through. It's not that we don't love you. We do. *Mami* has a lot to do now that I have to do by myself, and sometimes I don't have the time to play with you the way we used to."

Junito was looking at me hoping to hear an answer that would make him feel better.

"I love you, little man. You know I do, right?" I said, lifting up his shirt and poking his belly button.

Junito put his head down to hide the smile that was forming on his lips. He knew what was coming next.

"Okay?" I said, lifting up his T-shirt and blowing big air kisses into his stomach.

Junito laughed and it sent a warm feeling throughout my body. When I stopped, he asked for more. I loved hearing him laugh, so I kept going until he had had enough.

After I finished playing with Junito, we lay down on the bed with our feet hanging off the edge of the mattress, looking up at the fluorescent stars and moon on the ceiling.

"Mercury," I said, pointing to the first planet closest to the sun.

"Venus," Junito said next.

"Earth," I said.

"Mars," said Junito.

I was about to say Jupiter when Junito interrupted our game.

"*Mami*, is Daddy going to get married to somebody else?"

I didn't know how to answer that, because I didn't know what the future had in store for us.

"I don't think so, *pa*," I said. Then a second later I realized that maybe he asked because he knew something I didn't. "Why do you ask?"

"Because Daddy was on the phone with his friend and he was fighting and saying he didn't want to get married."

Get married?

"What friend was he talking to?" I said, still lying down, pretending that all was well.

"I don't know."

"Was he talking to Uncle Johnny?"

"No."

We kept staring at the ceiling until Junito leaped off the bed, remembering who it was.

"Jasmin."

"Jasmin?"

"Yeah, Daddy's new friend."

I closed my eyes and could feel the nerves in my body tighten up. Everything inside me felt twisted and tense. I felt dizzy.

"*Mami*, can you take me to the park?"

"Junito, *Mami* is tired. I told you that already. Who is Jasmin?"

"I told you, Daddy's friend."

My stomach was doing flip-flops and again my appetite disappeared. I told Junito to go on my laptop or to go build a Lego house. I really needed to be alone at that moment. He whined, but after I gave him the look, he ran and did what I told him.

I couldn't move. I was lying there, staring at Venus and Mars and noticing how Earth was in between the two of them. I never noticed that before. I mean, not in that way. Could that be why men and women didn't understand each other—was it because there is a planet between us?

Maybe Junito had gotten his wires crossed, like a bad game of telephone. But how could Junito misunderstand something like that? Why would his father, who was already married, tell someone he didn't want to get married?

I fought the urge to pick up the phone and call Manny. Instead, I walked into the kitchen to get something to drink. The overdue Con Edison bill was staring at me from the fridge and I realized I was supposed to go pay that in person like yesterday. Screw it. I didn't care. Let them turn off my lights. Besides, what was so bad about living in the dark all the time?

I could feel that hole in my heart aching again and I couldn't stop the tears from falling down. Even though my little miracle was here with me, I still felt alone—so alone that it reminded me of the time my *abuela* accidentally left me in the lingerie section of Gimbels Department Store. I remember being so small and looking up at the bras and underwear hanging over my head hoping that she would pop her head out from one of the racks. I waited there alone in the same spot for what seemed to be an eternity, feeling as though I'd never see my family again. I was afraid of walking away in case she'd come back to look for me. As I stood waiting alone, while strange big people walked past me, I was screaming inside, I want my *Mami.* I need my mother!

18 "Stop crying, Idalis, you're going to get a sinus infection. You know how sensitive your *nariz* is," my mother said, handing me a huge paper towel from above the kitchen sink to wipe my nose.

"*Mami*, what am I doing wrong? Why is this happening to me?"

"Well, *nena*, you haven't been to church in a long time. What do you think, that God doesn't know that?"

"The God I pray to doesn't make me go to church."

My mother made the sign of the cross, kissed her thumb, and asked God to forgive me.

"This is why things are happening to you. *Por qué* you create your own rules? Why do you do that? Why can't you make it easy for yourself and Junito?"

"Ma, it would be a lot easier for me to just do what everybody else does. It wouldn't be as much work."

I started feeling sorry for myself for being rebellious and I could feel my eyes watering up again.

"*Yo sé, mija.* I know. *No llores,* Idalis. Don't cry."

"Why is Manny being so stupid?"

"You have to talk to him, *nena.*"

"I can't."

"*¿Por qué no?*"

"Because I don't trust him."

"He loves you, Idalis."

"Really? Then why don't I feel that?"

The doorbell rang before my mother could answer my question and she suddenly looked nervous, as if she were hiding something. For some reason, I now felt I'd been talking to a conspirator.

"*Mami*, that better not be him," I said, standing up from the table.

"*No te vayas.* Sit down," she said, holding my elbow, trying to force me back down into the seat.

"You called him?"

"Yes, you can thank me later when you get back together."

"Ma, I came to you because I needed your help and you set me up?"

"*Ay, Dios mío*, Idalis, my goodness. Sit down!"

The doorbell rang a second time and I tried to figure a way out.

"Idalis, stop running away, okay?" she said as she left the kitchen to open the front door.

As I stood alone in the kitchen, contemplating my next move, I stared at the back door wondering how long it would take me to run through the neighbor's backyard to the front yard and into my car without my mother and Manny catching me. In my head the plan didn't seem to work, so I ran to the bathroom and locked the door behind me instead. I heard my mother and Manny walk through the hallway and into the kitchen, engaged in bullshit small talk. I felt like an addict caught in the middle of an intervention. I heard my mother call my name. I wanted to curse her out.

"I'm in the bathroom, Ma."

"You have a guest. Manny came to see you. Isn't that nice?"

I wanted to throw up right into the toilet next to me. My mother was so manipulative. So controlling. So wanting everything her way. Why couldn't she be more like Mrs. Brady? Mrs. Brady never would have forced Marcia into staying married if she didn't want to. What was her obsession with me working out my marriage? It wasn't her marriage. It was my marriage and my life.

I looked at myself in the mirror and I wished that I could catch a glimpse of a younger version of me staring back. The younger me would have fought a little more for my independence. She would have been able to ask for respect and get it, but she wasn't there. Somewhere in the last ten years she lost her ability to be true to herself.

My mother offered Manny a beer, he passed on it, and I could hear them walk into the living room. I waited a few minutes for the redness on my nose to fade back to its natural color before joining them in the living room. I didn't want Manny to think that he was worth even one of my tears.

As I made my way past the kitchen, I could clearly hear Manny's voice. Again, I could feel my nerves twisting inside me.

"Hello," I said, trying hard to act confident and strong as I entered the living room.

He smiled, almost as though he were sincerely happy to see me.

My mother excused herself and went upstairs to her bedroom. But before leaving, she gave a look as if to say, "Here, *nena*, this is your chance to make things work with your husband."

"You okay?" he asked, settling deeper into the old tapestry chair.

"I'm good," I answered, sitting across from him on the love seat.

"Your nose is red."

"I've got allergies."

"You look good, though, as always."

His comment made me want to roll my eyes in disgust, but instead I glanced over at the clock on the mantel over the fireplace.

"Thanks."

"So your mother wants us to talk."

"She does, doesn't she? I guess you've been talking to her."

He nervously tapped his fingers on the arm of the seat, as if tapping would help him through this.

"I try to stay in touch."

He tapped again.

"Junito is with Selenis?" he asked.

"Yeah, Ralphie took the boys out to Clove Lakes Park to play baseball."

"Yeah, your mother just mentioned that to me. You could've told me."

"Well, I hadn't heard from you, so I assumed you were busy."

"Yeah, sorry about that. I have different hours at work now that I have to pick up Junito."

We sat for a moment not saying anything, but I couldn't stand feeling so out of control.

I pretended to recheck the time and glanced over at him. Our eyes caught. We said nothing. He looked around, and started tapping his fingers again. I sat there waiting. This was ridiculous now. Why was I being so quiet and so polite?

"Listen, Manny, I think it's time we make a decision."

"About?"

"About the obvious. We can't be separated forever. I need to make a move or do something here."

"We've only been separated for three months, Idalis. I know people separated longer than that."

I felt like crying in his arms and smacking the shit out of him all at the same time.

"Why would you want to be separated longer?"

"See, you hear what you want to hear. I said I know people, I didn't say us."

"But you were insinuating that we should be separated longer before we make a decision."

"No, but maybe we *should* think about things a little longer first. That's all I'm saying. I don't know if we're ready."

"Really?"

He tilted his head and shrugged one shoulder to the side, as if to say, "Right, that's what I think."

"I guess the other night was just a test, then," I said.

"The other night was mutual, I thought."

"You said you missed me."

"I did and I still do."

"But you're not ready to get back together?"

"I don't think you are either, Idalis, because you would have said something sooner."

"Okay, then I don't think that more time is gonna help either one of us. I think we both know the answer right now."

"So you're ready to make things work again?" he asked, nervously untying and retying his shoelaces on his Jordans.

The question threw me for a loop because I seriously didn't know the answer to that; part of me was unsure, the other part wanted to believe that we could salvage what we had started a decade ago, but I couldn't trust him the way I used to.

"Let me ask you a question. Are you seeing someone, Manny?" I asked, looking directly into his eyes.

"What?"

"You heard me."

"Idalis, come on."

He removed a stray hair from his jeans and flicked it on the floor.

"Junito heard you talking to someone on the phone."

"When?"

"I don't know when. He heard you saying you didn't want to get married."

"Junito probably heard the television on."

"It wasn't the television, Manny. He heard you talking to your friend."

The surprised look on his face gave it all away.

"Now, why would I be talking shit like that to a person who is just a friend?"

"Right, that's what I want to know."

"Don't you have friends, Idalis?"

"Yeah, I have friends."

"Okay, then."

He went back to his tapping, but this time it looked like he was thinking hard, probably trying to find a way out of his web of lies. Either Manny was a chronic liar or he didn't know squat about communicating.

I needed to get real. I needed to face him head-on and stop letting other people tell me what to do with my life. Finally, I thought I was ready to hear the truth.

"Manny?"

"Yeah?"

"Do you love me?"

"Do I love you?" he said, crossing his legs and smoothing out the wrinkles in his jeans. "Come on, Idalis, you know I hate being away from my son. How can you ask me such a silly question?"

"I know you love Junito, but are you in love with me?"

After I asked the question, I thought of the motivational speaker at the library that day: ". . . You can tell when something just ain't right . . . when things ain't working, but y'all still hanging on."

He settled back into his chair and straightened his jeans again. He was either nervous or his jeans were making him uncomfortable, or both. He slouched down on one side of the chair and moved his arm onto the armrest. He held his hand to his mouth, playing with his lips. After twisting his lips around once, he moved forward in his chair. He started talking with his hands in a prayer position, pointing them at me.

"Idalis, I do love you. How can I not love my wife? We've been through it all. I miss the way we used to be and the things we used to do together. But all I keep thinking about is how you push me. You push too much sometimes."

"How do I push you, Manny?"

"You don't let me be. If it makes me happy to sit and play video games, then leave me alone. It's not like I'm those dudes that go drinking and come home drunk all the time. I go to work, and I work hard, I come home, and I want to rest. That's it. Why you gotta go mess with me all the time? If you ask me, I don't think you're happy with me."

"It was never about how I felt about you, it was always about you not helping me. I needed you to do more things around the house and to be there to support me. I was doing everything by myself and you took me for granted."

"That's because you like doing everything by yourself. You like getting up at six o'clock in the morning to start cleaning the house before you go to work. I don't tell you to do that. So I clean the bathroom twice a month; at least I clean the bathroom, right?"

"I had to get up that early because it was the only time I had to do that, and the bathroom should be cleaned every week, Manny. Especially because Junito pees all over the place sometimes."

"But the bathroom gets cleaned."

"Only when you feel like doing it."

"No, when I can do it."

"Manny, if you got off the video games and stopped watching TV for an hour, you could clean the bathroom every week. You could even take those stockbroker classes at the college. You're always complaining about your job, but you never do anything to move forward. I think you like being stuck. How is life going to get any better for us if you can't move forward?"

He laughed. "You see, this is what you do. You push and push and push."

"I'm not pushing. I'm talking. Do you think it's right that I go to work all day, take care of Junito, and maintain every detail of our lives by myself?"

"My mother did it."

"I'm not your mother."

And there it was, the answer to all our problems. His mother. I didn't have anything to say at that point. It was as if our words had hit a brick wall. I could not compete with his idea of perfection. From the corner of my eye, I could feel that he was working it out in his head, trying to figure out why I couldn't be more like his mother, and I was sitting there trying to understand why I couldn't be more like her too.

It was awkward and painful to sit and wait to see what would happen next, but I purposely didn't make the first move. I challenged myself to see if I could stop controlling things.

The doorbell rang.

I decided to get up myself and get it.

"I got it, Ma!"

I opened the front door and a sassy young Baby Phat–wearing chick snapping her gum in my face stood there holding her gaudy little pleather purse around her shoulder. Her super-large hoop earrings stuck out from behind her long brown hair.

"Can I tawk to Manny?" she said in a nasally pissed-off voice.

I could feel my heart surrender. It was tired of doing flip-flops, it was tired of fighting, and it was tired of being picked up from the floor and put back in place.

I opened the door wider and pointed in the direction of the living room. I grabbed my pocketbook from the floor in the hallway, looked up, and saw my mother looking down at me from the top of the staircase. There was no look of disappointment on her face. She wasn't saying anything to me. I wanted to tell her off, but I couldn't. I felt as though I were fighting the world.

As I left the house, I could hear Manny's friend ask him why he left her in the car so long. Her voice was trembling and I could tell that she was more than just a friend.

19

"*¿Cómo estás, idiota?* How are you, idiot?" Selenis's mom asked as I walked into the house, trying to hide the fact that I was crying.

"*Estoy bien,* and how are you, Doña González?" I answered, realizing that I was getting used to the name-calling. I thought, What the hell, what's one more abusive relationship anyway?

"*Mami,* go to sleep," Selenis told her mother.

"*Yo no soy un perro,* Selenis."

"I know you're not a dog, Ma, I'm just letting you know it's time for a nap."

"*Qué mierda.*"

Doña González walked back to her room.

"Your nose is red. What's wrong?" Selenis asked as she picked up her mother's tray of food and placed it in the sink. She then sat next to me at the kitchen table.

"Manny finally did it. He's moved on with someone else. And she's so young."

"Is this one for real?"

"Yes, this one is for real. She had the nerve to show up at my mother's house asking for him. I'm tired of his bullshit, Selenis. I'm tired of the constant headaches, the crying. The bullshit games he plays. Why can't he let me go?"

"Maybe 'cause you can't let him go yet?"

"But I am ready. I'm not hanging on to him."

"*Chica,* I know you. You haven't let go of him completely. Half of you has, but the other half isn't sure."

"You're right, I'm not sure. I'm so confused."

"Well, you know what? It's time for you to start seeing other people too."

"Well, I did. Kind of."

"You keeping secrets now?"

"I wasn't ready to say anything 'cause I wasn't sure what to say."

"Who is he?"

"He lives on Staten Island. He's professional, never been married, no kids, and he owns his own house, but I don't know."

"It sounds too good to be true."

"He seems so sincere, though."

"They all seem sincere. Shit, Ralphie cried when we got married, at our wedding. Don't you remember? The same dude that was bawling like a fucking baby is now jerking off to some make-believe bitch. Believe me, they're all sincere in the beginning."

"So what happened with the pictures?"

"What happened? I found more."

"You haven't talked to him about that?"

"I'm so pissed, Idalis, that I don't know what to do. It's like I want to catch him in the act so I can make him feel like shit. It's getting ridiculous because he's doing this on the family computer. I was using it the other day and I get an instant message from some chick named Coconut Flavored Mami. The minute I saw that shit I knew she wasn't selling *piraguas*. And what if Carlito or Symone were on the computer? Doesn't he think about that?"

"But is it like *Playboy*-type shit, Selenis? Because you know back in the day guys used to read *Playboy* and women used to go crazy, like they were cheating or something. But look at *Playboy* today. It's nothing. They show more in R-rated movies now."

"I don't care if the Internet is supposed to be the new *Hustler*. He's spending money on jacking off when he could do that by himself in the bathroom, for free."

"Well, that's kind of hard to do. Don't you think?"

"Whose side are you on?"

"Sorry, I'm just saying, I know that every so often Manny would check stuff out too, but I didn't let it get to me."

"Oh, really, well look where that got you."

"No need to get nasty."

"Well, I'm sure that Manny wasn't doing it every day."

"No, he wasn't."

"Why does he need to be on that thing all the time?"

"Selenis, it's time we get the fuck out of here. Let's just take a ride. Screw everybody. Well, except the kids. They have nothing to do with this."

"If I could leave right now, I would."

I sat there thinking about a possible escape. I held on to my car keys, staring at them. Selenis was cleaning up the crumbs that landed in between the sofa cushions.

"What are you doing tonight?"

"The same shit I'm doing now."

"Let's go to the Bronx."

"You crazy," Selenis said, trying to dismiss me.

"I'm serious. Let's just get the hell out of here."

"What about the kids?"

"I'll take Junito to my mother's house and you let Ralphie watch the kids."

"I don't know, Idalis."

"We do everything for everybody else all the time. Let's just get in the car and get out. Have our own fun."

"My mother needs to get washed tonight and I'm gonna tell you right now that Ralphie ain't doing that shit."

"So let him figure it out."

"She needs help going to the bathroom, Idalis."

"What you need is a nurse here to help you. You can't be doing this by yourself all the time."

"Right. With what money? That ain't happening."

"Listen, we have to show these assholes how to appreciate what they got. Let's disappear for a few hours. Besides, we need to find us again. What the hell, we'll be back tonight. Fuck 'em."

Selenis looked at me and I could see her serious expression turn into a devilish grin.

20

As I drove over the Willis Avenue Bridge into the Bronx, the initial anger was fading and I wondered if I had made a mistake. I was starting to feel stupid, but Selenis was singing along with Sa-Fire and I'm not sure she wanted to turn back.

Boy, I've been told leaving you is the thing to do.

"Hey, what do you think ever happened to her and that other singer, Corina?" Selenis asked.

"Oh, man. 'Temptation' was one of my favorite songs. I don't know, I read somewhere that Corina was acting now. I don't know about Sa-Fire."

"Good for her," she said.

Selenis held a pretend microphone and started singing into it. She sang outside into the air, without a care in the world. It didn't matter to her what the drivers passing by thought of her vocal ability. Yeah, she was loud and off-key, but she was letting herself have a good time, finally.

"So where we going?" she asked.

"I don't know, I figured we'd ride up to the old *cuchifrito* stand, grab some *pastelillos* and *alcapurrias*, and then we can walk around and reminisce."

"Whoop-dee-do! That sounds like fun."

"You don't miss the kids?"

"Don't ruin my good time with your negativity. I don't want to go back home right now, okay?"

"Okay."

"It was your idea to do this anyway," she said, biting her pinkie nail.

"I said okay."

She was right. I was only a few hours away from home, but I was finding it hard to let go of the responsible mom in me.

I drove up to the Grand Concourse and hung a left at Mingo's Bodega.

"It looks a little the same, doesn't it?"

"There's a lot more Dominican flags out here now."

"Isn't that the place we used to cop weed at with Trisco and Kique?" Selenis said as she pointed to a church.

"Oh, my goodness, it's a Pentecostal church now. Wow."

I glanced at the new brick church where the old dilapidated tenement building once stood. It was strange to see a cross hovering above the same place where I smoked my first joint.

"You think they sell it inside now?" Selenis said.

We both laughed and then made the sign of the cross.

"You think Ruben still lives in the same place?" I asked.

"I would be surprised, 'cause as gorgeous as that guy was, he had a big future ahead of him. I picture him living in some luxury condo with a *Playboy* playmate."

Selenis gave me a look. I guess saying the word *Playboy* was a reminder of why she was escaping.

"He used to live on a Hundred and Sixty-third Street. Let's just go see," Selenis said.

"There's Yankee Stadium!" I said, feeling proud to be a New Yorker, although I had never actually been to a baseball game there.

When I drove up to 163rd Street there was a block party going on and it wasn't the kind of block party I'd ever seen on Staten Island. There were at least a hundred people and half of them were dancing. The other half congregated around the DJ or in small groups, some nodding to the music, others heavy in conversation. A police barricade blocked the incoming traffic, so I parked on Concourse Village West, a block away. Selenis and I got out of the car and walked through the nondancing crowd that had formed a circle around the DJ. As we walked farther up the block, we dodged kids on skates, a group of young boys rapping along to the song that was playing, and we almost got run over by an old man pushing his ice-cream cart through the crowd. The music was blasting from humongous speakers. The young DJ, wearing a Dominican flag baseball cap, was getting ready to spin his next song. A few old women had their heads stuck out of their apartment windows to watch the party, and some people were sitting on fire escapes trying to catch the action from above. I thought, Now, this is a block party.

I noticed Selenis looking at her cell phone. She showed me the text message from Ralphie. It read: WHEN ARE YOU GETTING HOME?

She didn't text back and put her cell phone back in her purse. I watched Selenis and wondered if she was fighting any guilty feelings. If she was, she was hiding them well. I guess it was the Gemini in her.

As we approached Ruben's building, we could hear a guy across the street trying to get our attention. "*Yo, mami, mami, pssss. Mira, gordita,*" a pockmark-faced, bandanna-wearing older dude yelled out.

Selenis pulled her shirt down to cover her stomach and her behind.

"*Vete pa'l carajo.* Go to hell!" Selenis yelled.

"Only if you come with me," he replied. It's amazing how guys can insult and compliment a woman in the same breath.

Selenis and I walked up the stairs to the front door of Ruben's building. We glanced at the names and apartment numbers next to each bell.

"He still lives here!" Selenis said.

But before she could ring the bell, a group of teenagers left the building. We decided not to ring the bell and snuck into the lobby without announcing ourselves. What the hell, we thought we'd surprise him instead.

I was excited to see if Ruben still had that Benjamin Bratt look.

Out of all the guys we'd met at Club 90, Selenis and I voted him the prettiest guy of all; Ruben never had to go after women, they came to him. His women were the cream of the crop. He even dated one of the models in that liquor ad that hung on the storefront window at Mingo's Bodega. He liked his girls tall, super-beautiful in the face, and small in the waist.

When Selenis and I stepped into the elevator, I could smell sizzling *sofrito* in the air. It reminded me of the times I used to visit my cousins in the projects back when I was a kid making the family rounds on Christmas Eve. I could hear Marc Anthony's old ballads playing in one of the apartments. It clashed with the Ludacris track that was playing outside. There was something about coming to the Bronx that always reminded me of my own childhood back on the Lower East Side, before my parents trekked to the suburbs. It made me realize how far my family had journeyed from their origins. I wondered if I would have been the same person had I grown up in the city instead of the suburbs.

"You think he's married?"

"Ruben, married? I doubt that," I said, stepping up to apartment number 405.

When I got to the door, I didn't knock right away because I was distracted by all of the bumper stickers on his door. There were at least ten stickers on the top portion of the door and a scattered ten or so on the bottom with quotes and sayings about the army and war. MAKE LOVE NOT WAR, BUSH SUCKS DICK, THE APOCALYPSE IS NOW.

"I guess he was in the army," Selenis said.

"You think?"

I hesitantly knocked on the door.

We could hear footsteps inside approaching the peephole. Someone was staring at us. We were waiting. No one answered.

After a few seconds, I looked at Selenis and she looked at me. Selenis knocked on the door this time, a little harder than I had.

Finally the door opened, and it wasn't Ruben on the other side.

It was an older woman wearing an old housecoat, like the ones my *abuela* would buy from Woolworth's. Could she be Ruben's mother?

"*Sí?*" she asked.

"Does Ruben Diaz still live here?" Selenis asked.

"*Sí.*" She held on to the door. Not letting us in.

"Is he home?" I asked.

She still held on to the door and gave us a blank stare.

"*Nosotras somos amigas,*" Selenis told her.

As soon as Selenis told the old woman that we were friends she let us in. I think it was the Spanish that did it.

When I walked into the apartment, a strong odor hit me hard. It must have hit Selenis too, because she turned to look at me. It smelled like a combination of roach spray and cooked cabbage.

"*¿Tú eres la mamá de Ruben?*" Selenis asked.

The old woman said that she wasn't his mother. She was Ruben's aunt. This was the point of introduction where you would usually tell the person how nice her home was, but we couldn't find one nice thing about it, so we just followed quietly behind her. Besides, I was trying to hold my breath so I wouldn't inhale the stench. I couldn't imagine why Ruben would live in this mess. The apartment was a total wreck and from what I remember, he used to be a neat freak. The place looked completely different than it did back when I hung out with Ruben. It was the same old red corduroy sofa, but it was ripped and faded near the armrests and none of the chairs in the room matched it. The room was cluttered with unopened boxes labeled by content, like someone was moving out. There were no blinds or shades on the window, and the living room was so bright that Selenis and I could actually see ourselves walking through the beam of dust particles in the air. We passed a small hallway and noticed a black cat staring at us from the bathroom.

The old woman knocked on the back bedroom door.

"Yeah?" I heard a familiar voice answer.

Selenis walked in front of me and into Ruben's room. Ruben was sitting in a chair facing the window.

"*Ruben, tienes visita.*"

Ruben turned around in his swivel desk chair to see his visitors, and I tried hard not to let my jaw drop. What a shock to see how much he had changed. He looked much older than he actually was. In fact, he looked ten years older than I did. His beautiful curly hair was completely gone from his head. He was heavy. Not fat, just less muscular than he used to be. His face brightened up as soon as he saw us and I could see a missing tooth in his smile. Had I not been so shocked to see the massive transformation, I would have run to him. But seeing the new Ruben stopped me in my tracks.

"What the hell? Look at this. It's Laverne and Shirley. Whatchu doing here?" he said as he got up from his chair and gave Selenis and me big bear hugs.

"We were in the neighborhood and we thought we'd stop by."

As he pulled away from me to hug Selenis, I could smell his body odor. It was strong and musty; I wondered when the last time was that he had taken a shower.

"Looking for herb, huh?"

Selenis and I laughed.

"No, not really. We're not the cheeba-heads we used to be. We just took a ride and figured we'd come by to see if you still lived here," I said.

He turned to Selenis. "You put on a little weight, didn't you?"

"Uh, excuse you, you don't look like a Bally's member, *maricón.*"

We all laughed.

"So what are you up to, Ruben?" I asked, glancing around the room at pictures of seminaked Asian women adorning his walls.

"Trying to live, girl, just trying to live."

"You were in the army?" Selenis asked.

"For a minute; I got shot in the thigh three times, almost died and shit, and they sent me home."

"Oh, sorry, Ruben," I said, realizing that that was probably the reason he was sitting back down.

I could see his hands trembling as he got up again from his chair and limped over to a nearby night table. He pulled out an enormous ziplock bag filled with weed and began to unwrap a Phillies blunt.

"You can't get no better than this shit," he said, removing a few pinches of weed and laying it on the desk in front of him.

Fifteen years ago, the presence of an illegal drug never would have fazed me, but the mom in me was freaking out, especially since I kept hearing police sirens in the background. I wasn't sure how Selenis felt, but for a second I felt unsure about being in that room. It wasn't like Ruben was the same guy I knew. The pretty boy with the bright future had disappeared, and a darker, less fortunate man with obvious problems was now sitting in front of me. I didn't know what to expect.

I watched him as he placed the weed in the blunt.

"Listen, we just wanted to see how you were doing. We don't want to bother you or anything," I said, trying to find a way to leave.

"You leaving?"

"Yeah, you leaving?" Selenis echoed, like she had a way of getting home herself.

"You can't go. I haven't seen you two in a long time. Listen, I smoke 'cause I don't like painkillers, okay? If the weed bothers you, I'll put it away."

"Ruben, do you. Don't worry about us, just do you," Selenis said as she walked up to his dresser and looked at a photograph of him. "Oh, how funny, I remember when you took this picture at the club. Remember when we used to profile on Forty-second Street in the city?"

"Yeah, it was me, you two, and I forgot those other brothers' names," Ruben said.

"Kique and Trisco," Selenis and I said in sync.

"Yeah, you married them?"

"No, we didn't," I said.

"Remember that Japanese girl that used to dance on the speakers at the old Club 90?"

"Yeah, the one that was going to college to be a dentist?" I said.

"Yeah, I had two kids with her. Those little guys right there," he said, using his nose to point at a large picture on the dresser.

Selenis picked up the picture.

"They're beautiful, Ruben," Selenis said, handing me the picture.

"They look like you," I said, checking out the two little boys that slightly resembled Tiger Woods.

"Thank you," he said with extreme pride in his eyes.

Something told me he hadn't seen them in a while.

"Don't you miss Club 90?" I asked.

"I heard they reopened that joint. They got this thing they call Reunion Thursdays."

"And the old crew goes there?" I said, getting excited.

"I don't know. Haven't been down there or out much lately. You know?"

I suddenly thought of the possibility of seeing Trisco.

"You got kids?" Ruben asked us.

"Yeah, I have one—" I answered.

"And I have too many," Selenis said, finishing the sentence.

"Kids are beautiful, man. They change your life."

"Yeah," Selenis and I said at the same time.

At that moment, I thought of Junito and wondered if I should give a quick call to my mother to check up on him. I couldn't call her then, though. She'd ask me a million and one questions and make me feel like I was up to no good again.

Ruben finally lit up, took a huge toke of the blunt, and passed it to me first. Even though I didn't want to take it, I did. It felt big in my hand compared to the little joints I used to smoke. It brought me back to the old me, the me that I'd been trying to become again. What surprised me was that I was so busy trying to relive my past, it never occurred to me that there were some things I didn't want to revisit. Like the getting-high, making-out-with-strangers, and having-sex-with-more-than-one-guy-at-a-time me.

I looked at Selenis, who was anxiously waiting for me to pass the blunt to her, so I did.

"You go first," I said.

"Go ahead, girl, don't be shy," Ruben said.

"Let her go first, that's okay."

Selenis inhaled, and to my surprise she held the smoke in the back of her throat like a pro, swallowed, and let some flow out through her nostrils.

"Damn, girl, you must give good head too," Ruben said.

Selenis laughed, trying to keep her mouth closed so that the smoke wouldn't escape too soon.

I could tell by the way Selenis was staring at the blunt in her hand that she thought it would take her to a place much better than where she was at the moment. I looked over at Ruben, and I felt he was stuck somewhere in his past too.

Selenis passed it to me.

I looked at the blunt again and dared myself to go all the way, regardless of the proceed-with-caution sign flashing in my head.

"What happened to the little joints we used to smoke back in the day?" I asked Ruben.

"Nah, that shit is wack now."

"I don't know. I have to drive back home."

"*Chica, mira,* that stuff will wear off in a couple of hours. Didn't you say that this is what you wanted to do?" Selenis said.

I gave her a look as if to say, "Have you lost your mind?"

"Idalis, didn't we come out to have 'me' time?"

You know what? She was right. This was about me. Was Manny worrying about the way he was acting and the decisions he was making? Not one bit! Why shouldn't I be able to have one worry-free moment in my life without having to think about how I wasn't acting my age? I needed to do me, damn it! Even if it meant I looked stupid doing it. I wrapped my lips around the large cigar, inhaled, and as the heavy smoke hit the back of my throat it hurt so bad, I choked and started coughing it up. After I passed the blunt to Selenis, I heard a police siren in the background, but this time I didn't panic.

"*Cójalo con calma*, take it easy," Ruben said, laughing.

I tried to laugh, but I was still coughing.

"You girls must be pissed at your husbands or something. 'Cause after fifteen years, why would you come visit me?"

"Uh, yeah, we did escape, and yeah, we hate them," Selenis said.

"I hear you. I got divorced, lost my job, and shit. But I'm gonna get my kids back."

"Wow, that was heavy," I said, trying to catch my breath.

"You blew it all out, stupid," Selenis said.

"Shut up," I said, passing the blunt to Ruben.

When Ruben brought the blunt to his lips and inhaled, I could see that he liked getting high. That's why it wouldn't have surprised me to know he lived his life stoned all the time.

"Love is a fucked-up thing sometimes," Ruben said.

"That's what I say. How the fuck do you get up and decide that you want to separate after ten years of marriage?" I said.

"Damn, ten years?" Ruben said on the inhale.

"No, I got one better—how the fuck do you go on the Internet and jack off to some picture of a *pendeja* that's not even real?"

Ruben looked at Selenis for a second with a serious look and then busted into uncontrollable laughter. He laughed so hard that I started to laugh too.

"You serious? You think a picture is a threat to your marriage? Nah, girl. That shit is about you and how you feel about yourself."

"Whatever," Selenis said, rolling her eyes again.

I could feel myself letting go, drifting in and out of the room, trying hard to hold on.

"Ruben, what is this shit?" I asked.

"They don't make cheeba no more, girl, this shit is hydro now. That shit you used to smoke back in the day was wack compared to this."

"And what do you mean about me? I'm not insecure," Selenis said, continuing her own conversation with Ruben.

"So then why would a naked picture of a girl bother you? It shouldn't. We don't fall in love with pictures. We fall in love with real women."

"But why do you have to look at those pictures if you have something real at home?"

"'Cause it's obvious, the shit is fun to do."

I could see that the more Ruben smoked, the more normal he became. I could see glimpses of the confident and suave Ruben that I knew back in the day.

"Let me tell you a secret about men. Here it is: We want our women to adore us, to love the shit out of us. Feed us good, suck our dicks till we go blind, and we won't go nowhere. You suck his dick till he goes blind?"

Selenis took another hit of the blunt and rolled her eyes.

"See, that's why he's jacking off to some picture. You women don't get it. You just got to give us enough love so we don't go nowhere else."

Selenis laughed. I knew the weed was getting to her too because she couldn't stop laughing. When Ruben passed the blunt around a third time, I turned it down. But Selenis didn't.

"Selenis, that shit is strong, take it easy," I told her.

"Hey, Idalis, you know I had a crush on you, right?" Ruben said.

"Really?" I answered, trying hard to remember the fly Ruben I knew so that I could feel good about his comment.

"Yeah, but you were always into that dude."

"Trisco?" I answered.

"Yeah. You were on him. I really thought you two would get married. What happened?"

"I don't know. I guess I met my husband."

The memory of the day I met Manny made my heart flutter, but the fluttering stopped when I saw Selenis fall on the floor.

"Selenis? Selenis?"

"You girls can't handle your weed, damn," Ruben said.

"What?" Selenis asked, trying to lie back down.

"You okay?" I said, lifting her head up.

"I'm tired, Idalis. Can I take a nap?"

"Selenis, no," I said, slapping her in the face to wake her up.

She found the strength to slap me back and said, "Can you wake me up when we get there?" before nodding off again.

I could see that Ruben had moved his chair closer to the window, away from us. He was staring out at the tenement building across the way. Right about now, I wished I didn't feel so high.

"It's nice to see you girls," he said, still staring out.

"It's nice to see you too, Ruben," I said, trying to hold up Selenis's head.

Ruben's aunt knocked on the door and offered to have us stay and eat, but it was getting late, so we passed. Besides, I had to get rid of the high I was on and get back before my mother called me. I knew that I could never act my way out of a serious high.

"Ruben, I think I better take her home."

He kept staring out of the window and I realized how fragile life could be. In just fifteen years, the person I knew to have so much ahead of him was dying, and not from a terminal disease.

"Yeah, yeah, I understand."

I slapped Selenis on the face so hard, her eyes opened and stayed open. "That hurt," she said.

"I know, stupid, we have to go."

"I can't walk."

"No, you have to walk."

Ruben got up from his chair and passed me a postcard. I stuffed it in my bag without looking at it; I was too busy trying to help Selenis. Ruben and I stared into each other's eyes and I gave him a big hug, knowing that this would probably be the last time I'd ever see him.

"You take care of yourself too," he said, with sad eyes.

Selenis and I walked down the hallway and to the elevator. We heard Ruben close the door behind us. I pushed the elevator button and waited for it to reach our floor. Selenis was rubbing her temples and I was trying to focus on the numbers above the door.

"I have a massive headache and I need three Reese's Peanut Butter Cups," Selenis said.

"That weed was ridiculous," I said, pulling out the postcard that Ruben had handed me. It was the Club 90 invite.

"Let's go there," Selenis said.

"Check you out. Ralphie's not gonna let you out again."

"Excuse me, but he didn't give me permission tonight. Besides, I don't give a shit what Ralphie thinks."

The elevator arrived and we both stepped in. Even though we were higher than we had been in a long time, we felt in control. We made a selfish choice to enjoy ourselves and it actually felt good.

"He's the same, isn't he?" Selenis said, talking about Ruben.

"Yeah, I guess."

"Chubby and bald but the same."

When the elevator doors closed in front of us, Selenis and I looked at each other and we laughed. Running away from home was the best thing we could have done. It had only been a few hours, but we remembered what it was like to be free. And we knew we needed to escape again soon.

21 The next morning the industrial drums in the water looked like white lily pads and the Bayonne Bridge looked like the Golden Gate. I opened my closet door and I swear I saw a beam of sunshine piercing through the clothes. I removed a giant trash bag from the back of the closet, the save-it-till-I-can-get-back-into-it bag, and browsed through it. There it was. The black bolero jacket with the big red heart on the back and white graffiti lines scribbled all around it. I put the jacket on. I looked in the mirror. Today was going to be a good day.

While I was setting up the ironing board to fix the wrinkles in the back of the jacket, Junito dragged his feet into the living room.

"Hey, what's wrong, *pa*?" I said, straightening out the jacket on the board and gently smoothing the wrinkles out.

"School's almost over," he said, plopping down on the sofa.

"And then you become a second-grader. That's so exciting."

"No, it's not. I like my friends in the first grade."

"You'll see them again."

"And I won't see Mrs. Jackson either."

"It's okay, *pa*, that's what happens in school. You say good-bye to some people, but then you say hello to new people. It can be a lot of fun."

"I don't want to say good-bye. I want them to stay my friends for a long time."

I sensed the seriousness of his sadness and I rested the iron upright on the board. I sat next to him. Sometimes I forgot that however small Junito's problems seemed in my world, for him those same little problems were the ones that would inevitably screw him up in his thirties.

"I know that saying good-bye to some of your friends makes you sad. It makes me sad when I have to say good-bye to people I like, but then God gives me more people to like."

"I don't want them to go away. Everybody goes away all the time. Like Daddy. He went away and now he's not coming back."

I sat quiet for a second, thinking about my answer. This was big for him. This wasn't about going into the second grade. This was about being afraid of change. My poor child took after his father in so many ways.

I sat there thinking about how my own mother used to help me get through my difficult kid moments. She never sat and talked to me. She never patted me on the back and told me that everything would work out fine. No, she would whip out the all-powerful golden *chancleta* to help me with my problems. She believed a good swift smack would snap me right out of my misery.

Good thing I was here and she wasn't. She'd probably hit him on the backside and tell him to stop being such a *sángano*. She was so not evolved. That old-school parenting of the I'm-the-boss-you-do-what-I-say method didn't make sense to me. I couldn't hit my son over the head with a slipper for inconveniencing my life. I brought him into this world and I was responsible for his personal and emotional growth. Unlike my mother, I didn't blame someone or something else for what he said or did. It was up to me to inspire and empower my son because at six years old what could he possibly know about solving problems? I didn't expect from him what my mother expected of me. "Ay, *Idalis, tú eres muy exagerada.*" Exaggerated? I remember when I accidentally broke the two front wheels off my Barbie's camper and she got so angry that I was crying about it, she snapped the remaining back wheels off and told me to make it a house instead. I didn't want a house! I wanted a camper that would travel across the country, so that Barbie and Ken could take make-believe exotic family vacations to San Juan like we never did. But no, because of my mother's inability to handle any of my little stresses, Barbie and Ken were stuck living in a trailer park for the rest of their lives. I would never be that insensitive toward Junito. I would always listen to what he had to say and be there for him, no matter how long it took him to get over it.

"Junito, *pa*, I know exactly how you feel. *Mami* hates saying good-bye to things too, but sometimes God closes one door and—"

"It's your fault that Daddy left!" Junito blurted out like a rich white child gone mad on *Diff'rent Strokes*.

I realized that he was hurting, so I tried to stay calm and tried to remember the section on parental love in the book *The Road Less Traveled* as I followed him to his room.

"Junito, don't yell at *Mami*, okay? I understand that you are angry."

"I hate you!"

"What?"

"You're so bossy!"

"Junito, calm down, *pa*."

"You're stupid."

"What did you just call me?"

He didn't repeat it.

I was trying to keep my emotions in check because I knew that I needed to be the bigger person here. I inhaled and slowly exhaled and as I reached out to hold him in my arms, I heard Junito say something in the smallest voice that he could muster up: "You're an asshole."

I stood there with my head tilted to one side, like a dog trying to understand what his master has just said.

"Did you say I'm an asshole?"

Junito didn't move. I didn't move. Okay, the lily pads had now turned back to industrial drums. I was pissed. I could hear my mother and grandmother telling me, "I told you so." I could feel my mother pushing me to go into the closet and pull out the belt, but I fought the urge and the voices as much as I could. I knew that when my mother kicked my ass, it did nothing but shoot my self-esteem down, only to leave me trying to build it back up for the rest of my life—alone, because I couldn't afford therapy. But how should I handle this? Manny's voice always straightened Junito up. Maybe I needed to call Manny. No, because then Manny would think I needed him. I didn't. I had to think on my feet and fix this problem now. I couldn't let Junito think that he could walk all over me.

"You're in big trouble," I told him.

"Whatever," he said.

My blood was rising, and my veins were thumping hard. I was ready to give in to the old-school method of tough love. But I couldn't.

"If you don't say you're sorry right now, I'm going to start getting rid of your favorite toys," I said, firmly placing my hands on my hips.

"So?" Junito answered.

"So?"

I didn't know what to do. My plan was backfiring. I looked around the living room for clues. Wait. Television. Take the television away. Entertainment, yes, that too. I walked into his room and he followed me. I scanned the room for ways to punish him. Maybe I should pull a *Supernanny* on him and take all his toys, throw them in a garbage bag, and hide them. But that was too much work and I was not in the mood to clean his entire room of toys. And suddenly, there it was. Like a sign from God, there was the one thing that I knew would straighten Junito right up. That little black box of evil was staring back at me. I got you now, sucker!

I walked toward Junito's TV and I yanked the PlayStation out from the wall. I brought it into the living room with me and thought, Oh, this feels good.

"You want to call me bad names? Okay, here! See this? This is why Daddy isn't here. This evil thing is why we are not together. Not me! This is the real mistress, the evil that has destroyed this entire family. So you know what, here it goes. Say good-bye to the devil right now!"

"I'm sorry, *Mami!*"

I held the PlayStation in the air, above my head.

"I won't do it again, *Mami*."

"That's what you say all the time, Junito. That's it, no more chances!"

Like a Teenage Mutant Ninja Turtle, I used one hand to remove the garbage can cover and with the other hand I shoved the black box down into the garbage can so far, I could smell the two-day-old rice and beans sitting on the bottom.

"*Mami!*"

"I'm sorry, did you say something?" I said. I could feel the sinister laugh coming up like a burp, but decided not to use it and held it in.

Junito stood there looking at me. He started to cry and ran back into his room.

I listened to his little feet run away and I stood in front of the garbage feeling as though I had finally conquered the demon. I should've done this a long time ago. I could hear Junito's soft sobs from the other room and the strange thing was, it didn't affect me one bit. What I had just done was for our own happiness. A two-hundred-dollar piece of equipment was now covered in leftovers and was about to lie dead in a dump somewhere in Brooklyn later this week. I thought every mother and wife in America should experience the pleasure of destroying the real reason families couldn't eat or be together at the same time anymore. We wouldn't have to hear those three irritating words our kids and our husbands said every time we called them to the dinner table. We would never have to hear them say "After this level" ever again.

22 The next morning I walked into my cubicle to find a pile of work on my desk and a sticky note stuck to my computer screen that read: "Need to see you regarding new campaign." I ripped off the sticky note and walked into Samantha's office.

"Idalis, good morning. Sit down," Samantha said, grinning from ear to ear.

The bitch was chipper this morning; I wondered what she wanted from me.

"I have really amazing news. We just acquired the Linda Maria doll account."

"Who is Linda Maria?"

"Who is Linda Maria? Well, it's the first Latina doll ever to be mass-marketed. Created by Edgardo Levy, the vice president of the Levy Toy Company. Edgardo is Latino." Samantha smiled and waited.

I didn't know what she was waiting for, so I said, "Really?"

"Yes, isn't that exciting for you?"

Did she expect me to react like E.T. did when he recognized Yoda on Halloween?

"Where is he from?" I asked, as though I cared.

"I don't know, actually, but that doesn't matter, because he is very excited to know that we have Latino talent on our staff."

"We do?" I said, surprised and excited that maybe my little activist message the other day inspired new hirings.

"Of course we do, Idalis."

Hmmm, I could swear that when I did a head count of all individuals in the creative department who I thought had ancestors in South America, Central America, Cuba, the Dominican

Republic, and Puerto Rico, I only came up with one: me. And Geraldo Manuel, the janitor.

"I thought that this would be the perfect opportunity for you to lend us your expertise. Would you like to work as a junior creative executive on this campaign?"

"You're offering *me* a promotion?"

"Well, in a way, yes. I am offering you a chance to baby-step into management."

There had to be a catch here.

"I don't know what to say."

"Well, it's pretty obvious. It's either yes, I will accept, or no, I will not accept, but I can't imagine that you would say no to the chance of working closely with our client."

Management had never let their secretaries get too close to their clients. This couldn't be real, but hell, I decided to take it before she realized her mistake.

"Well, okay, yes, of course I will accept."

"Great. Now, as I stated before, this is an opportunity to possibly become management," Samantha said, putting emphasis on the words *opportunity* and *possibly*.

I was so excited and shocked that I didn't care to know anything more about it. Who cared? I was on my way to becoming an executive.

"Idalis, I think working on this project could make you into the person you've always dreamed of being."

I could feel butterflies in my stomach as I imagined the possibilities of sitting in my very own corner office. My mother would die.

"Samantha, thank you so much. When do I start?" I said, shaking her hand.

"We are actually going to move you out of the secretarial pool today and move you to the creative executive area."

I couldn't contain myself. How had this happened? Did it happen this easily?

"So who will be taking over my secretarial responsibilities?"

"Oh, actually, you will. For now, until we can get someone else in. Your title will change in three months, once we see how it all comes along. You know how that goes. We want to give you time to make sure this works for you as well."

"Oh."

Bubble was now bursting.

"If all works out well, this can be a life-changing moment for you."

"I see."

"We all had to start somewhere, Idalis."

She was right. I had to pay my dues. Hell, she was looking to promote me without a degree—that was pretty big. I should be thankful.

"Thank you, Samantha."

I walked out of her office and back into my cubicle, feeling as though I'd hit the lottery but I wouldn't be getting the payout until the year 2050. But hey, this would be a big test for me. It was a big day. I was on my way to becoming an executive, so I'd better start dressing like one. I guess if I worked a few more overtime hours I could get that Donna Karan suit that I wanted at Macy's.

"Oh, by the way, Idalis . . ." Samantha popped her head back into my cubicle. "Now that you're an executive, you're considered an exempt employee. Isn't that great? Now you're a true professional."

Exempt? Exempt! I was going to be working more hours and now I couldn't collect overtime? There had to be a pay raise here.

"Samantha, uh, I guess I'll get an increase, then, right?"

"Now, Idalis, let's not put the cart before the *caballo*. Employee evaluations are yearly, you know that. And you just had one a few months ago. Don't you want the promotion?"

"Of course I do."

"Then be a little patient for now; things will materialize the way you want them to. As long as you concentrate your efforts on making Edgardo Levy a happy client, everything will work out."

I guess she was right. The nerve of me, to ask for more money when I didn't even have a degree. I should have been on my knees.

"Thank you again, Samantha."

"You're very welcome. And Edgardo will be happy too."

When Samantha left my cubicle, I put my head down on the desk and I cried. I guess they were happy tears. Who the hell knew?

23

"So let me get this straight: you work the same hours but get paid less," Selenis said as she used the tines of her fork to seal the edges of the uncooked empanada.

"But I'm an executive now," I said, trying to believe that myself.

"Then that should be good, right?"

"I guess."

"I don't know, Idalis, I always thought that when you got a promotion you get more money too."

I could hear Ralphie walking in the front door. I heard him say hello to Junito and Carlito before walking into the kitchen.

"Hey, Idalis."

"Hey, Ralphie."

Ralphie gave Selenis a light kiss on the cheek. I could tell that Selenis wanted it on her lips.

"Listen, I'm going to be in the office, I need to do some work. I'm locking the door. Don't let the kids upstairs," he said, leaving the kitchen.

I couldn't help but wonder if he was going to do work, or the other thing.

Selenis dropped the fork onto the countertop, purposely calling attention to herself.

"Since when do you have to lock the door to do work? Just tell the kids not to come in," she said, talking to him but looking at me.

Ralphie walked back in, "Did you say something?"

"You're getting ridiculous," Selenis told him.

"What?"

Oh, lord, I thought, here it goes and I'm in the middle of it now.

"What's ridiculous?" Ralphie asked.

"It's just weird to me that you need to lock the door to do work. We won't go in. We never just walk in," Selenis said, placing the empanada into the frying pan.

"All I want to do is lock the door. I'm not asking to stay out until almost midnight like you did the other night. Coming into the house at all hours smelling like weed."

"Idalis, was I smoking weed?"

"No," I answered quickly, feeling the rush of blood coming to my face as I attempted to lie. "Listen, I'm gonna go in the living room with the kids."

"No, Idalis, stay," Selenis said. Then she turned to Ralphie. "First of all, I never get out of this house. I should be allowed out from time to time."

"Well, that's your choice, you could've gotten a job like Idalis did, but you wanted to stay home with the kids."

"I had no choice, Ralphie, you don't make enough for me to send three kids to day care."

"Well, that's because your mother couldn't handle them all."

"My mother is old."

"Whatever, I got work to do. I don't have time for this."

Ralphie walked out of the kitchen again and went upstairs into the office.

Selenis and I stayed quiet for a second and I could hear her sniffling.

"I hate him," Selenis said.

"No, you don't."

"He's addicted to that shit now, Idalis."

"It's just a computer."

"No, it's sex. How do I compete with a computer?"

"I don't know, *chica*. Just don't compete."

Selenis placed the last empanada into the frying pan. I could see her looking at her reflection in the glass of the microwave. She was fixing her hair. I could tell that she needed to feel attractive again.

24

"*Mami*, what's inside farina?" I asked, browsing the shelves in the international aisle of the Super Food Supermarket.

"Ay, Idalis, cornmeal, *qué estúpida tú eres.*"

"I didn't know, Ma. Geez. That can't be very healthy?"

"You used to ask me to make you that before you went to school in the morning."

"Well, what do I know? I have to trust that you're feeding me the right foods."

"I took good care of you, okay?"

"I don't know, sometimes I think about the stuff you used to feed me, like an egg yolk and sugar in malta. What was that supposed to do for me?"

"Nothing. It tasted good, *verdad?*"

"Whatever," I said, throwing the bag of cornmeal into the cart.

I browsed the aisle checking out the variety of Latino goods on the shelves. Maybe if she had fed me healthier foods as a kid I'd have a better body today.

"Ma, why don't you ever make black beans?"

"*Porque no soy cubana.*"

"Uh, you don't have to be Cuban to eat black beans."

"Is black your favorite color, Idalis? I noticed that you like that color."

"What's that supposed to mean?"

She didn't answer.

"Oh, and what about the *galletas de manteca?*" I said, trying to make a point of how careless she was with my diet.

"And what about them, Idalis?" my mother said, pushing the cart past me.

"You used to give me these crackers with mayonnaise on them. These are butter crackers, Ma! You put mayonnaise on butter crackers, and fed this to me as breakfast? If I have clogged arteries, it's your fault."

"*Mira*, Idalis, *cállate* and go get me four mangoes. Make sure they're not too ripe."

As I walked through the aisles toward the fruit and vegetable section, I kept browsing the shelves, looking at the Italian-American selections. There was so much more for them than there was in the "international" aisle. I guess because there were more Italians than there were Latinos on the island. It's funny how my mother didn't allow the lack of choices to stop her from cooking her own traditional foods—even if it meant that she had to merge the two cultures. She used to make her own version of what she called "espaguetti." I think we were the only family on Staten Island using *sofrito*, a Caribbean-Latino concoction meant for beans and stews, in our spaghetti sauce.

When I got to the fruit and vegetable section, I picked up a mango and inspected it. The label said it was a product of Puerto Rico. How ironic. I could get these for free in *Abuela*'s backyard, but here I had to pay over a dollar for just one and they weren't even that good. I inspected it with my thumb, pressing in lightly, but the mango was too soft. As I picked up another one, I could feel someone standing next to me.

"Hi, that's actually my second-favorite Caribbean import."

It was Cameron and he seemed to be in a playful mood.

"Technically, my mother's the import, not me," I answered back playfully.

"Nice to see you again," he said with those beautiful full lips.

"How are you?" I picked up another mango, trying hard not to let his overwhelming sexy aura make me nervous. I dropped the mango on his foot.

I guess he wanted to talk through the pain.

"I'm good. Busy with work but good. I was thinking about you the other day."

When I bent down to pick up the mango, I noticed that he had sandals on a cute pair of feet.

"I'm sorry. Did that hurt?" I said, straightening back up.

"Don't worry, I have another set."

We laughed a little.

He was standing so close to me that his arms rubbed up against the side of my breast for a second. I felt a slight shiver throughout my body.

"So you were thinking about me?" I asked.

"Yes."

"Really?"

"Don't you believe me?"

"Idalis! Idalis!" I heard my mother's moose calls and knew that this beautiful moment was going to turn into something a little less fun.

"I'm here, Ma," I said, waving her my way.

"Oh, I get to meet your mother? I'd say this is my lucky day."

It was funny to see Cameron excited about meeting my mother. Especially since meeting her could ruin anything we had—he had no idea what he was in for.

I stood there waiting for her to find me. I waved my hand again and when she finally saw me, she immediately gave me one of her annoyed looks. She combed her fingers through her hair and approached Cameron and me.

"*Mami*, this is my friend Cameron. Cameron, this is my mother, Mrs. Bonilla."

"It's very nice to meet you, Mrs. Bonilla." Cameron shook her hand.

"Thank you," my mother answered in her pretending-to-be-nice voice.

Instead of trying to make conversation, my mother stood in front of us with her cart, looking at the coupons in her hand. It was so awkward that I felt I had to interrupt the moment.

"Ma, is this mango okay?" I said, trying to save her from look-ing completely rude.

My mother snatched the mango from my hand. Then in her very happy American voice she said, "Oh, very good, this one is very good. Okay, Idalis, let's go." She handed me back the mango.

She turned the cart around to start walking toward the check-out counter, but Cameron tried hard to impress her.

"Mrs. Bonilla, if you like mangoes, you should go to La Mar-keta. It's a new place in Stapleton. They have a great selection of fruits and vegetables from the Caribbean."

"Oh, *sí*, thank you, Camarones, but this supermarket is good for me."

Oh, Lord, she just called Cameron the word for *shrimp* in Span-ish. I wasn't correcting her; let her figure it out. Why didn't she think before she spoke? For God's sake, didn't she even wonder why someone would name their kid after a fish? When I looked at Cameron, he was trying hard not to laugh.

"*¿Idalis, me voy?*" my mother said.

"Yes, Ma, go. I'll be there in a second."

"*Adiós*, Mrs. Bonilla," Cameron said.

"*Sí. Adiós*, Camarones."

My mother pushed the cart away from us and toward the cashier section.

"Your mom is a hard sell, huh?"

"She's just weird when she meets new people."

"I know the deal. I've been down this road before."

He smiled confidently. The fact that he understood how igno-rant some people could be, even my own mother, didn't faze him. I liked that about him.

"It was nice seeing you again," I said.

He didn't answer me right away and I knew he had something more to say.

"Listen, I'm sorry that I cut our walk short the last time. It's just that I didn't want to be the transitional guy, you know? I know what it feels like to be in relationship limbo with someone who isn't ready to move on and I don't want to be caught in the middle of that again. Especially when it's someone that makes me feel the way you do. Anyway, if I could get another chance, I'd like to take you to dinner. That is, if you're still available tonight."

I held the lone mango in my hand, wondering how much time I had to answer him. I knew that if I went out with Cameron on a "real" date, I would know for sure if my love for Manny was a thing of the past. The thought of that scared me.

"If you're busy, I understand," he said.

I looked into his eyes. The man was beautiful. Seriously gorgeous on the inside and out, and I had no idea why he didn't give up on me. We stared at each other long enough to feel the electricity between us again. We both knew that there was something going on that we couldn't control.

"Okay," I said, feeling my heart being pulled in different directions. Something in my gut was telling me that after tonight my life could change. What if I fell in love with Cameron? Could you fall in love with someone new if you were in love with someone else? I didn't know, but I guess I was about to find out.

"Is six o'clock good? I can pick you up at your place, if you'd like."

"Actually, I could meet you at the restaurant, because I have to drop my son off at my mother's."

"Let's meet at L'Astrance in Great Kills at seven."

He raised his hand, brought it close to my face, and removed something from my right temple.

"You just had a little something on your forehead."

"Thank you."

I could feel that neither of us wanted to leave.

"I guess I'll see you later," I said.

He kissed me on the cheek.

"Later," he said, smiling.

This man always made me feel beautiful.

I quickly bought the mango and headed for the car. When I got there, my mother was leaning over the shopping cart waiting for me to open the trunk.

"What's wrong, Ma?" I asked while I opened the trunk of my car and placed the grocery bags inside.

"*Nada*," she said.

She was lying.

"Why so quiet, then?" I asked.

My mother didn't answer and got into the passenger seat. As I placed the last bag into the trunk and returned the cart to the cart bay, I dreaded the ride home. I didn't understand what my mother's problem was with anyone darker than us. She had no right to be racist; her own mother was dark-skinned.

"*Mami*, why are you so quiet?" I said, putting on my seat belt.

"*Nada*, Idalis, *nada, coño.*"

"Okay, now I know there's something wrong."

She gave me a look that said, "Start the damn car and let's go home already." I started the car and began driving out of the parking lot.

"You know what, Ma, this is really stupid. When are you going to get over this whole black thing?"

"*Ay*, Idalis, be quiet, *por favor*," she said, looking out the window.

I stopped the car.

"*Mami*, I don't know what version of Christopher Columbus's trip to the New World you learned in school, but obviously it was the one without the slaves. If you didn't know, the Spanish, that you so want to be like, brought African slaves in to do the work that the natives used to do, so whether you like it or not, we've got some black blood in us too. You act like Queen Isabella is your second cousin."

She didn't say anything to me. She just kept staring out of the passenger-side window. As I looked her way, I could see Cameron riding by in his BMW. He didn't see us.

"I don't understand why you, *Papi*, and *Abuela*, of all people, have a problem with black people. I really don't. It's so hypocritical."

She still didn't say anything.

"Okay, you know what? I'm going out with him; nobody is going to stop me. I don't care that Manny and I aren't divorced yet, and you know what, Ma, I may even—"

Before I could finish my sentence, she turned to me, looking directly into my eyes, and without saying a word, she dared me to say it. But I didn't say it. I didn't say that I might even sleep with him and get married. What I wound up saying was, "And another thing, his name is Cameron, not Camarones."

25

I drove up to the entrance of the restaurant with butterflies in my stomach. The thought of being out on a real romantic date, while still married, was making me nauseous. The restaurant had valet parking only, but I didn't have valet parking money, so I parked the car down the street and walked a block toward the restaurant. If only Manny could see me in my sexy black wraparound dress and my Isaac high-heel sandals. He used to love this outfit. I placed another emergency call to Selenis on my way down the block.

"Is Junito playing nice with Carlito?" I asked.

"Yes, and would you stop calling? Just go out and have a good time," Selenis said. I could hear Symone in the background asking for vanilla ice cream and telling her mother to make sure that there was no chocolate or strawberry in it.

"But it's been such a long time since I've been out on a real dinner date."

"It's a date, Idalis, he's not proposing to you. And whatever you do, don't start comparing him to Manny."

"You're right. Listen, don't give Junito too much ice cream, he always gets a stomachache."

"Go have fun, Idalis, and don't worry about Junito."

After I hung up the phone with Selenis, I felt a little better. Truth was, Manny and me were almost over. I guessed I'd better get used to the idea of being out on the market again.

When I walked up to the front door of the restaurant, I noticed that it was not a typical Manny and Idalis hangout. It was French and I doubted that *plátanos* were the common side order at L'Astrance.

Cameron surprised me when he appeared at the entrance and held the door open for me.

"Thank you," I said, checking out his fierce Jay-Z-inspired suit. It was hard for a dude to pull off wearing a pink shirt, but Cameron knew exactly how to sport it with his white linen suit.

I felt my body quiver from the excitement of being next to him and my hands started trembling. Why did this man make me feel this way?

"Wow, Ms. Rivera, you look deliciously beautiful."

The funny thing was that legally I was still Rivera and suddenly the reality of being married chipped away at my fantasy for a second.

"You look really handsome," I said, realizing that I had just complimented him. Now I knew he was special, because I had never done that, for no one, not even Manny. I guess it was something I learned while watching the women in my family. I never heard *Abuela* compliment *Abuelo,* or my mother compliment my father, or *Tía* compliment Uncle Herman. When I really thought about it, I had never heard Selenis compliment Ralphie. I guess it was something I never thought I should do or had to do. There were so many times I wanted to tell Manny how much I loved his legs, his eyes, and especially his sense of humor. There were times when I felt so lucky to have him that I would cry. He never knew that, though; I would never tell him.

Cameron held my hand. It was soft. Not girly, just manly and meaty. I could feel his thumb caressing mine. He brought our clenched hands up to his mouth and kissed the back of my hand.

An attractive brunette interrupted and escorted us to a table on the outside balcony, where we could see the Verrazano Bridge in the distance. When we came to the table, Cameron pulled out my chair. I stepped in front of it and waited for him to push it in. As I sat down, I realized that Manny had never pulled out a chair for me. Well, as a joke, but not seriously.

Cameron stared across the table and into my eyes as he opened the wine list.

"I don't know, Ms. Rivera, there's just something about you. I can't stay away."

He was making me nervous.

"Are you a merlot kind of girl?"

Oh, lord, what the hell was merlot? Wasn't he a magician or a warlock or something?

"Or would you prefer a cabernet sauvignon?"

My stomach turned, because I wasn't sure if I should know these things. I knew just two types of wine: sangria and Thunderbird.

"Whatever you pick is fine with me," I said.

He smiled. "Idalis. Idalis. Idalis. You know, I love that name."

I could tell.

"Thank you."

"So, tell me more. I want to know everything there is to know about you. What do you like to do in your spare time?"

I laughed at the word *spare*. "I usually spend any spare time with you-know-who."

Damn, I sounded just like Manny.

"How is the little guy?"

"He's good. He's so funny. The other day he tried to use this big word in a sentence. What was that word again . . . ?"

As I was trying to remember, I could feel that Cameron was maybe losing a little interest or uncomfortable with the kid talk, because he straightened his fork and knife on the table.

"Oh, yeah, it was *ridiculousness*," I said, realizing that the word *ridiculousness* might not seem like a big word to someone like him. But then again, I was talking about a little boy, so he should appreciate it.

"That's cute. It reminds me of my niece. When she was three she tried to use the word *implausible* in a sentence. It was hysterical."

I wasn't even sure if I knew what *implausible* meant.

The waiter arrived and took our wine and soup order. Cameron ordered in French. I thought guys like this only existed in movies and romance novels. When the waiter left, Cameron extended his hand across the table. Maybe he needed the salt? I placed the salt in his hand. He laughed and placed the salt down on the table and extended his hand again.

"I wanted to see your hand," he said.

"Oh," I answered, offering him my sweaty palm.

He looked at the palm of my hand.

"Don't tell me you're a palm reader too."

"Well, an amateur one. I wanted to look at your life line."

Suddenly I got this vision of us, married, on our honeymoon; while I'm in the bathroom I overhear his phone conversation. The only words I can make out are about our insurance premium.

"It's long."

Well, thank God for that.

"Hmmm," he said, using his finger to trace a line on my palm.

"What?"

"Your fate line, there's a small line going through it. I've never seen that. I've read about it, but I've never actually seen one in person."

"What does that mean?"

"It means there will be or have been obstacles in your life. But it looks like once you get past them, it's smooth sailing."

The waitress broke up the moment as she placed the wine bottle and glasses on the table. Cameron stared at me while she uncorked the wine and poured a bit into a glass for him to taste. After he nodded his approval, she filled both glasses. He picked up his glass and met mine already in midair.

"To beginnings," he said, clinking my glass.

"To beginnings," I repeated, sipping the wine and feeling that even though I was enjoying the newness of getting to know Cameron, the other part of me was longing for something more familiar and comfortable, like Manny.

The waitress brought us a second menu and I couldn't make out anything on it because it was all in French. Even if it were in English, I'd have no idea what the hell kind of food I was eating.

"I've had the *emincé de volaille* a few times. It's delicious. It's sliced chicken with a Roquefort sauce served with potatoes."

"That sounds good to me," I said, knowing that when in doubt, choose chicken.

"Have you ever had French food?"

Yes, at Epcot in Disney World.

"I think so, but either way I always like to try new things," I said, realizing that I sounded like a ten-dollar whore for a second.

"I like that," he said, looking back down at the menu.

"So I thought that Spanish was your favorite thing?" I asked, wondering if he had played a French girl the same way he might have been playing me.

"Well, since I travel a lot, I do get to taste the world. So I try to eat new things, but never down under."

Did my whorish comment create this sudden sexual overtone?

"I won't eat Australian food. Don't ask me why, I just don't have any desire to try it," he said, turning the conversation back to normal again.

He stared at me and grabbed my hand so he could hold it across the table again.

"But as they say in the hood, I love me some Spanish, you know what I'm saying?" he said, suddenly turning into a romantic watered-down 50 Cent.

"I hear you, homey, I feel you." The ghetto talk for some strange reason turned me on.

We laughed.

The waitress arrived with the soup. Cameron waited for me to take the first taste. I looked at the five pieces of silverware in front of me and I had no idea which spoon to pick up.

"You okay?" he asked.

"Yes," I said, knowing I really wasn't and I was ready to have a panic attack.

I was thirty-five freaking years old and didn't know what spoon to use?

He continued to wait, but I had no idea where to start. He stared at me. I couldn't let him know that I didn't know what spoon to use.

"Listen, I just remembered, I forgot to tell my girlfriend something. I'll be back in two minutes."

When I placed my napkin on the table and stood up, I felt like the room was spinning. I tried to get my balance. What the hell was happening to me? I ran into the restroom. I wanted to be alone, but of course this restroom had an attendant. I stood near the window to get away from the little old lady in the white smock and dialed Selenis on my cell phone. I could feel the sweat starting to bead up on my forehead and drip down my face. This date was stressing me out. Pick up, *chica*. Pick up. She picked up.

"Again, Idalis. Why didn't you just bring me with you?"

"Shut up. Listen, real fast, which is the soup spoon?"

"The one that doesn't look like the fork, *pendeja*."

"Stupid, I'm talking about the two spoons. There is a big spoon and a smaller spoon on the table. Which is the soup spoon?"

"I don't know."

"You have to know."

"I don't. Just pick one."

"What if it's the wrong one and I embarrass myself?"

"If he likes you, Idalis, it shouldn't matter."

"No, this guy is all class. I can't do that."

"We all fart and pick our noses, okay? I'm sure he does too."

"Great help you are, I'll figure it out myself."

I clicked off the phone and leaned over the sink. The sweat was dripping down my face. I could see the attendant in the mirror's reflection. She smiled at me. She looked Latina, but I didn't want to assume anything.

Funny thing was that she did.

"*Buenas noches*," she said, holding a paper towel in her hand.

"*Sí, buenas noches*," I answered.

She handed me the hand towel.

"*¿Está caliente?*" she asked.

"No, I'm not too hot," I answered, patting my face dry.

I could feel her staring at me, trying to figure me out. Maybe she could help me.

"Do you speak English?" I asked her.

"*Sí. Perdón.* A little."

"*¿Qué cuchara* do I use for soup, *la pequeña* or *la grande?*" I asked, hoping she would know which spoon I should use.

She laughed and said, "*La grande.*"

"*¡Gracias!*" I wanted to jump up and down and hug the woman to death. I reached into my pocketbook and realized that I had no tip money for her.

"I'm sorry, I only have a twenty."

She stared at me, probably thinking, Of course it would be one of my kind to stiff me.

I walked back to the table, feeling like someone who had been in a time capsule for ten years. I hated feeling stupid. It's funny how I never felt this way when I was with Manny. I never felt that Manny was out of my league. Maybe because we were playing on the same team.

When I came back to the table, Cameron was not eating his soup, he was just patiently waiting.

"Everything okay?" he said.

"Yeah, sorry. I hope the soup isn't cold."

I sat down but I couldn't fight the feeling that I was in the wrong place at the wrong time with the wrong guy. I suddenly missed Manny and I realized that I couldn't trust my heart to know what it really wanted. As I placed the napkin back on my lap, I watched Cameron take the first taste of his soup. Instead of just bringing the spoon to his mouth, he moved it away from him and then into his mouth. Why was he scooping it up and over? Just scoop it straight up into your mouth. I'd never seen anyone eat soup like that before.

Now it was my turn and I wasn't sure if I was supposed to be eating soup my way or his way. I didn't know if I even knew how to eat soup anymore. This guy's proper etiquette was really stressing me out. Didn't he know I was just a Corona-beer-drinking, all-you-can-eat-buffet girl? Now if I ate the soup the way he ate his, he'd know for sure I didn't know what the hell I was doing because I'd look like I'd never eaten my soup like that.

I didn't belong here. I had no idea what the hell I was doing. Manny and I didn't eat our soup like that. Who besides Cameron ate their soup like that? Maybe people in France did. Shit, I was not from France and I didn't do merlot and I didn't like that I had too many fork and spoon choices. Couldn't we have gone to Applebee's?

Out of nowhere, I felt this ache in the pit of my stomach. This lonely aching feeling like I'd just made the biggest mistake of my life. I felt like Bogart in *Casablanca*, Meg Ryan in *When a Man Loves a Woman*, Tom Hanks in *Sleepless in Seattle*. I had to get to Manny and tell him how I felt before it was too late. I missed him! I missed the way he didn't care if he had bleu cheese all over his mouth. I missed the way we licked our fingers after we had buffalo wings. I missed the way he would burp out loud and make the kids in the next booth giggle. I missed us.

I picked up my napkin and placed it on the table.

"You okay?"

"I have to go home, Cameron," I said, getting up from the table and walking away.

"Wait, Idalis." I could hear him getting up from his chair. "What happened?"

"Nothing, I'm just . . . I don't know. Maybe I'm just not ready for this. I'm sorry."

"Did I say something to offend you?"

"No, you didn't. It's me."

He grabbed my hand before I could get a lead on him.

"You're killing me right now. I want to know what's wrong."

"It's not you. I'm so sorry."

He gradually let my hand go and I walked out of the restaurant and ran to my car. I had to get Manny back. What was I thinking? Who did I think I was? My mother was right. I wasn't Elizabeth

Taylor. I was average folk. Like Manny, the man I missed more than anything else right now. I missed being with my husband. I missed having a husband. I had to let Manny know that I still loved him and that we had to work this out.

I drove across to the other side of the island in ten minutes when it should have taken me twenty. I got to Manny's place and his Durango was parked outside and the lights were on in his room. Thank you, universe! This must be meant to be.

I knocked on the door. No one answered. But the lights were on. I paced back and forth and finally, after a few seconds, he came out in shorts and no shirt.

"Idalis?"

"Listen, Manny, I need to talk to you."

"Now?"

"Yes, now."

"Hold on, I have to get something from my car, give me a second."

I waited outside while he got his car keys. It took him a minute longer than I thought it should've taken, but I didn't say anything because I didn't want to ruin anything. I wanted to let Manny know that he meant the world to me. I wanted him to know that I'd learned from my mistakes and I never wanted to lose him again. He was my soul mate, the love of my life.

"¿Qué pasa? What's wrong, and why are you so dressed up?" he said, stepping out of his apartment. We both walked down the stairs to his car.

"I went out on a date."

"You came to tell me that?"

"Yeah, well, no, I miss you. I miss us. I was thinking that we should try everything to make this work. I know that I've nagged you a lot and I haven't been able to trust you lately, but I promise that's gonna change. You're the one for me, Manny. I knew this ten years ago and I know it now. We have to stay together."

"What happened on the date?" he asked, as if I were hiding the real reason for my sudden visit.

"Nothing."

"Something happened."

"No," I said, and I hugged him, the way a kid hugs his favorite teddy bear.

He broke the hug. "Who is this guy?"

"You don't know him. He's a friend."

"You don't dress like this for friends."

"He took me to a fancy French restaurant. That's why I'm dressed like this."

"Oooh, a French restaurant. What the hell do you know about French food?"

I didn't like his tone of voice. It reminded me of the times we had fought. Out of the corner of my eye, I noticed someone looking out of the window, but the curtains were drawn the moment I turned my head and looked up.

"Is someone in there?"

"No. It's just . . . Johnny."

Why would Johnny be sneaking peeks out of the window?

"Then why doesn't he say hello to me?"

"Because he's busy like he always is."

"Do you have someone in there?"

". . . No."

I didn't know why, but my intuition was telling me to run up those stairs and barge into that room. So that's what I did. I started running up the stairs and I didn't look back, because I knew that Manny was lying. I barged into that living room thinking that I would see Jasmin. But no, it wasn't Jasmin, it was a different girl, older than Jasmin, lying on the couch watching television. There was no sign of Johnny. She smiled at me.

"Who are you?" I asked.

"Jessica, and you?" she said with a seductive air.

"I'm Manny's wife."

"Well, I'm Manny's friend," she said proudly.

I ran out and looked over the porch railing. Manny was leaning with his back against the passenger-side door, holding his forehead in his hand. I ran down the stairs so fast that I tripped off the last step and almost broke the heel of my Isaacs. I managed to catch myself and ran to my car.

I didn't want to hear my name; I didn't want to turn around. I was beginning to feel really stupid and desperate. I kept coming back and running away and coming back. I just wanted to pick up Junito at Selenis's and go home and move on with my life. But I needed to know why. Why he wasn't trying harder to keep me. Why he wasn't trying to keep our little family from completely fading away, and why he wasn't afraid of losing me forever when I was still afraid of losing him. I knew that being separated meant that we were supposed to be away from each other, but couldn't he just be alone, like I had been all this time?

"How could you be mad at me when you were out with some dude tonight?" Manny yelled.

I walked back toward him.

"First of all, it's the first time I've been out with anyone. Second, I don't bring different guys to my house all the time. This is the second girl I've seen you with. Why do you need all these women in your life? Is this why we separated? So you can sleep with every whore you meet? I chose not to have anyone serious in my life because I wasn't ready for that yet. I didn't want to share my bed with anyone but you."

For a second he just stood there with a blank expression on his face.

"What kind of separation did you expect, Idalis?"

"The kind where you stay alone and think things through before getting back together."

"Was tonight the first time you saw that guy?"

"No. But I stopped it before it went anywhere serious."

"So it was serious?"

"No. Obviously I left him, in the middle of dinner, to tell you how I feel about you."

"You're here because you feel guilty."

Maybe I did feel a little guilty, but that wasn't the reason I wanted Manny back. He made me so angry I wanted to slap him. Instead, I took a step forward and pointed my finger in his face.

"All this time, I've been sitting in my house waiting for you to decide whether you want me back or not. I've always wanted you back, but you've never made me feel that's what you wanted. And you know what I just realized? That you're the biggest ass I've ever met in my entire life and I'm sorry that Junito is your son because I hate for him to know how fucked up you really are. You had the opportunity to tell me months ago it was over. Instead, the night you came over you chose to take advantage of me. Your wife! You took advantage of your wife! The same person that has been with you through it all, the good times and the real fucked-up ones, which were many. You treat me the same way you treat these other women in your life. I never imagined you to be this type of person. Just tell me to move on. It's really easy, Manny, you just have to say it. That's it. I can't move on until we end this. I mean, really end this. What is so wrong with you that you can't tell me it's over?"

"I love you," he said.

Again I wanted to slap him hard across the face, but instead I stared into his eyes and tried to find that safe place I'd always felt with Manny, but I couldn't find it and I realized that I might never find it again.

"It's over. Let's just get the divorce," I said.

He looked at me. It seemed as though he wanted to say something to me, but he didn't. I think he was surprised that I was the one that actually said those words.

"I do love you, Idalis," he said.

I didn't respond. I couldn't. I felt numb.

I got into the car, ignored every speed limit, and just cried my eyes out while George Benson told me that "nothing stays the same." The lyrics made me cry harder than I had ever cried before. I cried for me, for Junito, for the last ten years that seemed like a total waste. I cried for the little girl inside me who had so many dreams. I cried so hard and so much, I couldn't catch my breath. Finally, I just sat in the car, staring out the window, waiting to go into Selenis's house to pick up Junito. My eyelids were heavy and my eyes stung. I wanted to rub them and I couldn't because of the mascara and I didn't want Junito to know that I had been crying. I turned the engine off and let my body rest for a moment. There was nothing left inside me. I felt like a lump, hollow except for the pain.

I stared at Selenis's house. It was such a nice house. So white. So pretty. Little black shutters on the windows and colorful flowers in the front yard. No one knows what goes on inside of pretty homes. I always thought pretty homes were happy homes. But maybe ugly homes are happy homes. Everything I thought was right, was wrong. Everything I knew was my truth, was no longer the truth. I felt like I had to relearn everything I'd ever learned because it all seemed wrong.

Things had to change. I had to change.

When I got to Selenis's front door, I heard her yelling. I wiped my tears before ringing the bell. Carlito opened the door and Ralphie was in the middle of the living room doing nothing but just standing and looking up at the ceiling.

"If you don't stop this shit, I'm telling you right now, you're going to lose me," Selenis said from the top of the staircase.

"Hi, Idalis," Ralphie said, trying to make this all look normal but doing a bad job.

Junito and Symone were playing Connect Four and seemed oblivious to everything around them.

"Why is she so upset?" I asked Ralphie.

"I have no idea."

"What are you doing, Selenis?" I screamed, looking up at her from the bottom of the staircase.

"Fuck him, Idalis. I hate him. This shit is going to stop now," she said, walking away from the top of the staircase and into Carlito's room.

I walked up the stairs, hoping that this wasn't going to turn ugly. I just didn't have the energy for this. When I got to the top of the stairs, I saw Idalis walk out of Carlito's room with a baseball bat.

"What are you doing? The kids are in the house. Don't do anything stupid."

She didn't say anything to me and she walked down the hallway.

"Selenis, listen!"

"Idalis, not now," she said, holding the bat up in the air.

My stomach dropped. I could feel something bad was about to happen. She had finally lost it. Selenis had had all she could take. There was no rolling off the shoulders anymore, because everyone had a breaking point and this was it for her. She moved down the hallway with the bat in the air. But instead of going downstairs where Ralphie was, Selenis walked into Ralphie's office and slammed the door shut. Before I could get to her, I heard her hit something in the room. She hit it again and again and again. I knew what she was doing.

"Selenis, I'm coming in."

She didn't answer.

As soon as I opened the office door, she stopped hitting the computer. There were bits and pieces of plastic and metal on the carpet and on top of Ralphie's desk. I could hear Ralphie cursing her out downstairs. He knew he was guilty, which was probably why he didn't go after her.

"Give me the bat," I said, grabbing the bat away from her.

She looked at me and ran away into her bedroom. I followed her down the hall, leaving the bat behind.

When I entered the bedroom, she was crying. I sat on the old rocking chair I had given her when Carlito was born.

"You calm?"

Selenis didn't answer. I looked around the room and noticed how messy it was. There were open boxes of clothes on the floor and old photo albums, a few scattered crayons and coloring books, an old sweater I'd given her five years ago. It was the only room in the house that was unorganized and filled with junk. At the edge of her bed, I noticed a brand-new forty-inch television set. How did they expect to get romantic with that in the room? I could see that her eyes were bloodshot and I wondered about how far she would have gone if I wasn't here.

"Why did you do that?"

"Because I was tired of wondering what he was doing in there."

"You have to talk to him."

"I'm not talking anymore."

We sat there quietly. Manny popped back into my mind and I tried hard to push the thought away so I could be there for Selenis.

"How was your date?"

"I left the date and ran to Manny's."

"Manny's?"

"I can't talk about that right now, Selenis. Really. I just can't."

"Idalis, what is happening to us? Is this normal? If it is, I can't take it anymore. I need to get out of here. I'm losing my mind. This is not how I pictured my life. All I do is take care of people. Wipe asses, clean the house, make meals, and eat Oreos and ice cream all day long, that's all I do. Look at me, Idalis, I'm not happy and I'm fat."

"I know how you feel, Selenis."

"I try. I do try to do it all, but I can't."

"I know."

"The other day I went to JC Penney and bought a sexy red nightie to surprise Ralphie. I thought, You know what, maybe I haven't been doing enough to keep the fire in my marriage burning. I have to try to turn my husband on again. So I blow-dry my hair really nice and I put on some red lip gloss, like I did back in the day for him. I put on that sexy little nightie and I tell him to turn off the lights so I could surprise him. And he says to me how can I surprise him in the dark? But I feel like if he sees me he's going to laugh or something, because I know I look fat. It's hard to be sexy when you're fat. So for the first time in a long time, I gathered up the nerve and decided that I can't let my insecurities get in the way of my marriage. I come out of the bathroom, open and ready. I even model the outfit for him. I felt fat, but I didn't care, I was doing it for him. I walk around the bed and show him my whole body. I didn't think I could do that with the lights on, but I did, and I thought, Man, this is the person I had three kids with. He's seen everything. Why have I been hiding all this time? And then he lifts his head up from the pillow, looks me up and down, and says, 'You look like shit.'"

Just saying the words made Selenis cry again.

"I would never tell him he looks like shit, Idalis. No matter how fucked up he looked."

I walked over to the bed and sat down next to her and held her. Selenis needed so much to be held. Shit, we both needed to be held.

I pulled back and I looked directly into her face and I said, "You're beautiful."

"No, I used to be beautiful. I'm fat and I don't know what happened to me."

"That's because you take care of everybody else. We need to do us," I said, wiping the tears off her face. "We never just do us."

We sat for a moment, not saying anything. I knew that we were both probably thinking the same thing—how it was impossible to do us with the schedule we had. Then Selenis looked up at me and she wiped her tears and said with a little bit of renewed energy, "Remember back in the day whenever something happened that threw us out of whack? Like a guy said something stupid, or we couldn't find a job for the summer, we would get up and just take ourselves out to Club 90. And after a few rum and Cokes and a few dances, we'd bounce back somehow. We would forget all the shit that we went through and the next day it all seemed so much better."

As I listened to Selenis, I could see us, back in the day, dancing our problems away at Club 90, without a care in the world. It didn't matter that we didn't have a set career, or a man in our

lives, or even a complete picture of the future, we just kept dancing, believing that everything would turn out fine for us. We had
faith that whatever tomorrow brought us would be so much better
than what we had at that moment. We lost our faith along the way
and we needed to get that back.

At that moment we looked at each other, with smiles starting
to form on our faces. We knew what we had to do. Now we just
had to do it.

26 On our way home from Selenis's house I noticed that my little man had fallen asleep. I didn't want to wake him up, he looked so rested. I drove around for a few more minutes to avoid waking him up. I took peeks at Junito through the rear-view mirror, staring at his perfect little face, feeling so lucky to have him. Then the thought of Manny leaving me and asking for custody of Junito unexpectedly entered my mind. I would die if I had to be separated from my little miracle. I could feel my nerves twisting inside me again, the way they did when I thought about how out of my hands my life was right now.

I stopped the car on Richmond Terrace across the street from the Staten Island Ferry. For the first time in a long time, I took in the tall steel buildings across the harbor. It was the sight that every tourist marveled at and it was the first thing native New Yorkers were so happy to see when they returned from being away—those beautiful buildings that were lined up perfectly at the water's edge. But today, as I looked out across the bay between the water and the sky, I was reminded of how life was so unpredictable. Those two buildings missing from the skyline constantly reminded me of how long I really had on this earth. I felt the urge to hold Junito in my arms forever. I never wanted to die, so that I could be with him whenever he needed me. Who else on this earth was going to love my son the way I loved him? Who was going to take care of him the way I did? What would happen to him if I was no longer here? Would Manny remember to read to him every night? Would he remind Junito to brush his teeth every morning, would he be there to tell him that he shouldn't laugh and jump while he was eating or he shouldn't run with a lollipop in his mouth? Would he kiss him and hug him a hundred times a day so that he could grow up to become a loving tender man? I hung on to the steering wheel; I could feel my heart racing, my mind racing. I felt like I was on top of the highest peak of the Rolling Thunder roller coaster ride at Great Adventure. I was high up on that damn thing, and I knew that any second now I was going to feel my stomach drop. I hated that feeling. I gripped the steering wheel and I waited for the feeling to pass. I couldn't move and I felt paralyzed. What the hell was going on? My body was trembling and I felt like I was diving off a cliff. Was I having a nervous breakdown or was this a panic attack? I started the car, but I couldn't move the gearshift. I waited to see if the feeling would pass. I prayed for it to pass, and as soon as it did, I put the car in drive and turned the corner. I checked Junito again, this time turning around in my seat, making sure that he was really there and not a reflection in the mirror. I found a parking spot in front of my apartment and sat in the car. I tried to catch my breath. I pulled the sun visor down and looked at my face in the compact mirror, when something tapped the side of my window. At first I thought that I had somehow hit the window, but then I spotted the long nails. It was Jasmin and she was crying.

I rolled the window down.

"Can I tawk to you?" she asked.

"How did you know where I live?"

"Listen, I'm not stalking you, okay? I just need to ax you a question, that's all."

I didn't answer. I just stared at her. I could feel myself coming back to reality.

As Jasmin took a second to think about her question, I turned around to check on Junito in the backseat. His body was slumped over the seat belt and onto the next seat. He looked uncomfortable, but it obviously didn't bother him, because he was knocked out.

"I need to know if you and Manny are still married."

I couldn't believe he hadn't told her the truth.

"Yes, we are."

She started bawling.

I didn't want to get out of the car. Why let her think that I cared? So I grabbed a tissue out of the glove compartment and stayed inside.

"Here," I said, handing her the tissue.

"Thank you."

I watched as she blew her nose. Her nails were long and in the way. She had big palm trees painted on each finger and a sunset on each thumb.

"Is that it?" I asked, getting ready to roll the window back up.

"Yeah," she said. But she just stood there not moving.

I started rolling up the window.

"Wait, yeah, I do have another question," she said, feeling a little more confident.

"Yes?"

"Do you still love him?"

I took a second to think about it. Her anxiety suddenly became mine, I guess because we were both feeling the same way. I looked into her eyes and I could remember what it felt like to be her, at her age, playing pretend grown-up with grown-up men who didn't really care about you but who just needed their egos stroked by a young attractive woman who looked good and didn't know better. But I sensed that for Jasmin, this wasn't a game. I knew that this was real for her the way it was real for me. Although I could've played big sister to her, I chose not to. I had to start drawing some lines in the sand for myself. Besides, she was playing the grown-up game with someone who still meant something to me.

"I don't know. Listen, I have to go, I have to take my son upstairs."

"I'm sorry, I won't bother you again."

As I watched Jasmin walk away, I saw a glimpse of myself in her. Those high-heel shoes and tight pants, that newfound twenty-one-year-old sexiness, the inexperienced I-want-to-be-a-woman strut. I remembered that walk like it was yesterday. Sometimes I still felt exactly like Jasmin, a little girl trying hard to act like a grown woman.

27 The following night it was time for Selenis and me to take that leap into the Grand Canyon. She begged her cousin Cuca to come over her house and take care of Doña González and the kids. It cost Selenis ten dollars an hour before Cuca would agree. We didn't wait one minute after Cuca arrived, and we quickly snuck out of the house before Ralphie got home from work. I thought Junito and Selenis's kids would be too much for Cuca, and I didn't have an extra fifty bucks, so I brought Junito to my parents', where they could take care of him. All the important details were in order and we were finally ready to break out.

As we drove up the New Jersey Turnpike toward the George Washington Bridge, we listened to one of our favorite old-school CDs and we promised ourselves that tonight, and every Thursday from now on, would be "do us" night. We were going to bring the fun back into our lives—or die trying.

"Is my hair okay?" Selenis asked as she raised the window up to the halfway point.

"Yeah, what about mine?"

"Yeah, yeah, yeah."

"I'm so fucking nervous."

"Nervous? I need Pepto, girl."

"You so stupid."

On our way there, we bopped our heads to the music, shimmied, bit our nails, thought quietly, searched for a better song, told jokes, tried not to talk about the kids, did the "Car Wash" clap, pumped each other up between songs, sang off-key, flirted with a couple of very young guys at a traffic light, tried not to call the kids, sang some more, and finally we thought quietly as we pulled up to an empty parking space across the street from Club 90.

I couldn't wait to get in. We could hear the bass thumping as we crossed the street.

"Okay, we don't call home no matter how much we want to."

"Yeah, but what if they call us?" Selenis asked.

"Then we pick up, because God forbid it could be an emergency."

"Okay," Selenis said.

We both hesitated. I knew what she was thinking. Imagine being out partying while one of our kids was in desperate need of help. I pictured Junito's arm broken and my parents trying to help him, trying their best to communicate to the doctor in the emergency room what had just happened while he was screaming for his mommy. I could feel a little panic attack coming on, but I pushed it away with the selfish thought of having a good time.

"You ready for this?" I asked.

"I've been ready. Ralphie is going to be so pissed off. I love it."

We finally made it to the entrance of Club 90 and stopped to stare at the outside of the warehouse.

"Is this the most amazing thing you've seen?" Selenis said.

"It looks exactly the way it did back in the day, girl."

"The same sign and everything."

Walking into Club 90 felt like we were on a time-travel mission. It was a high without the munchies. We abruptly stopped at the door, like we had crashed into an invisible force field. But there was nothing stopping us; we were just trying to figure out the song playing before the song could tell us.

"No, I want to guess the song," I said as I tried to rush ahead of the lyrics to get to the chorus so that Selenis wouldn't beat me as she always did.

"*Cállate*, shut up, *pendeja*, I'm trying to listen. Besides, you know I'm better at this than you," Selenis said, holding her hands over my ears.

Selenis and I had always played this game back when we were

club-heads. We could be in the middle of a nice dance and we would hear the DJ mix the next song and we'd rush to guess it before he finished mixing.

"'Bango'!" Selenis screamed out first, as always.

"To the Batmobile, let's go," I said, before the old Todd Terry mix gave away the rest of the lyrical clues.

Selenis and I walked past a muscular Latin-looking dude who was flirting with two young girls. One of the girls was wearing a tight pair of jeans, a cutoff shirt, and a pair of kick-ass leopard-print high heels, and the other was in a tight black dress and pink stilettos. They both looked like they could be aerobics instructors. Selenis and I tried not to let the bulging arm and leg muscles on these chicks ruin our mood, so we did a little shoulder shimmy past the bouncer—who wasn't giving us the time of day anyway—down the stairs, and into the black-lit staircase. When we finally got inside, I was surprised to see that the club was packed with young people. For a second, I doubted that we would run into anyone from our past.

"Why isn't anybody wearing stretchy pants?" Selenis asked.

I didn't answer and quickly scoped the place in hopes of finding another bolero-jacket-wearing thirty-something woman with black stretchies on. Nope. We were the only two who were doing it up old school.

"Oh, well, now we know," I said.

We walked farther into the club and the music sounded loud to me. I could feel the bass thumping in my chest. I had forgotten how loud club music could be.

Selenis and I took baby steps toward the dance floor, taking in every ounce of detail and trying hard to somehow get our groove back. Anyone looking at us could tell we weren't regulars. It wasn't the clothes that gave it away, it was the way we reacted to everything seeming new but still familiar.

We slowly took everything in. I didn't know what Selenis was thinking, but I swear that being in Club 90 revived something inside me. I felt that young girl trying to emerge.

"Oh, my God," Selenis said, "it's exactly the way it used to be."

I couldn't believe what I was seeing. Usually when they re-open a club, like when the Copacabana was on Fifth Avenue and they reopened it downtown on Eleventh, they kept the name but built a completely different club. This was Club 90 the way I had remembered and experienced it. It was wide and long with two levels of mirrored walls. When I stood at the center of the dance floor on the first level and looked up, I could see the other club-bers leaning over the railing looking down at me. Four speakers that were taller than me were located at every corner of the dance floor. The disco ball above the dance floor was the only thing missing. In its place were a bunch of little high-tech lights rotat-ing back and forth and shooting off colored beams to the beat of the music. Selenis and I just stood there with big smiles on our faces.

"I died and went to heaven," Selenis said.

Even though it seemed like the same club, the new breed of dancers took away that old-school feeling. They were grinding up against each other so hard that they might as well have been hav-ing sex. That was not how we danced back in the day. Back then it wasn't about the grinding, it was about the dancing.

From the corner of my eye, I spotted a familiar face.

"Selenis, Selenis, don't look. No, I mean look. Oh, my God, is that who I think it is?"

Selenis squinted for better focus.

"Holy shit," Selenis said. She pretended not to see him and turned to face the dance floor.

"You gotta go say hello."

"No, he's gonna think I'm fat."

"He's looking over here," I said. "He still has the freckles."

"Okay, that was stupid. Like people lose their freckles when they get old?"

We both waited to see if Roland would recognize us. I could see him looking our way, but then he turned back around like he wasn't sure if it was us or not. Then he looked toward the dance floor and then back at us. I guess the curiosity started to kill him and he finally walked toward us.

"Okay, I know I'm not bugging right now, but I swear you look just like this beautiful girl I used to know," Roland said.

"It's me!" Selenis gave Roland a kiss on the cheek and wrapped her arms around him. Roland hung on to the hug a little longer than she intended.

"Remember Idalis?" Selenis asked.

Roland's eyes looked even bigger than I had remembered. I was laughing inside thinking about how Selenis must have felt kissing him. I smiled at him.

"Ms. I-can-dance-by-myself-all-night-if-I-want-to Idalis?"

I laughed and gave Roland a hug. It was weird to hear him say that about me, because that girl he described was trying to come back to life.

I listened to Roland and Selenis catch up with each other. I could see that Selenis needed this moment now more than ever. I was happy that she was out of that house, even if it was just for a few hours.

"Groove Is in the Heart" started playing in the background and I knew that Selenis used to love that song. She looked at me, hoping I'd want to dance with her, but instead Roland took her hand and led her to the dance floor. She looked back at me.

"Go, enjoy yourself," I said.

I looked around the club to see if I could spot other familiar faces. I wondered if Trisco knew about the club being reopened. What were the chances of that happening? For all I knew, Trisco could have moved to Iowa. Who knew? I guess I should just enjoy the moment, because sooner or later I'd have to get back to the real world.

I walked to the bar to get a beer. I stood there taking in the music, the people, and remembering the times I walked into this place feeling like I owned it.

The DJ mixed the next song; it was one of my favorites, "Silent Morning," and the only Latin freestyle song I really liked to dance to. I could feel myself trying to move to the beat, but I quickly stopped because not only did I feel stupid, but my body's dance memory was stuck on old-school choreography. I guess that's what happens after you turn thirty. The last dance you did well is the dance that stays with you forever. In the way that Michael Jackson is still stuck on that grabbing-his-balls move and how Madonna still dances like she did in that *Truth or Dare* documentary. I guess after a certain age, it's hard to keep up with the latest dances, or maybe it's not a big deal to know them. So instead of trying to compete with the younger crowd, I nodded my head to the beat of the music and tapped my foot. It was funny how often I dreamed about tearing up the dance floor if I ever got the chance to come back here. I imagined the crowd staring at me, wishing that they could dance like me. Yeah, right.

As I stood there trying to talk myself into getting on the dance floor alone, someone grabbed my hand from behind. When I turned around I got the surprise of my life.

"Kique!" I yelled, hugging him so tight that I made him spill a little of his drink on the floor.

He held my arms out to check me out.

"You look fly as hell; the same, girl. Exactly the same."

Kique was better-looking than he'd been back in the day. He used to be skinny and short. Now he was heavier, more muscular, and he let his Caesar grow out into a longer, more normal-looking hairstyle. A thicker mustache replaced the peach fuzz he used to have, and the salt-and-pepper highlights made him look a little Richard Gere-ish.

"Where's my girl?" he asked.

I pointed to the dance floor.

I watched him as he watched Selenis dancing. She had no clue that she was being watched. I could see something in his eyes. He was taking her in, enjoying her. It was as if his heart had stopped for a second and he needed to catch his breath.

"That dude was always trying to take my girl," he said.

I couldn't tell if he was serious or not.

Kique handed me his drink, stepped up onto the dance floor, and beelined toward Roland as if some stranger were dancing with his wife. The thing was, though, that Roland and Kique knew each other, so Roland knew he'd always be second to Kique when it came to Selenis.

Selenis was so busy watching her feet move to the rhythm that she didn't notice Kique standing behind Roland. Kique tapped Roland on the shoulder and gave him the cutthroat sign. Roland laughed it off and walked toward the opposite end of the dance floor toward a group of young girls he apparently knew. Selenis finally saw Kique and gasped as she held her hand to her mouth. Kique spread his arms out, waiting for her to jump on him. Selenis jumped on him and they both fell down to the floor, one on top of the other. I laughed along with them as they continued lying there, laughing and holding each other. I could see their laughter turn into something else—something more serious. I knew that there was still something there between them.

Kique helped Selenis up from the floor and they started dancing like nothing had ever happened. I was getting a little jealous because I wanted to have as much fun as Selenis. I should have asked Kique where his boy was.

"Idalis!" a female voice called out nearby.

"Renee!" I yelled back, and I ran over to her.

I thought she'd get up from her seat and greet me with the same excitement, but she didn't. I wondered if that crazy party girl I knew was gone.

"Let me tell you, I must've talked you up, girl. It's so good to see you," she said.

She was sitting with three other women, and it looked like they had all been friends for a while.

"You look the same, *chica*."

"No, bitch, you do," she said, making her friends laugh.

"These are my girls, Geneva, Willy, and Brigitte."

I didn't notice at first that Willy was a little masculine around the edges. She kept eyeing me.

"Is this place a trip or what?" Renee asked.

"That's what I said when I walked in here. Did you see Selenis?" I pointed to the dance floor.

"Ooh, girlfriend put on some weight."

"Yeah, but you know she had three kids," I said, defending my best friend.

"That's why I didn't bother getting married, girl."

"That's not why," Willy said.

Renee looked at Willy as if she didn't want to let me know some truth that she was hiding.

"Anyway, you married?" she asked.

Two months ago I would've said yes.

"Not really, I'm separated."

"See, girl, that shit isn't worth the stress."

I felt Willy staring at me.

"You got any kids?" I asked.

"Yeah, a girl, Vanessa, she's twelve. She lives with her father."

Willy was making me feel uncomfortable because she was checking me out the way dudes check me out.

"You want a drink?" Willy asked me in a kind of macho way.

"No, thank you," I said.

"You want to dance?" she asked.

"Leave the woman alone. Don't you see she don't want to be bothered?" Renee said.

Willy looked like she got a little embarrassed. She stood up, grabbed Geneva's hand, and took her to the dance floor.

"Butches can be just as stupid as men, girl. Ain't no difference," Renee said, finally revealing the truth.

"I hear you. Don't know firsthand, but I hear you."

"I got tired of men, boo. I just got tired of the bullshit. I mean, women can be just as hard, sometimes even harder 'cause, well, you know how women can be. Bitchy and just raggy sometimes. But you know what, it's a lot better than the bullshit I had to deal with back in the day with some of these brothers."

As I sat there talking with Renee and catching up on changed times, I realized that George Benson was right. Nothing stayed the same. I didn't know why I thought that if I had the chance to meet up with the old crew, things would be the way they had been. I wanted to be happy and enjoy the moment, but I couldn't. I realized that no matter how much I wanted the past to remain intact, what was would never be again. We all got older. We all moved on. And maybe things were supposed to change.

Renee used her nose to point at someone behind me. I turned around. There he was: the person that had been on my mind and in my heart for the last fifteen years. He was standing right behind me with his back toward me as he watched Kique and Selenis dance.

I couldn't believe that Trisco was standing less than a foot away from me. Life is truly amazing. If you want something bad enough, it will happen. Just keep asking.

I smiled at Renee and she told me to go do my thing. She seemed to want to be alone with her girls anyway. I got up from the chair and stood behind Trisco. I couldn't see his face, but I could smell his cologne. It was sexy and soft. I could see that he had put on some weight, but it looked great on him. He'd always been a little on the skinny side. He had on a pair of dark slacks that made his butt look bigger than I remembered and a tight rust-colored T-shirt that showed his bulky but muscular physique. I wanted to just stand close behind him for as long as I could, but I was anxious for him to see me, so I placed my hands over his eyes.

"I know those hands," he said.

He turned around, and before I could look at him, he hugged me—really hugged me, as if he had found what he'd been searching for.

"Trisco Mendez, you just don't know," I said in his ear. I pulled away to check out his face. I noticed a few new lines on his forehead, and the small hoop earrings on his ears were gone. His hair was short and curly, with two short sideburns. His face was fuller, older, and more mature. He was checking me out.

"Damn, how did I let you go? I screwed up, didn't I?" he said.

"Did you?" I said, flirting with him.

He put his arm around my neck and kissed my right temple. He smelled sweet and clean, and when he kissed me, I felt a tickle, like the way soft hair brushes up against your skin.

"So where have you been hiding, love?" he asked.

"In Staten Island, with my little man," I answered.

"You married a midget?" he said with a smile on his face.

"No, I have a six-year-old son."

He pulled his arm away and bopped his head to the music, creating a gap between us. I think my answer seemed to bother him.

I watched Kique and Selenis dance like they were the only ones on the dance floor.

"And you?" I asked, wondering if he was single or married or in limbo like me.

"I'm a free agent."

"What?" I yelled, getting close up to hear him over the music.

He showed me his bare ring finger.

"You're not married?"

"Well, the one I wanted to marry got away."

I just smiled. I wasn't sure if he was talking about me or someone else. Trisco was always like that. He always said just enough to keep me guessing.

The DJ scratched a record so loud that the crowd on the dance floor started to boo. He took the microphone and yelled out, "Shut up, people! Don't you see the fire? The roof, the roof." That was all we needed to hear. Without any music playing, the crowd on the dance floor swayed back and forth with their hands in the air and chanted back in unison, "The roof is on fire." And then we heard the first few beats of the old old-school record Parliament-Funkadelic's "Knee Deep," but it was actually the sample track on De La Soul's "Me, Myself and I."

"Hmmm, I wonder if you dance as good as you still look."

"You challenging me?" I said.

"*¿Qué si qué?* Please, there is no challenge," Trisco said, wearing a big grin.

"Oh, okay," I said, making my way to the dance floor, feeling my best old-school groove coming back. Trisco laughed as he took me by the hand and whispered in my ear, "Let's see if you still got it." And I felt that same little tickle I felt back in the day, that you-make-me-feel-so-sexy tickle.

From the way Trisco was dancing, I could tell that he still did the club thing a lot. He always knew how to dance his ass off and I always wondered if he was as good in bed as he was on the dance floor. He took me by the arm and turned me around, pulling me into his body so that my ass lay right on his crotch. We grinded and I felt like a hypocrite, but I guess I had no choice but to go with the flow. I could feel him—all of him. If his foreplay in the sheets was as good as his foreplay on the dance floor, I couldn't see why he was still a free agent.

Life was amazing. All this time I had been waiting for this moment, the chance to see Trisco again. I had thought about this man for the last fifteen years and now, completely out of the blue, here he was. Did I do that? Did I make this happen? Or was this meant to be?

After thirty straight minutes of dancing, my feet started to burn; the balls of my feet felt like I had been dancing on sandpaper. My bolero jacket was drenched in sweat, but I didn't care. I was dancing my stress away with the man of my dreams. Yes, the man of my dreams. Okay, so if he was the man of my dreams, why hadn't I felt my heart flutter the way it did when Cameron looked at me or when Manny spoke Spanish to me? I wasn't trying to be ungrateful for what the universe had offered me, but I must have missed the I-found-the-love-of-my-life fireworks display when I hugged Trisco. How could that be? How, after all this time, could I have only felt a tiny, tender, soft tickle? So did that mean that there was never anything between us? We always acted like there was. Could I have imagined that relationship in my head? Maybe real love was quiet and tender like this? How could I hang on to the memory of Trisco for the past fifteen years and not feel bombs exploding now that we were getting a second chance?

After "Mandalay" started playing, I knew it was time to stop. For one, I hated that song, and two, my feet felt like they had their own heartbeat. The throbbing was really starting to slow me down.

I glanced at my watch and it was a little past ten. I thought about Junito and wondered if my mother had remembered to pull the covers over him. That thought brought me right back to the present. During my dance diva days, I didn't have responsibilities or worries. I didn't have a little man that I had to take care of. I was free to come and go as I pleased.

I walked off the dance floor toward the bar and Trisco followed me. Selenis and Kique were sitting much too close to each other on the love seat where Renee had sat earlier. Trisco and I sat in front of them on two small black cubes.

"Hey, dude, be careful. You got your arms around a married woman," Trisco said.

"So? She was mine before he married her. Finders keepers," Kique answered.

"You're so stupid," Selenis said, hitting Kique on the chest, then smoothing out his shirt to cop a feel of his stomach. I could tell that they were hot for each other. Kique started playing with Selenis's hair. Selenis caught me looking at my watch. I used my lips to point toward the bathroom to let her know that I needed to go.

"Don't leave me," Kique said.

"I'm not," Selenis said, trying to pry herself away from him. "I'm just going to the bathroom."

Kique wouldn't let go of her hand, but she managed to pull away.

We walked into the empty bathroom and stood in front of the mirror. We looked at each other and Selenis busted out laughing. She took her lip gloss out of her purse.

"*Chica*, this is so much fun that it's sinful. And the funny thing is, I don't even want to go home," she said, sliding the wand across her bottom lip. "In fact, I'm not leaving until I feel like it."

"Your feet don't hurt?"

"Yeah, stupid, of course they do. But you don't remember how we used to work through that shit?"

She was right. We weren't able to walk the next day, but somehow we didn't care. It was one of the occupational hazards of being a club-head, but right now I couldn't stand the pain and I just wanted to go home.

"You know what's bugging me out right now?" Selenis slid her index finger under her eye to fix an eyeliner smudge. "That Kique and I are like how we left off."

"I know. That's some crazy shit."

"Makes me wonder why I got stuck marrying Mr. Pendejo, Maricón. So, any sparks with Trisco? He looks superfine."

"I don't know," I said, going into my bag and pulling out a small blush brush. I was getting worried that Selenis was seriously forgetting that she had to get back to reality sooner or later. "He's fun to dance with, but you know, there's no fireworks."

"You kidding?"

"No, I wouldn't kid about that. But then again, Selenis, when I think about it, there were never huge fireworks between us."

Selenis shoved her lip gloss back into her purse and entered one of the stalls.

"Well, I don't know what to tell you about that, but Kique just invited us over to Trisco's place and I wanna go."

Trisco didn't mention any of that to me.

"We can't go; we have to go home, Selenis," I said, staring at the bathroom stall. I put my blush brush back in my purse, zippered it tight, and waited for her to flush so we could leave.

"Somebody is a party pooper. I guess I'll be going by myself then."

"You would flat leave me?"

"No, I'm not flat leaving you, stupid. Come with me. You never know, maybe you and Trisco need to leave the damn club to see if you got anything going on."

I heard Selenis flush the toilet and she straightened out her skirt as she came out of the stall.

I stared at myself in the mirror knowing that I was about to do something, once again, that my intuition was telling me not to do.

"*¿Qué pasa?* I know that you're not thinking about Manny right now."

"No, stupid. I'm thinking about Junito more."

"That sounds like you were thinking about Manny."

"So, what if I was?"

"You know, Idalis, call me fucking *loca*, but I'm telling you, I'm so tired of the bullshit at home that I don't even care what happens. What the hell? We didn't get married and have kids to suffer. This is what life should be like. Fun. Besides, you don't think Manny is having his fun?"

"Okay, maybe he is, but don't you think we should head back to Staten Island? It's really late. I don't want my mother to start bitching at me."

Selenis gave me a long look and washed her hands.

"I told you what I wanted," she said at my reflection in the mirror.

I was always finding myself in these kinds of situations. The ones you knew you should stay away from because they would only make your life more complicated.

"One hour, Selenis, one hour and that's it."

Selenis wanted to drive with Kique, but I begged her to ride with me, because I wanted to talk to her alone before we got to Trisco's house. I felt that I needed to calm her down a little. I looked at her, bopping her head to Information Society. How ironic. I did want to know what she was thinking.

"Listen, I know we're out to have a good time and all, but we do have to get back to reality sooner or later. Right?"

"Right. But later."

Selenis raised the volume. I lowered it again.

"Selenis, I know you're amped about Kique, but let's not forget that you're married," I said, afraid of what reaction she would have to that.

"You're married too."

"Yeah, but I'm separated."

"So, you could say that Ralphie and I are separated."

"Not legally."

"When he decided to fuck the girls on the Internet, we automatically went into separation mode, whether he knows it or not."

"Selenis, you have to chill. Okay?"

"You're taking all the fun away. When you want to have fun, Idalis, you have to let the cork out of your ass. That's the only way fun knows how to work."

"The cork."

"Yes, the cork," she said, raising the volume.

I turned off the radio.

"I have no cork up my ass."

"Yeah, you do. This was your idea. 'Let's escape! Let's get out of here! Let's show them!' Okay, I'm here now, ready to let go, and you're putting on the brakes. Why is everything so heavy with you?"

She got me so heated I was about to turn the car around and go home. But up ahead I saw Trisco turning his Navigator into a driveway.

"You're just drunk."

"And you're not. Get drunk, Idalis."

"I can't get drunk. How will we get home?"

"So, drink some black coffee like everybody else does. I don't know."

Selenis was reckless. What the hell? She knew I wasn't going to drive home half drunk. And what did she mean, that I had a cork up my ass? Before I could ask her, Trisco motioned for me to park behind his car. Kique bolted out to open Selenis's door. I watched her get excited when he held his hand out. I knew that she was having a good time, but I didn't want her to do anything stupid that she would regret later. The truth was, Ralphie hadn't cheated on her. He just needed to get his rocks off a little.

I saw Trisco walk up to the front door of a duplex. From where I was standing it looked like he lived on the first floor. He swung it open and Kique walked in, with Selenis right behind him. Trisco looked down at me, smiled, and then walked in. I thought it was weird and rude that he didn't at least wait for me at the door.

I locked the car and walked up the brick steps and into the apartment. I was praying that Selenis would change her mind. I didn't know why, but something told me that I should have just driven us home.

"You mind taking off your shoes? I just got these floors put in," Trisco asked with a smile.

I kicked my shoes off onto the pile and I swear I heard my feet give a sigh of relief.

"Nice wood floors, Trisco," I said.

Trisco's place was gorgeous. It looked like the AFTER photo of one of those design shows on cable TV. The walls were painted a deep red, making the two large black and white mountain landscape photos stand out. I sat on the buttery leather sofa and put my feet up on the matching leather ottoman and started massaging my toes.

"What color is that sofa?" Selenis asked.

"It looks like mustard," I said.

"It's actually squash," Trisco answered.

I could see the pile of men's magazines under the coffee table in front of me: lots of girlie girls in sexy poses sitting on top of expensive sports cars.

"Damn, Trisco, this is nice," Selenis said. "See, this is what you can get when you don't have kids."

"Thanks."

"Selenis, you own a house, be thankful," I said, pissed that Selenis so conveniently forgot how lucky she was.

"Yeah, but you know it doesn't look like this on the inside."

"You own a house, baby?" Kique asked.

"I do. You don't?" Selenis asked.

"No," Kique answered, a little embarrassed.

"I don't either, Kique," I said, hoping to make him feel better.

"I should've went to school like my man here," Kique said, sounding extremely proud of his boy.

"You ladies want something to drink?" Trisco asked.

"Please," Selenis yelled out.

Trisco walked over to a large armoire in the corner of the room, opened the doors, and introduced us to his minibar.

"Trisco went to college?" I said.

"Yes, why?" Trisco asked.

"Oh, I guess you don't remember what you told me back in the day. You said you would never give a teacher that much power over your life."

"Well, I was stupid back then, I guess."

"We were all stupid back then," Selenis said, looking out the window. Kique wrapped his arms around her waist and rested his chin on her shoulder. He whispered something in her ear that made her giggle.

"Yo, Trisco, we'll be in the back," Kique said, dragging Selenis by her hand to a back room.

As I watched her walk away from me, I held up my index finger to let her know that that was all the time we had—just one hour. Selenis held up two fingers. Kique saw that and must have thought Selenis was giving me the peace sign, and flashed me the peace sign as he closed the bedroom door.

"I'm not a waiter," Trisco yelled out. He poured the vodka and apple-flavored martini mix into a shaker and then into a set of martini glasses.

Kique came back into the living room without Selenis, took the two drinks, and disappeared into the back of the house.

Trisco brought me a drink on the sofa.

"No, thanks, I have to drive."

"No problem, Ms. Responsibility."

"Somebody has to be."

He gently placed the drink back on the bar.

"You nervous?" he asked, sitting back down.

"Why would I be nervous? There's nothing to be nervous about. We're grown-ups now," I said, knowing that I was very nervous.

"Don't you think it's strange that we never did this? Not even back in the day."

"You mean, strange that we never took it out of the club?"

"Yeah, it's funny how that never happened," he said as he stared into my eyes.

"It's nice to see you again, though," I said. "Did you think about me?"

He started to play with my fingers.

"A lot," he said.

"It's funny, you don't know how many times I've thought about you."

"Then why did you marry someone you didn't love?"

"I did love him."

"But you thought about me."

"Well, yeah."

He got up from the sofa, put on some Marvin Gaye, and came back to sit next to me. I heard Kique yell out, "Oh, yeah, baby!" when "Sexual Healing" started to play.

"Does the guy you married know about me?"

"No."

"Oh, you kept me a secret, then."

"I guess."

We sat close to each other. He was sitting with one knee bent, and with his arm leaning on the sofa back behind my neck.

"You did okay for yourself, didn't you? I always thought you were going to be a famous break-dancer or something."

"Yeah, I know," he said, pausing before continuing. "But there's no real future in that. Besides, Mom passed away after Club 90 closed. So I did a lot of soul-searching, you know?"

"I'm sorry."

"It's gonna happen to all of us one day."

He grabbed a small remote and the lights dimmed.

"Player," I said.

"How do you know I'm a player?"

"You have a remote that turns the lights down. You're a player."

"Maybe I'm just lazy."

He gave me a smile that made my toes curl and I felt my heart skip, finally. He moved in closer and I knew that we were about to kiss.

"We were so young back then," he said.

"I know."

He touched my lips with his finger.

"What did we know?" I said.

"Not as much as we know now."

He softly kissed my lips and then I felt his tongue in my mouth. So this was what it felt like to kiss Trisco Mendez. He wasn't rough or hard, he was smooth and gentle. It was a nice soft kiss. I wanted more, so I kissed him back. He smiled and we kissed even deeper.

Marvin Gaye was making it even hotter for us, telling us to make love tonight. But I didn't want to go that far and if I didn't stop I knew that was exactly what would happen. I stopped kissing him.

"What are we doing?" I said, getting up from the sofa.

"I think they call it kissing."

"I know, but what are we *doing* doing?"

"You think I want to have sex?"

I gave him a look as if to say, "Duh."

"I don't want to have sex," he said.

"Right."

"Not that I'm not turned on or anything," he said.

I laughed and walked to the window.

"I think you're nervous," he said.

"No. It's just weird how I wished to see you and I did."

"So why can't you just enjoy it?"

I looked at him from where I was standing. There was no denying that he looked good. Trisco didn't have to try to be sexy—he was sexy. He had one of those faces that called out to be kissed; his lips puckered out a little and his deep brown bedroom eyes always had that come-hither look. I wanted to keep kissing him, but I could feel that I was rationalizing every move I made. I realized that that was the difference between the old me and the new me. The old me was impulsive and spontaneous and the new me questioned every move I made. Nothing was stopping me except me. If I wanted to find that spontaneous me again, I had to stop thinking about what I was going to do and just do it. I decided to go for it and I sat on Trisco's lap and straddled him. He didn't seem surprised or uncomfortable. It was as if he was expecting it to happen. I held his face, pulled his mouth to mine, and kissed him hard. I was in control this time. I made a choice on my own, finally. I guess that was one of the things that had changed about me since the separation. I'd learned how to make my own choices, as opposed to someone else making the choice for me. I now realized that the world was my candy store and I could buy what I wanted when I wanted it. I didn't want to stop kissing him and the more he sensed that, the harder he drove his tongue into my mouth.

I was finally thought-free, but that didn't last long.

Our kisses became softer after Marvin sang his last song. We ended our intimate moment with an embrace. Then we stared at each other.

"Don't you have a woman in your life?"

He sat back, surprised that I would ask that at a moment like this.

"Yes," he answered, boldly and without any hesitation.

"You do?"

"I have a few."

I was so surprised that he would admit that, I inched away from him. He felt me pull away, and pulled me back to him.

"But none of them do it for me."

"Oh, come on, that's hard to believe."

"It shouldn't be."

"Trisco, we're grown, okay? And if you felt that way about me, then why didn't you ever come looking for me?"

"How do you know I didn't try?"

"Stop playing with me."

"Okay, I'll stop."

There he went again. I didn't know if he was serious or playing.

"Don't you want to get married and have a kid or two?"

"For what? I like my life like this."

"You don't want kids?"

"No."

How could he not want kids?

"Have you always felt this way?"

"Yeah, pretty much so."

"Well, I always thought you'd make a good father."

"You trying to sell me on something here?"

"No, I just can't understand why you wouldn't want to have your own family."

"I come and go as I please. I don't need somebody coming into my life and telling me what to do all the time. Besides, from what I see with my friends, kids ruin everything. They get in the way of a relationship."

"How would you know, if you don't have any?"

"I just said I know people who do."

The look in his eyes suggested that there was once a child in his life. Whether it was his, I didn't know and honestly didn't want to find out. The truth would just disappoint me even more.

"I just know, baby, I just know," he said, picking up his apple martini and finishing it off.

"Okay, I'm surprised, that's all."

"Don't be."

He got up to remove the Marvin Gaye CD from the disc player and put on another CD. He grabbed my hand and brought me closer. "Always and Forever" started to play.

He held me tight as we slow-danced and kissed. It seemed like he didn't want to let go of me, but I was ready to leave. I could feel that there was nothing left for me to explore, that I was getting tired and whatever motivation I'd had before was now gone. There was nothing keeping me here. Again, I felt a void, that same old lonely feeling in the pit of my stomach. I wondered if Manny felt this way after he slept with me. Maybe Manny tested his feelings for me the way I was testing my feelings for Trisco. When Trisco cupped his hand under my breast to cop a feel, I knew this dance was over. I walked to the sofa and sat down.

"I'm sorry," he said, still standing in the middle of the floor.

"It's okay."

"Excuse me a second," he said.

He left to go to the bathroom and I sat and thought about what had just happened. All this time, I dreamt about what life would be like if I were married to Trisco and had his kids. Now to find out that he didn't ever even want children or to be married, it made my whole fantasy a waste. He was not the person I thought he was and now I felt stupid for having him in my heart all that time. I should have just kept him in the past.

When he came back, he sat down and leaned in to kiss me again. This time, I felt I had no reason to kiss him.

"I'm sorry, I think I better go."

"Don't go, Idalis."

"I'm sorry, Trisco, I have to get home to my kid."

I walked to the back room and knocked on the door.

"Go away," Kique yelled out. I could hear Selenis laugh.

"We gotta go, Selenis."

"Why?"

"'Cause we have to."

I went back into the living room and picked up my purse and shoes.

"Will I see you again?" Trisco asked.

"We're supposed to be at the club next week. That's what Selenis wants to do."

"Okay, I guess we'll do like we always do, right? At the club," he said.

"Yeah, I guess. Come on, Selenis!"

When I glanced at Trisco, I could see a hint of sadness. I thought, Maybe he does have a remote dimmer because he's lazy, or maybe my intuition was right, maybe he's just a player.

When Selenis and Kique came out of the bedroom, I prayed that she hadn't gone far with him. I wanted her to have fun, but I didn't want her to throw away her marriage. The wrong kind of fun could break up a marriage for good, and for as imperfect as Ralphie could be, I knew in my heart he'd never attempt to cheat on his wife. He deserved another chance.

Trisco stayed on the couch and Kique let us out. Again I thought that was rude, but hey, I guess we were both disappointed. Before we left, Selenis promised to keep in touch with Kique. For a moment, I wondered how she was going to do that with everything she had to do at home.

I thought for sure meeting up with Trisco would answer my what-would-make-me-happy question. But I guess I learned a valuable lesson. What happens in the past should stay there.

29 I walked into the office the next day super-tired, but I was excited to start working in my new "executive" position. Just saying it to myself made me feel more powerful. I heard Samantha walking briskly toward my cubicle with that urgent, it's-got-to-be-now march of hers. She popped her head into my cubicle and told me that Mr. White, the big boss and the head of the creative department, wanted to have a meeting with the team and our new client, Edgardo Levy. Thank God I'd pulled out the dress slacks today and not the hoochie mama dress.

I walked into the conference room a couple of steps behind Samantha and waved hello to the few folks seated around the long conference table. Marilyn and Levell were there. I'd be damned if I ever gave those two the time of day, so I took a seat as far away as possible. I noticed a dark-haired, nicely dressed guy sitting on the opposite side of the table, at the other end of the room. He looked like he could be Latin. He was young and wearing a nice light yellow button-down Ralph Lauren shirt, open collar, no tie, and was writing something down in a leather portfolio. When I took a seat, he looked up at me with his piercing green eyes, his goatee perfectly accentuating his lips. He smiled. I smiled back.

That must be Edgardo Levy.

Samantha sat across from him. I could tell that she had on extra blush and lipstick today. They smiled at each other. She crossed her legs and I noticed that she was wearing her favorite designer shoes, the sexy black ones that strapped around her ankles. I thought Samantha must have a thing for Edgardo. I could see why she might find him attractive. He had that Andy Garcia thing going on. Nice pleasant facial features, thick, shiny black hair, and a lean physique. Not my type, but he was cute in the way I found Sacha Baron Cohen cute when he was playing Ali G. Mr. White walked in behind me and took a seat at the head of the table. He didn't acknowledge any of us, but I still felt so important being there.

"Good morning, everyone," Mr. White said.

I was so happy about being included that I answered Mr. White the same way I answered Mrs. Lipton in kindergarten class. "Good morning, Mr. White."

I could feel my face turn hot with embarrassment at being the only idiot who did that. I took my pen to the yellow pad in front of me, pretending to write down important notes. When I finally looked up, I saw Edgardo looking over at me. He looked away.

"I would like to take this opportunity to introduce to you a wonderful person." Mr. White smiled at Edgardo. I noticed Mr. White's teeth for the first time. They were so small. No wonder he never smiled, it diminished his authority and made him seem human. "A talented businessman and the owner of the largest doll manufacturing company, our new client, Mr. Edgardo Levy, everyone."

We all applauded and Edgardo stood up behind his chair. I could tell from the fit of his shirt around his waistline that he had a six-pack and probably worked out every day. I could also see a huge bulge in the center of his black pants, but I tried not to look too hard.

"Thank you, Mr. White. I must say that I am extremely excited about having this very talented team, in the best advertising agency in the country, work on our new Linda Maria doll. I know that Linda Maria is going to be a huge success. It will be the first Latino doll to successfully cross over into the American market. We are so sure of this."

Suddenly I felt this implosion of pride inside me, the way I felt when I watched the ALMA Awards or when I was watching Carlos Santana or Marc Anthony at a free concert in Central Park.

Edgardo continued, "This doll is also special because she was created in honor of my mother, Maria Delgado. She left her birth-place in Panama when she was four, with her three siblings and her parents, to look for a better life here in America."

I saw Samantha give Edgardo a caring look. Edgardo didn't notice and continued speaking. Samantha crossed her legs and showed a little skin.

"But my mother's parents died in a car accident when my mother was eighteen, and she had to take care of her brothers and sister. She needed to get work fast, so she quit high school during her senior year and took a job as a domestic worker."

"Oh," Samantha said, followed by a few other sympathetic woes from the rest of the creative team.

"Yes, it is sad, but the irony is that I would not be standing here if it were not for that tragic event. Because my mother wound up working as a maid for my grandparents, and when my father saw her for the first time, he immediately fell in love."

"How romantic," Samantha said, straightening herself up in her chair.

"Well, for as lovely as that sounds, it wasn't easy for my father. When my grandfather found out that my father was fooling around with the hired help, he fired my mother immediately and told my father that if he had any sense and if he didn't want to be disowned, he would leave well enough alone. To my grandfather's surprise, my father left the next day and took my mother with him to build the Levy Toy Company. My mother was my father's inspiration for everything he created. This is why, when she passed away last year, I wanted to pay tribute to her with the Linda Maria doll."

I wanted to cry. Edgardo's story was so inspirational. I felt so lucky to be working on this project. It was exactly what I needed.

Edgardo pulled out a very tall doll, about three feet high, from a large plastic case. He turned her toward us and I swear I didn't know whether to gasp or to laugh my ass off. She was the ugliest doll I had ever seen. Her face was mud-brown with red freckles, and her hair was a brassy blond. Her eyes were green and she had thick eyebrows. Her lips were colored a bright red and she wore a maid's uniform. On second glance, the doll looked like Frida Kahlo on the *Like a Virgin* Madonna tour. Edgardo reached back into the box and pulled out a duster that he placed in her right hand. He then pulled out a very large plastic bowl of fruit. Actually, it was not a bowl of fruit but a hat made out of fruit.

"My mother loved Carmen Miranda," Edgardo said, placing the bowl of fruit on Linda Maria's head.

"Brilliant," Mr. White exclaimed.

Was it me, or was this doll the most offensive thing I'd ever seen? I got the impression that Edgardo had no clue about his mother's culture. If he had, he wouldn't be trying to market this monster to the average American kid.

"This doll is very important to me and I want to create the best advertising campaign we can," Edgardo said as he sat down and stood the three-foot monster up on the conference table next to him.

We all stared at her for a moment and I wondered what everyone else was thinking. Mr. White started talking.

"Well, Mr. Levy, this is very exciting and I would like to take the opportunity to go around the table and ask the creative team to share their initial thoughts and ideas."

No, no, no. I couldn't. There was no way that I could do that. I had to excuse myself and go to the bathroom. I couldn't lie with a straight face. I was the world's worst actress. The doll was staring at me as if the real Linda Maria could hear my thoughts. I had to excuse myself, but as soon as I tried to get up from my seat, Mr. White said something to me.

"Ms. Rivera, I am very curious to find out your thoughts on Linda Maria, since you yourself are a woman of Latin descent. I imagine that you must be very proud at this moment."

Edgardo smiled at me. I gave the group a nervous smile back.

Before answering, I took a look at Linda Maria *la fea*, trying to find an ounce of beauty in her ugliness. Edgardo saw me checking her out and quickly grabbed Linda Maria and passed the doll to Samantha. Samantha passed it to Levell, who stared at the doll in awe before passing it to the two account reps that were sitting between us. When she was passed to me, I pressed her little maid skirt down with my hands. I stared at her, still trying to find something good in her. Please, God, let me find something beautiful about her. I rubbed what appeared to be dirt off the top of her lip.

"She's a little dirty," I said.

I could feel the anticipation in the room.

"Well, Idalis?" Samantha tried to get me to give up my thoughts.

Levell and Marilyn were in my line of sight and I thought about how for every ass-kissing move they'd made, they'd some-how climbed up the corporate ladder, even if it was one rung at a time. I didn't want to be left behind in corporate secretary hell. I wanted to at least get the chance to come close to the glass ceiling, even if I had to squint to see it.

"I think she's beautiful," I said with a forced smile.

Edgardo smiled back and I could swear that everyone in the room just exhaled, as if hearing my feedback gave them the green light.

"Wonderful. Now let's get started," Mr. White said, rising from his chair and shaking Edgardo's hand. Everyone around the table started shaking hands and giving congratulatory pats on the back while I sat there alone.

I noticed Marilyn and Levell looking my way, smiling at me. Everyone was happy.

Wait, weren't they going to ask anyone else what they thought of Linda Maria?

I suddenly felt a weight fall on my shoulders, as if Linda Maria's legs were sitting on them. What did I just do? I went from being a secretary to setting my culture back by twenty years. How the hell did I do that? Why did I do that? I suddenly heard the singers in the old Broadway show *A Chorus Line* sing to me, *"Oh, God, I need this job!"*

Yes, that was it. That was the reason. I needed this job. Linda Maria was staring at me. I felt her calling me. She stood there on the conference table, unguarded. Suddenly, as if she were trying to communicate with me, she tipped over, fell onto the mahogany table, and her head rolled off her neck. Her head was rolling and it was coming right at me, but it stopped before it could fall on my lap. Everyone was silent. Linda Maria's face was facing mine and one of her open eyes closed. Then it opened again—like she'd just winked at me. I jumped back.

"I think she likes you," Edgardo said, and the whole room broke into laughter.

30   Later that day, Cameron told me to meet him at the new fishing pier near the boardwalk's kiddie park. It was a little chilly and overcast when I got out of the car, so I grabbed my velour hoodie from the backseat. I walked up the ramp and onto the boardwalk, where there were a few scattered walkers and bike riders moving in the direction of the painted arrows on the wooden planks. I saw Cameron, leaning over the railing and looking into the water. He was wearing a pair of long army-green cargo shorts and a sleeveless black T-shirt. He looked different, more casual, less intimidating. I could see a tattoo on his arm. He didn't seem the type to have a tattoo.

Cameron saw me and gave me a beautiful smile. He stared at me as I walked toward him and it made me nervous. I started concentrating on each awkward step I took. He met me halfway and put his arms around me. He then led me to a wooden bench that faced the water.

I folded my arms in front of me to warm myself—or maybe to distance myself.

"It feels like September weather," he said, making sure I was warm. I felt too close to him so I changed my position and sat facing him with one knee bent on the bench and the other one hanging off.

"Listen, I'm really sorry about what happened at dinner," I said, trying to feel comfortable.

"It's okay, don't worry about that. After that night, I realized that I have to check myself sometimes. We Leos can be a little showy."

"No, it wasn't anything you did, it was me. It was my first date in ten years and I didn't know how to act."

I watched him twist a sterling silver ring on his ring finger. He seemed nervous too. I looked into his eyes, he looked into mine, and he put his arm around me to warm me up.

"I'm warm," I said, pushing him away. He changed positions in his seat, moving farther away from me.

"Idalis, I have to tell you something," Cameron said, looking into the ocean. I turned to look at him. "I know you're going through a lot and I know that you're not ready to get into anything serious right now. And honestly, we don't even know each other that well for me to be talking this way. But I have to be honest with you. Whatever that thing is we have when we are together, you know, that feeling? I never had that before with anyone and I don't want to lose it."

I sat there looking into the water wondering how the universe could have sent me the most perfect person at the worst time of my life.

I watched him talk. He couldn't look at me. I guess he was afraid of looking into my eyes and finding out that maybe I wasn't feeling the same thing. But I did feel what he was feeling. I was just confused because of everything that I was going through with Manny. I couldn't deny that my feelings for Cameron were still there. Whatever crazy thing happened on the ferry the day I met him, I still felt it. It hadn't gone anywhere. For some reason, even after kissing Trisco, it didn't change. Was this what you felt when you met the right one? My stomach dropped for a moment as I thought about the last ten years with Manny. I remembered how excited we were when Junito came into our lives, and how little moments became beautiful memories. Was that all for nothing? Why did all that suddenly stop? Was it possible to live the rest of your life with one person? When did you know when he was the right one for sure?

A little speck of dust blew onto his face. I took it off with my nail. He looked at me. I wanted to kiss him and I knew he wanted to kiss me. I could feel something happening inside me. I wanted to tell him how much I *really* liked who he was. For the first time I wanted to give, really give, of myself, without being afraid of stroking someone's ego. I didn't want to let this moment go without letting him know that he was a beautiful man. And so I listened to my intuition and I kissed him, lightly, on the lips. I saw his eyes close as he gently kissed me back. I stared at him, he stared back at me, and we laughed a little. I felt the electricity again.

"Life is crazy, no?" I said.

Instead of answering, he pulled my hair away from my face.

"You hungry?" he asked.

I hesitated for a moment, starting to feel anxious again, wondering if I would make another stupid mistake that would make me feel like I was out of his league.

"We could do finger foods so that you don't have to stress out?" he said, laughing a little. I punched him in the arm. The man had dissed me and instead of getting angry, it made me feel at home, like he accepted me no matter what.

We walked to his car and decided to leave mine in the parking lot while we got something to eat. I'd never ridden in a BMW before and when I sat down in the leather seat it felt different. This new place was unfamiliar but safe and comfortable.

When Cameron put the gear into drive, I could see the muscle bulge in his arm and I felt a sensation inside me. I got excited. Once we started driving out of the parking lot, he turned on his CD player.

"You like old-school?" he asked.

I laughed at the irony. "I love old-school, you kidding?"

"Good, 'cause that's all I listen to."

He pressed PLAY and I heard a familiar Biggie song. He bopped his head to the "Juicy" sample, and that intimidating guy I'd sat across from the other night completely disappeared. I was sitting next to someone who I was feeling like I could really get with.

31

"Manny, I can't talk right now, I have to go somewhere," I said, holding the phone to my shoulder as I stuffed Junito's toys into his backpack and slipped on my new sexy black stilettos.

"Where you going?"

"Out."

"I wanted to talk to you about the other night."

"Listen, there's nothing to tell me. I saw all I had to see."

"Who you going out with?"

"None of your business."

He laughed.

"Just stop playing games, Manny, what do you want?"

"I'm not trying to play any games. All I did was ask you a question."

"No, you're trying to make me feel guilty for having a life."

"No, I'm just laughing at how when I come to you, you don't want to talk to me. It always has to be when you want it to be. It's funny, don't you think?"

"It's sad, not funny."

"Listen, the other night when you were telling me how you felt, I believed you. I feel the same way. I'm sorry, I was wrong for hurting you and not telling you the truth."

"Oh, my God, Manny the Macho Man is admitting he's wrong?"

"Yes, Idalis, I was wrong for not telling you that I've been seeing people."

"Well, now it's my turn."

"For what?"

"To see other people."

He didn't say anything for a second or two.

"Please, Idalis, both of us know the deal."

"Know what deal?"

"The deal we made ten years ago. That's the deal."

"You know what, this is getting really played. Why is it okay for you to have friends but it's not okay for me?"

"Who's this guy you're going out with?"

"You're joking, right? 'Cause you can't be serious right now."

"You know how I feel about you," he said.

I wished he could see me rolling my eyes.

"I have to go, Manny."

"Wait, I want to talk to you."

"Uh, talk to Jasmin or to your new 'friend' Jessica. Oh, but that's right, it isn't conversation that you really want from them, is it?"

He didn't answer.

"Where's Junito?" he asked.

"With his grandmother. Don't ignore my question."

He still didn't answer.

"What happened to the guy I knew back in the day? The nice tender loving father and husband I used to know. Or maybe I was imagining all that. You lie, you play games, this isn't the man I married."

"I'm no different, I'm just going through shit the way you are. You think this is easy for me? One day I have a wife and a kid, the next day I'm living with my brother, dealing with all kinds of shit."

"Then why bother bringing people like Jasmin into your life if you're not ready to?"

"I told you, we're just friends."

"Oh, yeah, is that why she showed up crying in front of my house the other day asking me if I was still married to you?"

He hesitated. "I didn't know she did that."

"Whatever. Manny, listen, I have to go."

"Where you going?"

"I told you, out."

"With who?"

"None of your business."

"Your mother told me you were talking to some black dude."

Now it was my turn to pause. My mother was amazing to me, she just wouldn't stay out of my business.

"I'm late."

"Since when are you into black dudes?"

"Since when are you into whores?"

"You may not believe this, but I do love you."

"Right, I know. Good-bye, Manny."

"Well, you go and do your thing with your little friend tonight. Make sure you get that shit completely out of your system, because I'm ready to come home now."

32 I thought that the day Manny decided he wanted to come back home would be the day I'd finally be able to exhale. I couldn't. Because in the time we had been apart, I had learned so much more about who he really was. He used to be so loving, caring, and sensitive. Now I couldn't trust him. He had changed. But what surprised me even more was what I was beginning to see about myself: I wasn't the woman I thought I was. I too was changing. I thought I'd be able to make my marriage work no matter what obstacles came my way. Yet when Cameron appeared in my life, he confused things for me. I didn't think I could be attracted to someone else so soon. I wasn't even over Manny yet and I was interested in getting to know someone else. How could that happen? Were those feelings real or was I just afraid of being alone for the rest of my life?

Why did I need a man in my life? What was I afraid of? I had to figure things out fast. I had major decisions to make. I seriously had to grow up. So I did the next best thing: I took Selenis to Club 90 and drank myself into a stupor—just to see what answers I might find.

"Look, Idalis, look how good I do the wop now," Selenis said, shaking her head to one side, then the other.

"Okay," I said, wishing the dance floor would stop spinning around so that I could catch my balance. "I can do one better, check out my running man."

We were drunk. Seriously over-the-legal-limit inebriated. We were rum-and-Coking our troubles away.

"Fuck Ralphie. I hate him and I swear I'll never suck his dick ever again," Selenis yelled out over Salt-N-Pepa's "Let's Talk About Sex."

I laughed so hard that I sprayed a bunch of nose mist in the air. Like a junkie, I wiped my nose with the back of my hand and kept dancing. At this point, I had no idea whether I was keeping up with the rhythm of the song or not. Hell, we were so high that I swore we were in Arizona with the police chasing behind my Jetta. I turned to Selenis and said, "I thought you didn't suck dick."

"Of course I do. What wife doesn't suck her husband's dick? Even if I did suck it like a lollipop, at least I sucked it."

I laughed again, picturing me pushing the gas pedal to the floor getting ready to fly over the Grand Canyon.

"Whoa!" I said, holding on to the air.

"What?" Selenis asked.

"I'm flying, girl. We're flying. Over the vagina of all canyons," I said, looking up at the ceiling of the dance club, imagining that the light show was the Arizona sky.

"You know how many times I sucked Manny's dick?" I said, counting the fingers on my hand and holding them up like a kid who was telling a grown-up her age.

"Seven times? Seven times in ten years? No wonder he did what he did," Selenis said, with such a truthful sting that I almost wanted to cry.

"Selenis, come on, what fucking chick likes doing that? Tell me. I don't know how sticking a big fat hard piece of flesh in your mouth and choking yourself is supposed to be fun. Shit, I choke when I brush the back of my wisdom teeth!"

"But, *chica*, we have to do that. We have to please our men. It's just something that comes with the territory. Sucking dick was part of the vows we took. Right?" she asked, unsure of the answer herself.

"Oh, yeah, I guess I didn't hear that one. 'Do you take your husband's dick in your mouth, in sickness and in health, and until death do you part?'"

We both laughed.

I could feel that Selenis and I were dancing to a different beat than the music, but we didn't want to stop. We just kept dancing.

"My feet hurt," Selenis said.

"My corns hurt. But ain't this fun!" I said. "I love you, Selenis. You're my best friend in the whole wide world. I don't know what I would do without you, girl."

"I love you too, mama. You're my sister."

We stumbled into a hug and I could feel a tear rolling down my face. I could also feel the sad trembling in Selenis's chest. When we separated we were strong again: warriors, using the music as a weapon against our pain. Our hearts may have been broken, but our spirits were flying over that canyon.

Out of nowhere Trisco and Kique approached us on the dance floor.

"Hey, you big corny motherfucker!" I yelled out.

"Someone's been drinking," Trisco said.

"Nah, this is me, disco motherfuckin' Trisco. This is me. Oh, watch your step. There's a canyon below your feet, bro."

Selenis and I both laughed. Kique and Trisco were staring at us.

"Come here, baby, I missed you," Selenis yelled back at Kique.

"You look sexy as hell, mama," Kique told Selenis.

"I love when you tell me that. You know why, because my husband never tells me that. Your wife is so lucky to have you," Selenis said, holding Kique's face between her hands. She kissed him on the lips.

We were flying high and we weren't worried about the consequences. Shit, we didn't care at this point. Why should we follow any rules or even bother caring about our lives when no matter what we did the universe kept shitting on us? As long as we didn't do anything stupid to hurt our children, Selenis and I should be free to act as stupid as we wanted to. The universe was a dark and lonely place sometimes, and right now we were both in a black hole, trying to climb out, searching for some sunlight. Fuck the universe!

"Trisco, can I ask you a question?" I said, rocking back and forth in place.

"Whassup?"

"Why didn't we ever fuck back in the day?"

"Excuse me?"

"I'm sorry, why didn't you ever make love to me back in the day? Why didn't we have a relationship outside of Club 90? Why?"

"Why?"

"Zee! Now I know my ABC's. Sorry. Yes, why? Because maybe I wouldn't've fantasized about you all this time."

"Because you didn't look like you were into me."

"What?"

"Idalis, you're a hard person to read sometimes, you know?"

"No, that was you, stupid. You're the one that's hard to read."

"Now I'm stupid."

"Sorry, it's just that I was there for you all the time. I didn't dance with anybody else. I was so loyal to you no matter what and you didn't show me any love. You're the one that fucked up, not me!"

"Why would I waste my time with someone that doesn't like to tell a man how she really feels?"

As soon as his words registered in the part of my brain that wasn't drunk, I realized what my problem was. The Jetta finally came crashing down on the other side of the canyon and when it landed I could see myself in the rearview mirror. I could see Manny running toward me with his arms stretched out, desperately needing to be held. The room was spinning out of control as I stepped one foot forward to gain my balance. I leaned into Trisco, pointing my finger into his chest.

"You know what, Trisco? That's a sorry-ass excuse. So what if I can't tell a guy what I really feel? So what? Why should I let go of my feelings completely when you're just gonna shit on mine eventually, anyway? Just being there should've been enough. I was always trying to make you see how much I liked you. Did

I dance with anyone else? Noooooo. I always danced with you. Always. If you would've told me that back then, maybe I wouldn't have wasted so much time thinking that we had something more. You know what? You remind me of that guy over there. The guy with the—"

I immediately turned to Selenis to see if she could see what I saw. I didn't know if it was a mirage from being in the desert that whole time, but I could swear I saw Manny and Ralphie standing near the bar.

"Selenis!"

"Yo, I'm busy," she said, grinding her ass up against Kique's private parts.

"Selenis, look over at the bar!"

She glanced over at the bar and I could tell she saw Ralphie and Manny. She straightened her skirt and in her most nonchalant way walked off the dance floor toward the ladies' room, leaving Kique alone. He started to follow her. I pulled Kique back and told him she had to go. I felt like I was running in a crooked line behind Selenis. When I finally could grab her arm, I pushed her into the ladies' room.

Selenis calmly stepped into the stall and threw up all over the floor, barely hitting the toilet. I watched from behind.

"We're in trouble," she said, trying not to gag again.

"No, you're in trouble. My trouble is different from yours."

"Ralphie is gonna kill me."

"No, he's not," I said, helping her off the floor and to the sink. Two young girls at the sink pinched their noses closed and backed out of the bathroom.

Selenis turned on the faucet and threw water on her face.

"Who's taking care of the kids and my mother?"

"You know that Ralphie wouldn't leave them alone. Maybe Cuca is."

"I'm so embarrassed."

"Listen, don't be. Maybe Ralphie will appreciate you a little more now."

"Can we stay in here?"

"Oh, shit, what if Ralphie got ahold of Kique?" I said, remembering we left the guys outside.

Selenis and I ran out of the bathroom and, as suspected, we saw Kique exchanging words with Ralphie, while Manny was trying to break it up. Trisco was standing near the dance floor away from everyone. I staggered toward Ralphie.

"Ralphie, Kique's just an old friend of ours," I said, trying not to sound too drunk.

"Oh, he didn't seem like a friend to me," Ralphie said, looking as though he were getting ready to punch Kique in the face.

"Listen, motherfucker, I am an old friend," Kique told Ralphie.

"Get the fuck out of my face!" Ralphie said, moving forward.

I was honestly surprised to see Ralphie jealous.

Kique looked like he wanted to pounce on Ralphie, until Selenis told him not to mess with her husband.

"Oh, it's like that?" Kique said.

"I told you I was married, Kique."

"So, I told you I was too; I thought we had something."

Ralphie looked over at Selenis.

Selenis couldn't look Ralphie in the eye and she ran out of the club crying. Ralphie walked out after her and Manny followed Ralphie. I walked behind all of them. I took one last look at Trisco and left the club.

"I'll call you," Kique said, loud enough for Ralphie to hear. Ralphie ran back and punched Kique in the face. Trisco didn't come to his friend's rescue. That surprised me.

When I got outside, I noticed that Selenis was throwing up the rest of her four rum and Cokes on the curb. I was surprised that I was holding my three down.

"Is this what you do when I'm not around?" Manny asked.

I didn't answer him.

Ralphie walked toward his car and Selenis stumbled behind him. Ralphie was angry for sure. But I knew he was more hurt than angry. I watched Selenis and Ralphie leave before getting into my car. As I opened my car door, Manny stepped up to me.

"You know I can't let you do that."

"I'm not driving it, I'm sitting in it."

"Until the morning?"

"Yeah, just leave me alone."

"Let me take you home."

"No."

"Listen, you need to be home for Junito. I'll take you and I'll come back tomorrow for my car."

Why was Manny caring all of a sudden?

I moved over to the passenger seat and let Manny take my keys. He didn't say a word. It was a long quiet ride to Staten Island and I wondered why Manny would take the trouble to come to get me. I didn't ask. I was too drunk to make sense of anything. When we arrived at my apartment, Manny helped me out, opened my door, and handed me the keys.

"Good night," he said.

For a second, I felt guilty about having had Trisco on my mind during the last few years of my marriage. I wanted to say thank you, but I didn't.

33

The next morning, my head was pounding like someone was trying to crack it open with a coconut. Before going to work, I got into my car and drove over to my mother's to check on Junito. I rang the bell and Manny opened the door.

"What are you doing here?" I asked.

"I wanted to make sure that Junito was okay."

"He's with my mother, of course he's okay."

"I'm spending the day with him."

"You didn't ask me."

"I don't have to ask you. You want me to tell your mother what you were doing last night?"

"I'm a grown woman, Manny. That doesn't scare me, and why am I even talking to you?" I pushed Manny aside and let myself in.

"You should be thanking me."

"For what?"

"For last night."

"I didn't ask you to come pick me up."

I walked into the living room, where Junito was watching cartoons. My mother was probably upstairs minding her business finally. Junito was happy to see me. He ran to give me the biggest kiss and hug I'd had from him in a long time.

"Come on, Junito, we're going to the park today," Manny said, walking in and interrupting our moment.

"The park! Yeah!" Junito said. He started doing ninja kicks to show how happy he was.

"Wait a second, I didn't say he could go."

"Oh, well."

"You're not taking him anywhere."

The ninja kicks stopped.

"Listen to me, Idalis. I'm serious. Junito is my son too. And after what you pulled last night, I don't trust that you're taking care of him the right way. You're lucky I don't report your ass. I'm taking him to the park. I'm his father and that's that."

"Let a lawyer figure that out."

"We don't need a lawyer."

"Why?"

"'Cause I told you, I'm coming back home."

"My house is not your home," I said, realizing Junito was there listening to us. "*Papito*, can you go upstairs and watch TV with *Abuela*?"

Junito left without a fight; he must have known this was serious.

"That apartment I live in, I found on my own. That's not yours," I said, pointing my finger in his face.

"Then we find another one."

"You can't bully your way back into my life."

"And when do you want me to come back, then?"

"I wasted a lot of time trying to keep this marriage together. I'm tired."

"Oh, so you lied to me when you told me you wanted to get back together."

"No, I did want to get back together. But after all the bullshit you've put me through, I don't know if I still want to."

"That's 'cause you're into niggers now."

"What? You got the nerve to call him a nigger when you have friends that are black? What is it with you people? You're all hypocrites."

"Yeah, it's everybody else, Idalis. It's never you."

I felt more alone at that moment than I ever had in my entire life. No one, with the exception of my best friend, made sense to me.

"You know what? Go ahead, take Junito. But you're not bullying your way back into my life. I don't care what shit you pull."

I took my bag and left the house, went home, and thought about my next move.

34 Later when I got to work, I sat and stared at the picture of Linda Maria on my desk thinking, What an ugly creation that poor doll is. I wanted to put her out of her misery. Poor Edgardo, no one would tell him the truth. How could a group of people pretend not to see the truth? Like my mother—why couldn't she see what was really going on with me and Manny? Why couldn't Manny see the truth? Why was I so afraid of living my truth?

I sat back in my chair and I felt myself floating above the cubicle. From a distance I could see the lie I was living. Starting with this stupid navy blue power suit I was wearing. For God's sake, it was no different than the plaid uniform I wore at Our Lady of Perpetual Help Elementary School. For the last ten years I'd been wearing a uniform. Actually, for the last thirty-five years I'd been wearing clothes that other people told me I had to wear. Like stretchy pants and bolero jackets, and the Victoria's Secret nighties that Manny gave me every Valentine's Day. Those black sling-backs weren't even my style. I hated sling-backs. I hated navy blue, I hated gray cubicles, and I hated that ridiculous stupid-looking freckle-faced doll staring back at me.

Someone needed to start telling the truth around here.

It was quiet in the office. I loved this time of the morning when there was no one around. It was just a normal empty office. No politics were being discussed, no games were being played, it was just the janitor and me. I finished drinking my much-needed Super Grande second cup of coffee and used my index finger to try and rub out the aching in my temples. My head was pounding again. Suddenly the coffee hit my bladder so fast that it made me jump out of my seat and run to the bathroom. I ran past the secretarial pool and thought about how just a week ago I sat there, next to the other secretaries, wondering when things in my life would change.

Before opening the door to the bathroom, I noticed someone sitting in the conference room across the hall. It was Edgardo, sitting and staring at Linda Maria. There must have been something wrong, because clients didn't usually hang around our office. Unless there was a meeting. He didn't look happy. I didn't want him to see me, so I opened the bathroom door quietly, but before I could step in we made eye contact.

"Oh, good morning," I said, waiting at the bathroom door.

"*Buenos días.* Can I speak with you for a second?" he asked.

Instead of telling him that I had to pee my brains out, I walked into the conference room. The double shot of caffeine made me feel like I'd just finished a thirty-minute step aerobics workout, so I was really fidgety. He asked me to close the door. I did and I sat down across from him and crossed my legs real tight.

"Hi," he said in a serious nonbusiness way.

"Hi," I said, trying to ignore the rush of coffee waves pushing against my bladder.

"Idalis, I feel like I can talk to you. I guess because I feel that we come from the same place."

"Thank you," I said, knowing that we really didn't come from the same place.

"You know, I told Mr. White it was very important to me to have a Hispanic person on the creative team. I felt I needed someone that would understand what I was trying to accomplish."

"Thank you, Mr. Levy, it's really an amazing opportunity for me," I said.

"Please call me Edgardo," he said. I glanced over at the Amazonian Linda Maria staring down at me. Edgardo got up from his chair and paced around the room a bit. I could feel that he wanted to say something.

"I had a dream last night about my mother," he finally said.

I didn't say anything. I just sat and listened.

"In the dream, my mother was trying to tell me something, but I couldn't hear her. She was yelling loud, with her mouth wide open, but I couldn't hear a single word. Then she grabbed Linda Maria out of my hands and stomped on her."

"Really?" I said, trying to act surprised at his dead mother's reaction.

"She told me to throw her in the garbage. That part I could hear. I know it was only a dream, but my mother always taught me to listen to the signs around me, no matter where they come from."

"Yes, I do the same thing. Well, I try to anyway."

"Idalis, what do you think?"

"About?" I said, crossing my legs tighter, hoping to stop the tsunami between them.

"About Linda Maria. Do you really think people will like her and understand what I'm trying to do?"

I could just lie again to save my ass and ensure that Junito and I would have a roof over our heads, or I could finally take a stand. I'd be risking everything, but I'd finally live my truth and help Edgardo live his.

"Edgardo?"

"Yes?"

I looked into his eyes. He was waiting for me to say something—maybe to validate his doubts. I wanted to save him.

"Can you excuse me for a second? I had two huge cups of coffee. I'll be right back."

He laughed a little, thinking I was cute, I guess.

As knock-kneed as I could, I walked across the hall and into the bathroom and ran into the stall. What was I going to tell Edgardo? I couldn't tell him the truth. If I did that, I'd probably be fired.

"Good morning, Idalis," Samantha said as she flushed the toilet and left the stall next to mine.

She must have recognized my shoes.

"Good morning," I said.

"Idalis, you know that Mr. White is raving about you."

"Really?" I said, trying to control the pee flow so that I could hear her.

"He told me he likes you. He says he can tell that you're hungry and passionate about your work."

"That's nice," I said.

"This is between you and me, but he said that if you do well on this account, he'll promote you to account management in another year, and as far as I know, he's never said that before. He thinks you're extremely valuable to us."

"He said that?"

"I wouldn't make that up."

I thought about how many times I'd dreamt about becoming an account manager and how it always felt so far out of my reach. I was curious to know more, so I flushed the toilet and left the stall.

"And just so you know, the position comes with a ten-thousand-dollar raise. I think if you play your cards right, this company could be your future. Sometimes it pays to be in the right place at the right time. I'll see you inside."

When Samantha left, I washed my hands in the sink and stared at myself in the mirror. Maybe she was telling me the truth. How could Mr. White lie about that? Ten thousand extra dollars would give me more freedom for sure. I could get a babysitter and not worry about Manny helping me out. I could pay my bills on time. I thought of Edgardo and his dream and his future. I guess this was why people pretended not to see the truth to save their own asses.

I thought about those people I'd read about who risked their security and their lives for the things they believed in, like Rosa Parks, Gandhi, and Mandela. Could I ever have done what Rosa had? Could I have fasted to make a political statement? I couldn't even stick to the daily points when I was on a diet. Could I have moved to Staten Island and started my own business in an unknown place the way Uncle Herman did without a college degree or any knowledge of how to set up a business? Why was I not made of what Uncle Herman and Rosa were made of? I guess I was destined for weakness instead of greatness. I was destined to live my life as a follower and to rely on men to define my existence.

I walked out of the bathroom and back into the conference room. Edgardo was sitting there, looking confused and lost. He was waiting for an answer, just like I was.

"Sorry about that. I should really cut down on the coffee."

He smiled.

"Edgardo, it was just a dream. I know this doll means everything to you and you want it to be a huge success. I wouldn't worry, if I were you. Linda Maria is beautiful and she'll be well taken care of here. I think you should go home and get some rest. You know things always work out in the end."

He thanked me and I wondered if he could decipher the bullshit in my words.

I left the conference room feeling like I had just walked to the back of the bus.

35 The weatherman was right: it was a clear, sunny, and breezy Saturday afternoon—a perfect day to start my summer tan in Selenis's backyard. I thought it would be an even more perfect day to spend with Cameron, but I hadn't heard from him in a few days and I had no idea where he was. Just in case he didn't get the first message I left, I called and left him another. The longer I didn't hear from him, the more I started to feel guilty about my little escapade with Trisco. Even though I knew that Cameron didn't know anything about what I'd done (I hoped), I couldn't fight the feeling that maybe karma was going to bite me in the ass.

When I got out of the car, Junito and I walked toward the side gate of Selenis's house and into the backyard. Selenis was exactly where she'd told me she'd be: laid out on a lounge chair in the backyard, alone. Junito ran ahead of me, kissed Selenis hello, and ran into the house to play with the other kids. I took off my T-shirt, pulled the straps of my bathing suit top down from around my shoulders, placed them under my arms, and lay back on the lounge chair next to hers.

"What's going on with you and Ralphie?"

"He won't leave it alone. He keeps wanting to know how far I went with Kique. I never thought that after all the shit we just went through, he even cared."

"What about Kique? Did he call?" I said softly, hoping that Ralphie couldn't pick up our conversation from inside the house.

"Three times on my cell. I don't want to call him back right now."

"Well, you know you're going to have to tell him to stop calling."

"Why?"

"Come on, Selenis. Stop."

"Why is it that men can have their little fun on the side and we can't?"

"But Ralphie is showing you that he really doesn't want to lose you."

"Oh, well, maybe it's too late."

"What do you mean?" I asked, hoping she hadn't done anything stupid the night we went to Trisco's place.

"Nothing."

"Please tell me you didn't sleep with him."

"I didn't," she answered, as if she wished she had.

"Did you kiss him?"

Selenis raised her sunglasses to her forehead, leaned forward in her chair, and gave me a look as if to say, "What happened in the Bronx will stay in the Bronx." She placed her glasses back on and lay back down.

"What happened with Manny?"

"He's acting like a jerk. He had the nerve to tell me that he wanted to come home. Do you believe that shit? After all this time, he wants to come back. Please."

"And?"

"I don't know if I want him to come home now."

Selenis laughed and said, "We shook these assholes up real good, didn't we?"

"I guess."

"Anyway, it's too bad things didn't work out with Trisco. He looks like he's doing all right for himself."

"The man doesn't want kids. What kind of man doesn't want kids?"

"A smart one."

"I just keep thinking about how much time I spent thinking about him all these years. Whenever Manny and I had an argument, I always imagined that the grass would have been greener had I married Trisco. What a waste of time."

"So there was no love connection after all?"

"You know what he had the nerve to say?" I said, sitting up in my seat. "That he never asked me out because he thought I wasn't interested in him. Now, what kind of crap is he talking about?"

"Well, you can act a little laid back sometimes."

"No, I don't."

"Yeah, you do. For as long as I've known you, I've never seen you bow down to any guy."

"Stop," I said as I moved down toward the end of my chair, facing Selenis. She was facing the sun.

"You know how you are. But I also know that when you feel right about something, you let go. So maybe you're right, you and Trisco weren't really meant to be. Maybe you haven't found your soul mate yet."

I thought about Cameron.

"Maybe I haven't found mine either," she continued.

"Listen, you don't know how things would be outside of that club, okay? In the club is one thing, you're all dressed up and sexy and you're drinking and dancing, but outside in the real world, it's a whole other thing," I said, stopping to realize that I sounded just like Manny the other night when he tried to share his insight about the single world. "Plus, Kique looks like he hasn't grown up much."

"That's what's fun about him."

Selenis sat up in her chair and fixed the top of her one-piece bathing suit. She put one hand up in the air, and with her other she adjusted under her bra. Her hand remained inside for a while and I wondered what she was trying to do.

"What's wrong?" I asked.

"I could feel something."

"Like?"

"Like a lump. Come here."

I sat at the edge of her lounge chair. Then she took my index finger and placed it on the side of her breast.

"Move it around," she said with a concerned look on her face.

"I don't feel anything,"

"No, over here."

Selenis repositioned my hand, forcing my finger under her right armpit. I felt a firm hard mass the size of a quarter. The minute I found it, I had a bad feeling. I didn't know anything about breast lumps, but something in my gut told me that whatever it was, it shouldn't have been there.

"Selenis, how long have you had that?"

"I felt it a few weeks ago, but it was smaller," she said, feeling the lump again.

"You need to get that checked out."

"It's probably just a cyst. They run in my family."

"That doesn't feel like a little cyst."

"Listen, God wouldn't give me any more than I can handle. I'm not worried."

But I knew she had to be worried because I knew my best friend. I knew that the minute she felt that lump, the first thing she thought of was what would happen to her three little angels if anything happened to her.

I moved back to my chair.

I watched Selenis as she straightened her bra back in place. She wasn't saying anything, as if she were heavy in thought. She lay back down on the lounge chair and put her sunglasses on.

"It's gonna be okay, Selenis."

"I told you I'm not worried," she said, with her voice trembling a little.

"Listen, if you need me, you know that I—"

"Idalis, stop being so dramatic, *por favor*, please! I don't want to talk about it. Everything is going to be fine."

"No, you stop! This is serious. You need to check that out. Stop being afraid of finding shit out. You did the same thing when you found those pictures on the computer. Instead of confronting Ralphie the right way, you go and take it out on the computer. Learn to deal with shit."

She took off her sunglasses and sat up.

"I'll learn to deal with shit when you start getting real about your own bullshit, okay? You've been hanging on to a dead marriage for over three months. If it's that easy to see the truth, then why do you keep chasing a ghost?"

"I'm not gonna fight with you. I'm tired of fighting with everyone in my life. Maybe I should've opened my eyes a long time ago. All I'm saying is that you shouldn't let this go. That's all. Just promise me that you will check that out right away."

She stared at me without saying a word. I knew that she was scared because she reached inside her bathing suit to check if the lump was still there. As if by some miracle in the last few minutes it had vanished or morphed into a pimple.

I hugged her and I said a little silent prayer, hoping that God or the universe or whatever person or thing made this planet rotate would cut us a break. But it didn't. A few weeks later, Selenis received the worst news of her life. She was diagnosed with stage two breast cancer.

36 I was tired, tired of the stress; tired of worrying about Selenis, tired of not being able to take off from work to help her when she got her chemo treatments, tired of lying about Linda Maria, tired of Manny bullying me into trying to make the marriage work, and tired of not knowing what role Cameron had in my life. Was he my soul mate or just another misdiagnosed crush? In the middle of all of this chaos and uncertainty, Uncle Herman called to ask for my help.

When I arrived at the luncheonette I was surprised to see that there was no CONSTANTINE'S WEBOS sign hanging above the storefront. I opened the front door and Uncle Herman was standing in the center of the floor wearing a dust mask over his mouth. He was pacing and taking in the empty space.

"Uncle Herman, what did you do?" I asked.

It was obvious what he had done—he had gutted out the entire place. There was no counter, no stools, no chairs or booths. It was a big empty space with a lot of white dust on the floor and walls. And Guillermo was no longer in the kitchen cooking delicious eggs.

"I'm not going to let some big-time breakfast chain run me out of business," he said, handing me a dust mask.

I placed it over my mouth and wrapped the thick rubber band around my head.

"So, what are you doing?"

"I'm building a nice big coffee bar with a little kitchen so that I can still make my famous *webos*. I did some research, *nena*, and I found out how to put computers in here. I'm going to make it very sophisticated but very Caribbean. Like if you were in the middle of Old San Juan."

I looked at the hole in the middle of the floor and the dust that lightly powdered the drab green walls. I didn't want to be a dream-crusher but I couldn't see it. I couldn't see his vision. At his age, maybe he should be selling the place. Perhaps he should retire, move to Clearwater Beach to spend the rest of his days. Was he crazy? How did he think he could compete against a huge powerful chain?

"*Tío*, how does *Tía* feel about this?" I asked, knowing that my aunt had a little more common sense than Uncle Herman had.

"She loves it! Now I just need to know that you can work here and manage it and I'll be able to die a happy man."

I stood there, not knowing what to say. My dream job wasn't working in a coffee bar. How did I tell Uncle Herman that I couldn't help him? Why did he keep trying to recruit me?

"*Tío*, listen, I love you, you know that. I just can't quit my job right now."

"I'll pay you thirty thousand a year to manage the place."

"But I need benefits."

"Benefits too," he said, wiping something off his eyebrow.

"You don't have thirty thousand a year to give me."

"Yes, *nena*, I do. And think about how convenient it would be for you. You could stay on Staten Island and not worry about leaving Junito when you go into the city. You could bring him to work whenever you wanted to. You would be the big *jefe*."

I could be my own boss? As good as that sounded to me, I had reservations. How could I walk away from the possibility of becoming an executive? And besides, what if Uncle Herman's little plan didn't work out? And why didn't he seem to have the same doubts I had?

"I don't know, *Tío*, I think you're pushing it."

"Pushing *qué*?"

"Pushing your luck. I think you should sell this place, get whatever you can for it, and retire. Amos's has been around for a while."

He gave me a disappointed look.

"Oh, I see. I thought you were more like me. But maybe not, maybe you're more like your Uncle Sammy."

"But you can't dream all the time, *Tío*. Sometimes you have to be realistic."

"*Realistic* is such a boring word."

"What if this idea doesn't work?"

"It will."

"But there's no guarantee that it will, *Tío*. Nothing is guaranteed."

"You are like Sammy, you need a life jacket."

"What?"

"*Nena,* let me tell you a little *historia.* Back in Puerto Rico, there was a pool *en la plaza.* It was ten feet deep. And *mi papá* took Sammy and me one day to the pool when we were six and seven years old. We didn't know how to swim. But he took us by our pants and threw us in the pool and he said, 'The one that makes it out by himself is the one that wins.' Sammy kept crying for somebody to throw him a lifesaver. But *Papi* wouldn't throw him one. Sammy almost drowned. But me, I learned to swim."

"And why are you telling me this?"

"*Mi papá* taught me a valuable lesson *ese día, nena.* You can't live life if you don't jump in the water without a life jacket. When you jump in without a jacket, you're the only one that can save yourself. And when you save yourself, you'll never depend on any-one to try and save you ever again."

I let the message sink in deep, hoping my mind would get it. But I guess, as always, I wasn't ready.

"Okay, but *Tío,* aren't you depending on me a little?"

"No, because I'll do this without you, *nena.* I have before. I just know you better than you know yourself. I know what will make you happy. I'm giving you an opportunity. You don't want it? *Vete.*"

I did leave. But I knew in my heart that there was a deeper meaning to Uncle Herman's persistence. I just wasn't sure what it was—yet.

37

Manny asked me to meet him at the bookstore on Richmond Avenue. I was nervous because he wanted me to make a final decision today. I wasn't ready, but I knew that I had to hurry up and decide what I was going to do with my marriage. Well, our marriage. It's amazing how all this time I was waiting for Manny to give me an answer and now I was waiting for my own answer. I decided to bring Junito along with me. I knew it was a dangerous thing to do, since when the three of us were together it made me long for the good old days.

Junito played with the train set in the children's section while Manny and I sat on the small wooden kids' bench nearby. Junito was happy that he didn't have to share the train set with any other kids that morning. Manny and I watched him roll the little blue train over the long track uphill and then down into the make-believe town and up the hill again. It felt strange with all of us in the same place. As I suspected, it felt like old times again.

"I miss this," Manny said, placing his hand on my knee.

I didn't respond. I shook my leg to get his hand off me and kept drinking my coffee. His timing pissed me off. If only he knew how long I had missed us.

"Well, at least Junito looks happy," I said.

"You're not?"

"Happy?"

"Sí."

"No, I'm pissed."

"At me?"

"Yeah, at you. All this time I wanted an answer from you and now you want me back and now I don't know what I want."

"Are you seeing that guy still?"

I gave him a look that told him to stay out of my business.

"If that's what you want, Idalis, go, I'm not holding you back."

I laughed. "Manny, you put me through a lot."

"We both went through a lot."

"I never thought that of all people you would be the one to hurt me the way you did."

We sat there staring at Junito, who was in his own world playing with the trains. A little girl much younger than him arrived to join in. She was so excited she grabbed a bunch of trains in her hand and let them drop to the floor.

"Those are mine!" Junito screamed, and picked all the trains up from the floor and placed them carefully on the track again.

"Junito, the trains belong to everyone, they're not yours," I said.

Junito handed the little girl a pink train and she was super-happy about it.

"I didn't go out of my way to hurt you," Manny said.

"But you did hurt me. So you can't expect me to feel the same way I did before."

"What did this guy do to you?"

"Nothing. If anything, he treated me with respect."

"You say you don't know me, but honestly, Idalis, I don't know you anymore either."

"Well, then why would you want to be with someone you don't know?"

He couldn't answer me.

I continued, "Listen, this isn't about some guy, because, honestly, I haven't known this person for that long. It's about what we've done to each other. We've broken each other's hearts. That's hard to fix."

"I know. You're right. I wish we handled things a little differently."

"But you know what, Manny? Maybe this is the way it was supposed to happen."

From where I was sitting I could hear a guest author reading from her book. I could also tell, from their response, that most of her audience was female. Her voice sounded familiar, so I stood up from the kiddie bench and peeked over the bookshelves. In the farthest corner of the store, I saw her. I told Manny that I would be right back and walked over to where she was standing. I never thought I'd see her again. I listened.

"You know why we dream, ladies? We dream so that we can believe in something bigger than ourselves. That's why we dream. It ain't easy to dream, sisters. It's a lonely thing, to dream. 'Cause you the only one that sees it. Nobody but you sees it. Well, let me take that back. Only you and the big sister who watches over you can see it."

The women in the crowd responded with an amen.

"But just because nobody else can see it, it don't mean it ain't there in front of you."

I thought of Uncle Herman.

"It's real easy to sit and watch your stories on the television all day, to stay inside while life passes by on the other side of your living room window. But today is a new day, my sisters. You will walk past that window and you will walk out the front door and you will follow your heart wherever it leads you. But don't turn back. You can't ever turn back, because if you want to find happiness, you gotta stop holding on. You gotta let go and follow that road in front of you no matter how crooked it gets or how many trees fall down in your path or how hard the rain falls. You will follow it, when you have faith and when you don't. And never step off that road for no one, because believe me when I tell you, you will find what you've been looking for. And you know what you use to help you down that road?"

No one answered. But I knew the answer.

"Your intwaition," I exclaimed proudly.

"Yes! My lovely beautiful brown sister, you are correct. Use your intwaition. And when your intwaition ain't feeling things are right, silence yourself and take a listen. And I'll tell you right now, that when things are right, your intwaition will tell you loud and clear. Get out of your own way, ladies! And just follow your heart. It's trying to show you the way."

I stood there with tears flowing down my cheeks. This stranger, this beautiful stranger, was giving me what I needed. Then I realized that so many people had been giving me what I needed. Uncle Herman, Selenis, Trisco, my mother, and even Manny, in his own way, were giving me what I needed to move forward. All this time I didn't want to move, but something was pushing me closer to where I needed to be. All these people were helping me, but I was afraid. I was afraid of being alone, so I kept returning to my past and holding on to things that weren't even there for me to hold on to, like the old me. All this time I thought if I put on a pair of stretchy pants, a size-four bolero jacket, and found my lost love Trisco, I could bring back that more independent, stronger, sexier, and younger part of me, but instead I was frozen in time and I wasn't allowing the future to happen.

I finally heard the silence. Inside me. It was me. I was what I was looking for and I felt stronger than I ever had before. I couldn't hide anymore. Now I knew for sure that the time I had with Manny was supposed to get me to this point. I knew Manny loved me and I loved him, but it was a different kind of love. We had to move on, for Junito's sake, for our sake. I finally started to see the truth about a lot of things in my life. My eyes were wide open and I could see better than I could ever see before. But I also knew that for Manny this was the beginning of his journey.

I smiled at the big beautiful lady with the burgundy braids, that beautiful lady who most people would write off as crazy. Who my mother would consider beneath her. Who Manny would just see right through. Who Samantha would just view as a "street person." Her message was meant for me, lucky me.

I made sure Junito was buckled up in the backseat of my car. I looked over at Manny sitting in the driver's seat of his car, staring at the steering wheel. He knew the truth. As I stood on the passenger side, I reached in and gave him my hand. He held and caressed it. He looked into my eyes and I saw a tear falling onto his face. *"Te quiero, Idalis."*

"I know you do. I love you too."

We held on to each other's hands. It was the last time we would do that.

The next day I walked into the conference room late for our meeting with Edgardo Levy. I apologized to everyone before quickly taking a seat. Edgardo glanced over at me. He wasn't smiling and he turned back to listen to Mr. White.

I watched Mr. White's lips move, but I couldn't hear anything coming out of his mouth. Everyone seemed to be moving in slow motion. I could feel the truth beneath their façades. I could feel who they really were. I could feel Samantha's lack of love and her overwhelming desire to succeed. I could feel Mr. White's ruthless commitment to keep his benefits and his job. He had to exert his power now because in a few years he would lose it to someone younger. I watched Levell and Marilyn, hanging on to every word that escaped from Mr. White's mouth. Hanging on gave them the strength they needed to believe that they too would sit in Mr. White's chair one day. I watched Edgardo. I could feel the warmth that radiated from inside him; he was the only person in the room who touched me that way. He still wasn't as happy as he had been before having that dream. Something had changed in him. He needed me.

"Excuse me," I said, clearing my throat and interrupting Mr. White's speech.

"Ms. Rivera, I'm not done speaking," Mr. White said.

"I know, but I can't sit here any longer without saying what I need to say."

I could feel Marilyn and Levell straighten up in their seats, probably thinking I had some nerve to interrupt the big boss.

"Idalis?" Samantha said, knowing I was going to say something that maybe I shouldn't.

"It's okay, Samantha. It's okay."

I hadn't realized the power I had in my hands—until now. In fact, I now realized that I'd had this power the whole time. I mean, my entire life I'd had the power to speak the truth and I never did. I was always scared of what would happen if I did. I took in a deep breath, exhaled, stood up, and finally said what I needed to say.

"Edgardo, I lied."

Mr. White stood up and said, "Ms. Rivera, you can sit down now."

"No, I can't sit down, Mr. White. Edgardo asked me for the truth, and for fear of losing my job, I lied. Edgardo, that doll is the ugliest doll I've ever seen."

Edgardo chuckled, softly keeping his composure while everyone in the room went berserk.

"Ms. Rivera!" Mr. White yelled, but I continued.

"I don't know any kid that would want to buy that doll. I think that there are many other ways to honor your mother, but this isn't one of them. I'm sorry I didn't tell you sooner."

I saw a smirk on Marilyn's face. Everyone was against me, but I didn't care. Edgardo wasn't. The minute he spoke, everyone got quiet.

"Idalis," he said. "*Gracias*, I appreciate your honesty."

Then he turned to Mr. White.

"Mr. White, I've had some time to think about this campaign and I want you to know that I will not be moving forward. I have decided to stop production on the Linda Maria doll."

"Is this a result of Ms. Rivera's outburst?"

"No. Coincidentally, I had already made my decision before Ms. Rivera shared her real feelings. She is an exemplary employee and I hope she is rewarded for her courageous and very kind effort." Edgardo picked up his briefcase, glanced over at me, smiled, and left the room. I felt good that I had been able to do something to help someone else, but I also felt a little unsure about what Mr. White thought. "I will be in touch to finalize all the details. Thank you."

When Edgardo left, Mr. White asked everyone to step out of the room, including me, but he asked Samantha to stay behind. The rest of us went back to our cubicles. When I sat down at my desk, I wondered if this would be the last time I'd be sitting in my gray cubicle. I couldn't see why; I hadn't done anything wrong. I'd just told the truth.

At the end of the day, Samantha called me into her office.

"Let me start off by saying that Mr. White has no intention of letting you go."

On the inside, I was ecstatic. I felt that my goodwill would pay off big-time.

"However, he is not happy about the outburst this morning."

"Outburst?"

"Well, think about it, Idalis. Not only did you advise a client without consulting Mr. White or myself, you rudely interrupted Mr. White while he was speaking. It was selfish and it definitely was not the behavior of a true team player."

The more she reprimanded me, the more I felt like I was shrinking in my seat. It was ironic that telling the truth could feel so good and so wrong at the same time.

"We've decided to move you back into the secretarial pool."

I didn't know what to say. Even though Edgardo Levy, an important client, was appreciative of what I had done for him, Mr. White still thought that I'd been wrong.

"Do you have anything to say, Idalis?"

I didn't have anything to say, but I felt had I said no it would have seemed out of line. And the last thing I wanted was to be out of line again.

"Thank you."

"I think you owe Mr. White an apology."

I sat there, quiet. I didn't feel the need to apologize.

"Well, I guess that's all, then," Samantha said, abruptly ending our session.

I stood up and left her office. I walked back to my cubicle and thought about what would be the right thing to do. I knew that I didn't want to apologize, but if I didn't apologize, then Samantha would make it so difficult for me there that I wouldn't want to stay. I wasn't sure if I could handle another ending, though. I needed time to think about it.

39 Almost a week had gone by since I'd spoken to or seen Cameron. I had no idea where he was or what he was feeling. Did he suddenly lose interest in me or was I so afraid of being alone that I imagined those romantic moments and intimate conversations? Why are men so hard to figure out?

But what if Cameron was Mr. Right? Part of me wanted to hang on to that possibility, but the other part of me, the one that was trying to grow up and take responsibility, was beginning to think that there was no such thing as a Mr. Right.

Of course, as soon as that thought crossed my mind, he called.

"Hey, sweetheart," Cameron said, as though he had spoken to me three hours ago.

I heard airplanes in the background.

"Hey," I said unexcitedly.

"I got your messages."

"Okay."

"Sorry I couldn't call back sooner. I was stuck in meetings the whole week."

"No problem."

I didn't have the energy to talk. I could feel that my heart wanted some time off. It needed a little vacation.

"What's wrong?"

"Nothing."

"You're not mad or anything?"

"No."

"Yes, you are."

"Cameron, I've had a really difficult week."

"I'm sorry. Do you want me to call back?"

I gave myself time to think about the right answer.

"Cameron?"

"Yes?"

"I can't do this right now."

"Then I'll call you later."

"No, I can't talk to you right now or next week or next month."

"You're angry because I didn't call."

"I'm not angry. I am a little disappointed. But this isn't about a phone call. It's about me needing time alone."

"Are you getting back with your husband?"

"No. Like I said, I need time alone."

"You don't sound like the happy Idalis I saw the last time we were together."

"Because right now it's really hard for me to be happy when I have so many changes in my life."

"Talk to me, honey. I'm here now."

"I'm tired, Cameron."

"I wish I would've called. It's just that I had this deal I was working on, and—"

"Cameron, you don't have to explain. It's okay."

"I should've called. I'm sorry."

I started to feel bad because he was feeling bad.

"Don't be sorry. It's not that. It's just that I have so much to think about. I have to think about where I'm going to go and how I'm going to take care of my kid."

"You've been doing that already, haven't you?"

"Well, yeah, I guess."

"You're going to be fine, Idalis. Listen, I'm coming back to Staten Island tonight. I'll pick you up and take you out. You won't have to cook or anything and we can sit and talk."

"I can't go out tonight and I can't handle a relationship right now. I can't see you anymore."

I heard the whirring of an airplane engine in the background; it stopped and then Cameron sighed.

"Cameron?"

"I'm here."

"Did you hear what I just said?"

"Yes, I did."

"Oh."

"It's just strange how quickly things changed. All I did was go on a business trip."

"You never told me you were going on a business trip."

"I didn't mention any of that?"

"No. If you did, I wouldn't have left two messages."

"So that's why you're angry at me."

I laughed. "No, really I'm not angry. But it's funny how you forgot to tell me that."

"Yeah, I had to come to D.C."

Of course, how convenient to have a meeting in the same place your ex-girlfriend lives.

"Oh, D.C.," I said.

"It's not what you think."

"What do I think?"

"That I came here to see my ex."

"I wasn't even thinking that."

"What were you thinking?"

"Nothing."

I had nothing to say. What could I say? That once again a man had disappointed me? It wasn't not like we had anything going on. Right? We had strong chemistry, that was it. I wasn't going to sit here and tell him how full of shit it all sounded and that I couldn't understand how someone could say, "I feel you. I've never felt like this before" and then not return a call for a few days or forget to mention that he was going on a business trip. I wasn't going to allow myself to go there again. Even if he was telling me the truth, I wasn't going to allow my heart to believe it. That was it. The heart was now officially closed for business—until I was ready to open it again.

"Cameron, thank you for everything."

"Everything?"

"Thank you for the time we've spent together."

He sighed again.

"But most of all, thank you for making me feel special."

"Idalis?"

"Yes?"

"I'm going to miss saying your name."

I laughed a little. "Good-bye, Cameron."

"*Adiós.*"

After I hung up, I realized that the reason I was having such a hard time making decisions was that once a decision was made, there was no turning back. I'd never know what it would be like to go down that other road.

40

"*Tío*, I have to leave in five minutes, where's Guillermo?"

"He's coming, *nena*, he's coming," Uncle Herman yelled from behind the light blue marble counter.

I turned the silver cup on the espresso maker to the side, removed it from the machine, and carefully poured the espresso into a small, light blue porcelain cup. I loved the cups that I had picked out because they matched the tiles on the service counter so perfectly. I added the milk froth, stirred, and handed the old woman across the counter her second cup for the morning.

"I didn't know that Spanish coffee could be so good," she said in her thick Italian accent. "It reminds me of home."

"Thank you," I said, proudly looking around the new place, thinking about how nine months earlier there were cracked concrete floors, ripped Sheetrock, and remnants of a broken dream.

Constantine's Webos was gone, long gone, but the spirit was still here. My courageous uncle wouldn't let anyone mess with his dream, so he built a quaint coffee shop called La Casita San Juan. It was the best little coffee shop in all of Staten Island and served, as one food reviewer put it, "the most delectable egg dishes in all of New York City." Not to mention the empanadas (my idea) were starting to cause a buzz with the younger crowd. The morning lines were so long that we set up a take-out window and had Selenis, on her good days, help us get commuters to their buses on time.

The place was beautiful, so I didn't mind working the six-days-a-week and fourteen-hours-a-day schedule. Anyway, I could always bring Junito whenever I wanted and he loved being there.

The floors were a dark wood with a glassy shine and the walls were burnt orange. After seeing a design show, I got excited and sponged the walls with a little red layer on top. That's what gave the place an Old World feeling. Each table had a different mosaic pattern that matched the seat of its chairs, and lots of exotic plants hung from the walls in long black planters. The place was so pretty that a local writer, who happened to work at a design magazine in New York, did a little write-up and we were voted one of the twenty prettiest little coffee shops in the country. It was so empowering to know that Uncle Herman and I, with no formal training, had accomplished so much on our own. I couldn't understand why I hadn't gone into business with him sooner.

Uncle Herman was right: when you know in your heart that something will work, it will. You just have to jump into the water without a life jacket. I had to be honest, though, I didn't jump in right away. It took a little time. After I got transferred back to the secretarial pool, things at work didn't feel right anymore. I felt like I had outgrown the corporate game-playing. I no longer cared to see what the glass ceiling looked like. The same way I was holding on to Manny and the past was the way I was holding on to my job. I always thought that if I were loyal to my job, I would be rewarded, the way my father was rewarded when he stayed in his job for twenty-five years. The days when corporations were loyal to their employees were a thing of the past, and I had to make the decision of whether I wanted to sell my soul for a frequent paycheck or take the risk to find a happier, simpler way of life.

It was when Uncle Herman called me for some decorating advice that I started playing around with the idea of changing careers. But it wasn't easy, because Edgardo Levy had made me a great offer. An offer that would have had my mother ecstatic, since the office was located in one of the tallest buildings on Park Avenue. That was the moment I decided to jump into the water. After spending time with Uncle Herman decorating and fixing up the coffee shop, I realized what I could do on my own and turned down the offer.

The coffee shop felt like my second home; a little taste of San Juan in the middle of Staten Island. Our little shop brought people together. And in my own way, I realized I was changing the world, one *café con leche* at a time. I knew that having so many cultures under one roof was not an easy thing to do in Staten Island, but on any given day you'd find a few Italians, Russians, Albanians, Puerto Ricans, or Mexicans sharing their personal stories with each other. I finally felt that I had accomplished something meaningful.

Uncle Herman and I came up with a cute little menu filled with a variety of coffees that he knew would make the customers keep coming back. I never realized that everything I'd learned at the advertising agency might be handy. I created all the advertisements and even started a little advertising campaign. I was finally able to use both sides of my brain.

Even though La Casita San Juan was a hit right away, I knew that there was no way we could run Amos's out of business. We had to stay on top of our game because Amos's had fifty franchises around the country. How could we compete with that? We didn't try to beat the chain; instead we just stayed true to our mission — to give our customers a place they could escape to, while offering the best in customer service. And from what I'd heard, Amos's wasn't big on customer service.

Unlike other coffee shops, we made sure that every person who walked through our doors was completely satisfied with our products. If they weren't, we would make sure that they were. We'd give out free refills to our most loyal customers and I started the Bring-a-Friend Day, when friends could try any of our menu items for half the price. We didn't have Amos's money, but we had heart and we believed that our little idea would survive, and it did.

As for my best friend, well, Ralphie wound up taking a leave of absence from work so Selenis wouldn't be alone when she had to go to her treatments. I guess the idea of possibly losing her — not so much to Kique but to cancer — was a stark reality for him. He loved his wife and he showed her by being there when she needed him the most. Especially since Selenis had to get a double mastectomy and had to wait four months before she could get her implants. I was the only one that could look at her bare chest, since I was also the only person she allowed to help her change her dressings. I knew she wouldn't let Ralphie go near her. Then one night Ralphie had a long talk with me and asked nicely if I could stop helping Selenis so much. Selenis told me that soon after, Ralphie walked into the bedroom, sat her down on the bed, and unbuttoned her blouse. She fought it, but he wouldn't stop. He wanted to let her know that he was there for her—for the long haul. He removed her prosthetic bra, and held her in his arms. Selenis said she'd never felt that kind of love before. She was able to finally let go of her insecurities and trust her husband.

Kique and his wife divorced a few months later. If only grown folks would find another way of moving on instead of cheating, endings would be so much easier.

As far as Trisco went, I never heard from him again.

How did I feel about Manny? I loved Manny with all my heart. There was no easy way to say good-bye and neither of us knew how to do it the right way. Manny did meet someone a few months ago, someone his own age who he met at his job. Did it bother me? Sure, I'd be lying if I said it didn't hurt. But she was a great person. I knew because Junito told me.

When Cameron saw our little coffee shop profiled in the local Staten Island paper, he came by to say hello and wish us well. When I handed him a cup of coffee, my hand touched his, and yes, the feeling was still there. We smiled at each other. It was funny, because he also came by to tell me he was moving to California. He got another promotion and was going to head the Los Angeles banking division. As I watched Cameron leave the coffee shop, all I could think about was how funny the universe was. No matter how much you planned and worked and dreamed, it would always offer you little surprises. I realized that you just have to go with the flow, or fight it and never find true happiness.

I was sure that I had somehow found my way and that all the little lessons I'd learned were finally hitting home. I was getting it, little by little.

But the one thing I still didn't know for sure was what the universe would offer my best friend. She meant the world to me, but she wasn't doing well. The cancer came back hard. I spent many days and nights with her, holding her, comforting her, putting together family photo albums, making videos with the kids, telling her how much I loved her, laughing out loud and then suddenly just breaking down into tears. Letting go of someone you love is the hardest thing in the world. But I had to learn to let go of the things that were not in my control and live life for my friend even if to just give her hope.

Selenis and I decided that we would go back to Club 90 to celebrate our lives, the good and the bad, and to say one last good-bye to the old Selenis and Idalis.

I looked over at my best friend and she looked at me, while we sat at the edge of the dance floor. We could see our spirits dancing above the music. I remembered what Señora Topacio had said, and she was right. I was finally dancing alone, freestyle, and I was happy—well, happy to have this moment with Selenis.

As we left the club, we could hear the voices of Boys II Men. They were speaking to us. I held my best friend's hand tightly, hanging on to her, hoping that I could keep her with me forever. But even if that didn't happen, I knew that at least I'd have the memories.

To be my sunshine after the rain
It's so hard to say good-bye to yesterday.

ACKNOWLEDGMENTS

I must acknowledge the angels who walked with me on my path to help bring this book to fruition. My agent, Jenoyne Adams, who believed more than I did that I could do this. I couldn't have asked for a nicer, funnier, smarter, and more honest agent. Jeff Rivera, without your generosity and kindness I never would have met Jenoyne. Amy Tannenbaum, my most brilliant editor, who believed in this project from day one, along with the visionary Johanna Castillo. I remember in our meeting I mentioned that what was most important to me was that I never compromise the Latina in me. And I never had to. Thank you both for making this a beautiful and rewarding experience. Diana "The Park Villa" Jimenez, for coming back into my life, making me relive our own pasts, and inspiring me to write this story. Lina Sarrapochiello, Antonia Marrero, Mercedes Vasquez, and the rest of the Latino Flavored Productions Inc. family, for always being the ultimate team players, especially while I wrote this book. My sisters Jennifer and Yvette, two words: Gidget and Midget. Jonathon and Jordan, don't let anyone ever tell you that you can't. *Mami* and *Papi*, for giving me so much love, encouragement, and never-ending material. I don't know what I would do without you. Tony, the love of my life; it started in 1995 at the Copa, you allowed me to be me then and nothing has changed since. I could not have lived my dreams had you not allowed me to fly freestyle. My little miracle, Matthew, before you came into my life I had no idea what it was to love someone to infinity and beyond. And now I do.

4-11